TWICE
UPON
A TIME

TWICE UPON A TIME

Book Two in the Half Upon a Time series

JAMES RILEY

SCHOLASTIC INC.

ISBN 978-0-545-81646-5

12 11 10 9 8 7 6 5 4 3 2 1   14 15 16 17 18 19/0

Printed in the U.S.A.   40

First Scholastic printing, December 2014

Designed by Jessica Handelman
The text of this book was set in Goudy Old Style.

This book is dedicated to YOU.
Every other reader will think I'm talking
about them, but you know better.

TWICE UPON A TIME

CHAPTER 1

Once upon a time, Jack knew better than to do certain things. You didn't waste time trying to find the perfect temperature of porridge in a bear's house. You didn't point out to your suddenly extremely furry grandmother how big her fangs were. And you definitely didn't walk through a creepy fog while music from magical pipes drifted in eerily. These weren't even questions, you just didn't do them—not if you wanted to stay uneaten by three bears, disguised wolves, or scary old musicians.

Except here he was—fog, magical pipe music and all, and he just wanted to find the stupid Piper and get on with things.

Unfortunately, not everyone was so goal oriented.

"Does anyone else want to follow him?" May asked, shivering in her oversize blue cloak as her head bobbed to the music. She shifted a backpack full of food—a gift from Phillip's mother—higher on her shoulder as she moved with the melody.

"I hope you are joking, Princess," Phillip said, shooting her a worried glance. "Remember, we are *not* to go into his cave. That is where the children from the village went, and they never returned."

As if to reinforce the creepiness, a blackbird crowed loudly, then took to the air from some tree hidden in the fog. Jack shivered, thinking the bird almost sounded like it was calling his name.

"I know, I know, no cave," May said, rolling her eyes before swaying to the music again.

Jack sighed and stopped her. "Maybe you should wait a little distance away. . . . You don't seem to be handling this all that well."

"The rhythm isn't going to get me," May said absently. "Besides, what's the worst it could do? Tell me my grandmother is a horrible tyrant who tried to take over half the world? 'Cause, too late."

Jack and Phillip glanced at each other, and Jack could see his own concern reflected in the prince's eyes. May caught their look, and shoved them apart. "What did I say about doing that!" she shouted a bit too loudly for Jack's taste. "I'm fine! It's been three months. I'm over it!" She glared at Jack. "Either that or I'm quietly going crazy and I'll hand you both over to the next giant we come across. Care to bet on which way it's gonna go if you keep giving Phillip those stupid emo worry looks?!"

"Seems like crazy's taking the early lead," Jack said, then quickly turned and continued on ahead, trying to ignore the glare she had just thrown at him.

"If this is too much for you, we could find another way–," Phillip began, but May shushed him.

"It took us this long just to find the Piper," she said. "I want to know who I *am* already! And besides, I for one am tired of rescuing you from various invisible gnomes."

Phillip smiled. "I thought you said that we would never speak of that again."

"Yet someone keeps bringing it up," May said, her face expressionless.

"Can we concentrate?" Jack said, dragging May forward and away from Phillip. "The sooner we pay the Piper, the sooner we get to the Fairy Homelands and find Merriweather, so that—"

"So that we can find out for *sure* that I'm completely alone," May said.

Jack sighed. "I was going to say 'so that we can find your family . . . and *I* can finally go home.'"

Phillip grabbed Jack by the shoulders and shook him gently. "Go home? Why would you ever want that? Look at where you are! We stand in the middle of a dark, fog-drenched field. Off in the distance a figure waits, known only to us in tales told to frighten children. Enemy or ally, we will not know until it is too late, yet press on we must!" The prince shook with excitement at the idea, while Jack just sighed and waited for him to finish. "What is the point of *life* without adventures like this?!"

"See, I like to think the point of life is to be happy," Jack said with a shrug. "Also maybe not almost dying every two minutes. But I can see how we'll have to agree to disagree here."

"Maybe we can agree to go talk to the man?" May said, and pushed on ahead of the two boys. As she approached the figure in the distance, the music began to slow, eventually coming to a halt just as they were finally able to make out a thin, stooped figure leaning against a gnarled, blackened tree stump. The man wore a tunic of dull red, belted by a green rope with several heavy-looking pouches hanging from it. And though the music had stopped, the pipes remained at the old man's lips, his eyes closed as if he were still playing.

"Good evening, sir," Phillip said.

The man didn't move.

"Um, we heard you could maybe help us," May said.

The man didn't move.

"See, typically this would be the moment most people respond," Jack said. Nothing. "This is creepy," he whispered to May and Phillip. "Maybe he wants his payment—"

"Payment?" the old man said, lowering his pipes and opening his eyes.

"I think he heard you," May whispered to Jack.

"I'm so glad you're here to point these things out," Jack whispered back.

The old man sighed. "Ah. *You* three. It's about time."

May cleared her throat. "You were . . . waiting for us?"

The old man snorted. "For longer than I'd care to admit. You think I have nothing better to do than leave my cave in one place while I sit here, playing my pipes? The longer my cave and I stay here, the more likely it is that the Queen will find me." He glared at May. "Thanks to you three, she probably will. And now you want my help."

Jack winced, trying not to make the mention of her grandmother a bigger deal by looking at May. Thankfully, Phillip stepped forward, taking a large bag from Jack's hand. "We seek passage to the Fairy Homelands, sir," the prince said.

"Of course you do," the Piper said, eyeing the bag. "And I see you've brought payment?"

"Sounds like you're not a man to let bills go unpaid," Jack said quietly, his eyes on the pipes.

The Piper smiled. "If I'm owed something, then I will collect. The Piper will be paid, children, one way or another."

"Yeah, we visited the last town who didn't pay," May said. "The youngest person there was like sixty."

"They promised payment if I removed their rats," the Piper said, absently sticking his pinkie into one of the pipes as if he were cleaning it out. "I delivered, yet they did not. So I took . . . another form of payment."

"Their children," Jack said, shivering from more than the fog's chill.

"None were harmed," the Piper said, standing up to grab the bag almost indignantly from Phillip. He looked inside, and his face lit up, a smile harmonizing with the sparkle in his eyes. "Yes, *yes*, whispering reeds from the Swamp of All's End! Which of you harvested . . ."

"I did," Jack said, glaring at the bag. "And I've still got the burns. No one ever told us they whisper *fire*."

"They will do nicely," the Piper said, ignoring him. "Now

you've paid, and royally so. Speak your wish, and I will do what I can."

May stepped forward, a bit nervously. "We, uh, wish to travel to the Fairy Homelands. Please. Thank you. Please."

The Piper looked at her for a moment, then, almost faster than Jack could see, he raised his pipes to his lips, blew one note, and lowered the pipes. Like magic (appropriately enough), May instantly relaxed at the sound, letting out a huge breath she'd apparently been holding in.

"That's better," the Piper said. "You have nothing to fear, children. Not from me, not anymore."

"I would if I were afraid of cryptic statements," Jack murmured. The Piper glared at him, and began to raise his pipes to his lips again, so Jack quickly added, "But of course I'm not, who would be, and we have nothing but the utmost respect for you. Sir. Your Highness."

"The Fairy Homelands," the Piper said. "Not the easiest destination."

Jack snorted. "Not exactly, no. We've been searching for a way to them for the past three months. And from what we've found, there *is* no natural way to get there. We need magic. And a very specific kind of magic."

The Piper smiled, then held up his pipes. "Music," he said. "It's true. The fairies don't think in words or pictures like you and I do. They think and talk in music . . . so that's how they perform their magic as well. That's why most humans can't understand the little ones, though the fairy queens are able to speak our language easily enough."

Jack glanced over at the golden fairy in May's hair, and the fairy winked at him. "He's right, stupid human," she said. "If your kind were smart enough to understand music, you might have fewer problems."

"We might have had fewer problems if *you'd* known where the Fairy Homelands were!" Jack whispered back at her.

"NO fairy knows!" the golden fairy shouted. "We're sent away at birth! But if we live by the code and spread more good than ill, we might eventually be allowed back in! YOU are the ones trying to take shortcuts!"

"So that humming is her talking?" May said, then turned to Jack. "And would *you* stop yelling at her? It's not like she can understand you."

"Yeah, stupid human. It's not like I can understand you!" the golden fairy shouted, sticking out her tongue.

"I hate you," Jack said to her, turning away. "So, so, *so* much."

"Regardless," the Piper said. "My music can take you to the Fairy Homelands."

"*And* bring us back, right?" Jack added quickly.

The Piper's eyes twinkled. "If you wish. For that you'll need something more." The Piper reached into a pocket and produced a wooden whistle, which he handed to Phillip.

"Nice catch," May whispered to Jack.

"I'm sure the fairy queens are nice and all, but I'm not spending the rest of my life stuck in a whole city of these things," Jack whispered back, glaring at the golden fairy, who made a face at him.

"Blow into this whistle when you are finished," the Piper continued, "and you'll return right to this spot."

"*Return* to this spot?" Jack asked. "Are we leaving soon—"

The Piper brought his pipes to his lips and blew a melody so quick and intricate that it sounded like three or four Pipers playing all at once. The mist began swirling around faster and faster as the music sped up, creating a whirlwind of fog that quickly obscured the Piper, the cave, and everything else from view. The music grew louder, filling Jack's head, obliterating his thoughts, taking over his mind, not letting him even think—

Only to stop abruptly, dropping them onto grass much

brighter than it had any right to be, on ground that was both softer and harder than any Jack had ever felt. He groaned, then pushed himself up, noticing a glowing paved stone roadway beginning just a few feet away from the spot where he'd landed. Whereas behind him . . .

Behind him was only mist.

"I think we're here," May said, matching his groan a little just to Jack's right.

"There does seem to be something . . . different about this place," Phillip said, then gasped.

Jack quickly followed Phillip's gaze, up the paved road to a gate that seemed to be made of silver latticework circles, then past *that* to . . .

"Uh-oh," Jack said.

"No uh-ohs!" May said, glaring at him. "NO! Not after everything we've been through! No more uh-ohs!"

"I do not think we have a choice, Princess," Phillip said.

May started to reply, then finally saw what the other two were staring at. "Uh-oh," she said.

On the other side of the gate, enormous tree-trunk-size vines blocked out all view of what lay beyond as the vines circled and intertwined with one another. Between that and the fist-size thorns growing out of them every foot or so, the overall effect was definitely "Uh-oh."

"Look," Phillip said, his voice choking a bit as he pointed. Just past the gate something lay crumpled over one of the vines. Jack stepped closer, and realized with a start that it wasn't something so much as some*one*.

"NO!" the golden fairy yelled. "My queen!" She leapt into the air and quickly flew at the tangle of vines, reaching out desperately for what appeared to be the body of a fairy queen.

Jack immediately launched himself out to grab her, knowing that it was too late but not being willing to just let the fairy fly headfirst into whatever curse had turned the Fairy Homelands into this overgrown . . . whatever it was.

Unfortunately, Jack was right. He *was* too late.

The golden fairy passed the silver gate and immediately dropped to the ground, landing hard on a vine, her body unmoving.

And a second later, unable to stop, Jack's momentum sent him tumbling past the gate as well, and into oblivion.

CHAPTER 2

A warm wind tousled Jack's hair as he opened his eyes, finding himself back in a familiar place. The oak tree behind him seemed to be made specifically to fit his back, and the grass gently swaying in every direction calmed him instantly, as it always did.

"Noooo," he groaned, driving a fist into the ground. "Come on. How many times do I have to say it?!"

"You cannot avoid me forever," said a man in a dark blue cloak from behind him. "I know you've been skipping sleep whenever you can, but eventually you must dream." Beneath the cloak the man wore black armor from head to toe, the only markings of any sort a white circle inside a white oval, the symbol of the Wicked Queen's Eyes, her inner circle of spies and assassins. "And when you dream," said the Charmed One, "you *will* learn."

"Better people than you have tried to make me learn," Jack told him as he pushed himself to his feet. "And they all failed too!" With that, he turned and sprinted off in a random direction. Glancing behind him, he saw the knight beneath the oak tree, just where he'd left him, which was good. At least the man wasn't chasing him. Jack turned back to look where he was going—

And found himself running straight toward the oak tree and the waiting knight.

Jack slowed to a stop, then glared at the man. "You have no idea how much that irritates me."

The man grinned. "And yet you keep trying."

"I'm not going to be trained by you!" Jack shouted. "You or your stupid sword!" He yanked the sword the knight had given him in a giant's mouth three months ago off his back, and then threw it straight at the knight.

The knight caught it easily, swung it a few times, then whipped it back, right at Jack's head.

Both of Jack's hands flew up of their own accord and slapped together, stopping the blade between his palms just inches from his face.

"It appears as if someone's learning whether they want to or not," the knight said, his smile growing wider.

"I don't have time to argue this again!" Jack shouted. "We finally found the Fairy Homelands, but there's some kind of curse . . . a curse that might have killed me, by the way."

"You wouldn't be here if you were dead," the knight said, but looked away as if distracted.

"Oh yeah?" Jack said. "Because last I heard, you were not so much in the alive category yourself. . . ."

"Shh!" the knight interrupted, raising a hand. "Be still!" He turned slowly in a circle. "Someone is here. No one should be able to get through my defenses into your mind, but someone has broken through. Someone . . . familiar."

Jack turned in a circle as well, accomplishing nothing, since no one was there. The only sign of life at all was a city a few miles in the distance, but even that seemed empty and abandoned, at least from here. But given that he'd never seen the knight look even the slightest bit concerned, let alone worried, Jack decided there was more going on than he could see.

Finally the knight seemed to relax. He shook his head, smiled, and turned back to Jack—then exploded into a million different pieces as a glowing white sword burst right through his chest.

In his place stood a girl in a midnight blue cloak, wearing black leather armor, complete with a white eye in the center. In her hands was a sword that matched Jack's exactly. And she was smiling.

"*First* of all," she said, "he really should have seen that coming if he's as good as he thinks he is. Or, thought he is. Thought he *was*? I never know what tense to use for dead people who come back in your dreams."

Jack leapt backward, immediately raising his own sword. "Yeah, grammar can be a real problem," he growled. "Like, how do you correctly say 'Who are you?' to someone who just killed a man right in front of you?"

The girl continued smiling as she slid her sword into its sheath on her back. "Oh, whatever, he's no more dead than he ever was. I just sent him away for a while. And as for who I am, I would have gotten to that if you'd let me get to my 'second of all.' You can call me Lian."

"Can I call you that because it's your name?"

The girl laughed. "In a way. Nice dream you've got here." She sat down beneath the oak tree and settled herself in. "You should probably get comfortable. You're not going to be waking up anytime soon."

"Shows what you know," Jack told her, not moving. "I'm a pretty light sleeper. I'm probably going to wake up any second now."

"Oh, sure," Lian said, rolling her eyes. "That's usually how magic curses work."

Jack narrowed his eyes. "And how do you know that? Who are you?"

"We'll be here forever if I have to cover everything twice," she said with a frown. "I told you, I'm Lian."

Jack shook his head. "You're an Eye."

The girl stood up and bowed with a deep flourish. "Proudly serving the Benevolent Queen of the World for almost ten years now. Why, is that a problem?"

Jack kept his sword between them. "I'm going to go with 'probably.'"

"*Someone* has trust issues," Lian said, sitting back down. "I'm not here to hurt you, just to talk. After all, you're already exactly where you're supposed to be, stuck in the Fairy Homelands under a sleep curse for the next . . . How many years is forever?"

Jack swallowed hard. "This is a bad dream, right? Some kind of nightmare? I'm gonna wake up and find Phillip getting attacked by invisible gnomes again?"

"Yeah, waking up isn't exactly in the plan," Lian said, picking some grass and twiddling it between her fingers. "In fact, I very much doubt you'll ever wake up before you die."

"You sound like my grandfather whenever I tried to sleep too late," Jack said, his sword still pointing straight at the girl. "So what, are you here to kill me, then?"

"Oh, not me," Lian said, throwing the grass into the air and watching it drift to the ground. "No. As soon as I told my Queen that I'd set the sleeping curse off, she sent four battalions of dragons on their way." The girl scrunched up her face. "I'm still a little unclear about how much a battalion is, so let's say it's eleventy-two. Which makes four times that many dragons on their way right now."

"That's some impressive math," Jack said, "but let's be honest. It took us three months to track down a way to get to the Fairy Homelands. Without the Piper's music—"

"True," Lian said with a shrug. "It does make traveling here a bit more of a headache. But dragons have a talent for going places other creatures can't, even if it takes them a while to get there. There are spells to break through, dimensions to crack, that sort of thing, so you've got some time." Her eyes brightened. "In fact, I'd guess you have until about sunset tomorrow night before the dragons arrive and set the entire Fairy Home-lands on fire."

Jack suddenly had trouble standing. "See, I have a problem with that," he said, his whole body going wobbly and all the blood draining from his face. "Not only because I'm part of the 'entire' you just mentioned."

"You, your princess, the hero prince, eleven fairy queens, and several hundred thousand fairies," Lian said, counting them off on her fingers. "And no offense, but it was the eleven fairy queens that necessitated this. My Queen can't have such all-powerful magic-users biding their time before they enter the upcoming war. No, it was better to just take them out quietly, and some bad decisions on their part made that extremely easy to pull off." The part of Lian's face not covered by her hood looked sad. "If it helps, it's unfortunate that you happened to get here just now, instead of after the razing. I never thought you'd be this early. . . . Figured you'd arrive to find a burned-out husk of a land."

"Why are you telling me this?" Jack said, any paleness now being replaced with the dark red blush of anger. "Are you just trying to torture me? Because talking to you is accomplishing that just fine on its own."

"Like I said, you're stuck here," Lian said with a shrug. "That is, unless you decide to take the intelligent option."

"Intelligent?" Jack said. "Someone's obviously never met *me*."

"You could join my Queen," Lian said, now playing absently with her sword. "Then I could wake you up and get you out of here. You'd be alive, at least. And I think you'll find that my Queen is a lot easier to deal with when you're not fighting against her."

Jack stopped to think for a second. "Lemme think how best to put this," he said finally, "because I don't want to offend you in some way. I'd rather walk naked through snow that's on fire while all my friends laugh at me than ever consider joining the Wicked Queen."

Lian glanced at him. "Wow, nice visual there. Someone's thought about this before! But there's no call to be nasty about it. I thought I was being nice."

"By killing hundreds of thousands of fairies?!"

"This is war, Jack," Lian said, her voice growing softer. "No one wants to see casualties, least of all my Queen. But if she didn't attack them, they'd attack her. She's just protecting herself, really."

"That's funny, because it sure looks a lot like she's the only one attacking."

"You're not . . . what's the word . . . *fun* to talk to, are you."
Lian sighed, then stood up and stretched. "Well, then, I'm not
going to waste any more time here with your grumpy pants. Good
luck with the whole sleeping till you burn up thing!"

Jack growled, then leapt at the girl, his sword raised high in
the air.

Faster than Jack could see, Lian whirled around and kicked
him in the stomach. Pain burst out all over his body as he dropped
his sword and flew backward, but before he could even land, Lian
was there. She grabbed him in midair, then threw him to the
ground twice as hard as he would have hit. The air burst out of
his lungs as more pain exploded in his head. He groaned loudly,
then opened his eyes to find her holding her sword to his throat.

"Here's the weird thing," Lian said, her voice entirely unconcerned. "My Queen, she thinks you're special. She thinks you're
smart. She's . . . *worried* about you."

"Worried about me?" Jack said as he tried to suck in air. "That's
so sad. Just tell her I'm doing fine, will you? I never wanted her to
worry or anything."

Lian rolled her eyes. "She's concerned you'll be a threat. They
all are. But I know better. 'Cause I know you."

"Oh, have we met?" Jack said, and before she could respond,

he threw himself to the side, rolling over. Her foot came down at him, but he grabbed it and yanked it out from under her—only she used his grip on her foot for leverage, kicking out with her other foot right into his face. Jack immediately released her as pain rocked through him, and her feet dropped to either side of his head, her sword now aimed at his nose.

"Yes, we have," Lian said, the smile back. "You're not where you're meant to be, Jack. You're on the wrong side. And I think you know it."

"I thought I was a threat," he said, his eyes narrowing. "You need to pick a point and stick with it." If he could just knock the sword away—

The sword slapped him in the side of the head. "Stop it," the girl said, apparently reading his mind. "And *I* don't think you're a threat. *I* don't think you're anywhere close to being dangerous. But my Queen does, and what she says goes."

The sword disappeared and the girl stepped back, allowing Jack to push himself back up to a standing position. A few feet away Lian tossed his sword into the air, twirling it almost faster than he could see, without the slightest bit of effort.

"Last chance to join us," she said. "You were always meant to, you know. That's why the Charmed One gave you his sword, and why you have such a natural talent. You're fast, even fighting the training. You're meant to be one of us, Jack." She stopped smiling, and her eyes looked almost sad. "You could even say you were born to be."

"Too bad I'm going to end up all burned to a crisp, then," he said, leaning against the tree for support.

Lian shook her head. "Fair enough. Good luck with that!"

And with that, the Eye disappeared, leaving Jack with less than two days to save an entire city full of fairies from a curse, with no idea what the curse was, or even how to wake himself up. Not to mention that whatever the girl had done with the knight, he hadn't come back yet. And if she could do that to a fully trained Eye, what chance did he have?

All in all, this *might* be a problem.

CHAPTER 3

As first her fairy, then Jack dropped to the ground just beyond the silver gate, something snapped hard in May. In the past three months she'd lost her home, her grandmot— her family, and her entire grasp on reality. And the only thing that'd given her any comfort in this fairy-tale world were two boys who'd stuck by her through magic and madness.

And now one of those two boys had just collapsed in a heap.

"NO!" she screamed, leaping forward, only to spin in a circle as Phillip grabbed her arm.

"No, Princess!" the prince said, his eyes fixed on Jack's unmoving body. "It is not safe!"

"Your *face* isn't going to be safe in a second!" May shouted. "Let. Me. Go!"

"No," Phillip said simply, pulling her backward despite her struggling.

"Stop it!" May shouted. "We need to save him!"

"Yes, we do!" Phillip shouted back, holding her tightly by her shoulders. "But first we need to figure out what type of magic caused this! It would do us no good to lose you as well!"

"Stop making sense!" May shouted, and squirmed her way out of the prince's grasp. Unfortunately, despite being hugely irritating, Phillip was right, so instead of running back to Jack, May just glared at the prince. "So, Mr. Rational, tell me what to do! What did this?"

"I have no idea," Phillip said.

"I will *smack* you," May said.

"It's a curse, you idiots," said a voice from behind them.

May and Phillip both whirled around to find a small girl sitting on a rock just inside the mist, wearing a midnight blue cloak pulled low over her head to cover almost all of her face. Beneath the cloak was some type of hard leather, all black except for a white circle inside a white oval right in the middle of her chest.

Phillip immediately drew his sword and pointed it straight at the girl.

And then his sword was in the girl's hand, the blade spinning like a basketball on one of her fingers.

May never even saw her move.

"Now *that* was kinda rude," the girl said, her frown the only thing showing beneath her hood.

"You did this," Phillip said, stepping away from May, something he often did when trying to draw attention away from her when they were threatened, which was way too often for May's taste, honestly. Though, seriously, being threatened even once was probably too much for May's taste.

The girl nodded slowly. "Partly," she said. "The magic isn't mine, but I set it off. Orders, you know."

May went cold, finally realizing what was going on. "Whose orders?" she asked quietly.

"She misses you, May," the girl said. "She doesn't admit it, but she does. We can tell."

And just like that, three months of purposefully ignoring any thought of her grandmother fell apart, and more than anything, May just wanted to run back to the woman and hug her. Also, maybe throw up.

"What is the curse?" Phillip asked, still circling around the girl as May struggled to not lose it completely.

"It's a sleep spell," the girl said, her eyes on May. "Don't worry. No one's permanently injured. Well, not till tomorrow night or so. No, we haven't really even started yet."

"Started?" May said, hating this girl more than anyone she'd ever met, which was saying a lot. "'Cause I can finish it right now. Just stand still long enough for me to kick you in the face."

The girl smiled. "This is going to be fun." She reached into her cloak and pulled out a coil of rope. "Oh, look. I've got some nice convenient rope here that you could use to pull Jack out of the range of the curse. Then all you'd need to do is wake him up." Her smile widened. "Any ideas how to do that?"

In spite of everything, May blushed. "Seriously, the kick in the face. Think about it. *I* am. Over and over."

"Nah, I'm not cruel," the girl said. "You wouldn't have a chance."

"Really?" May said, her eyes widening. "'Cause I'm giving your *face* a chance to get out of here before I kick it in *its* face. And that's the last chance it's gonna get."

"I know what you're here to do," the girl said, standing up. Behind her May could see a familiar-looking sword hilt poking out from her back. "As does my Queen, obviously. But she doesn't think you're quite ready to know where you come from. Not just yet."

"Doing what *she* wants kinda went out the window three months ago," May said. "She's welcome to try grounding me again, but she'll have to come tell me herself. And I can't make any promises about her face not getting kicked, either."

"That doesn't sound very loving," the girl said. "But I'm hardly one to judge about family. Still, it's your choice. I can take you to her right now and end all of this."

"You'll have to kill me first," Phillip said quietly.

The girl sighed. "Really?" Before May could even move to stop her, the girl reached out and grabbed Phillip by his shirt, then drove his head into her knee. The prince gasped in pain and tried to pull away, but the girl just kicked a foot into his chest, slamming him backward into the silver gate. He hit it hard and collapsed to the ground, not moving.

"PHILLIP!" May screamed, but the girl just held up a hand to stop her.

"You people have no idea how much of a favor I'm doing you," the girl said, almost sounding bitter about it. "Trust me. If the other Eyes had found you first, they wouldn't have given you the chance to even say one word. You'd be halfway to the Queen before you knew what happened. They all think you're dangerous, though."

"Dangerous?" May said, her eyes narrowing. "That sounds about right."

"Oh, you and the prince, you're not a physical threat," the girl said. "But that doesn't make you any less of a concern. Especially if you find out who you are."

"Ask my grandmother how she liked me being dangerous all over her old Magic Mirror," May said.

"You've had quite the easy time these last three months," the girl said, ignoring her. "That's all about to end."

"EASY?!" May shouted. "We almost died like fourteen thousand times!"

"That's nothing compared to what's coming here tomorrow night," the girl told her. "That is, unless you help me drag Jack out of the spell and join the Queen. I know that the rest of you follow Jack's lead, but I'm trying to appeal to you now as the voice of reason."

"See, there was your first problem," May said. "Thinking Jack was our leader. If you people had paper bags, Jack wouldn't be able to lead his way out of one."

The girl frowned. "I'm not fluent in whatever language you're speaking. Anyway. As I said, you won't have it easy. Let's assume for a second that you can escape from me. Which you can't. You still don't know what this curse is, or how to end it."

"Like we can't figure that out in all of two seconds," May said.

"Without a fairy queen to identify it?" Lian said. "Good luck. And I happen to know for a fact that eleven of the twelve fairy queens are right here. Think Malevolent's going to be willing to help? Even if you did figure it out, you'd have to find a way to end the curse before the sun sets tomorrow night, since that's when the dragons will arrive and burn the Homelands to the ground."

Dragons?! May gritted her teeth. "I've done more in a day and a half than most people do in *two* days—"

"And third," the girl said, smiling slightly, "there was that small matter of escaping from me."

May raised an eyebrow. "That was the first thing."

"It's such a big one, it deserves a second mention."

"Fair enough. So how do you want to do this? I'll make it quick, since there's a time limit."

The girl laughed. "Oh, you've got no hope against me. I can move faster than you can see. And don't even think about running. How far do you think you'd get? Ten feet? Fifteen?"

May glanced behind her. "I'm going to go with fifteen." With that, she turned and ran straight at the silver gate.

"What are you *doing!*" the girl yelled, but May didn't turn to stop. She could hear the girl starting to follow right behind her, so May threw herself forward straight at the gate—only to go completely limp, crashing to the ground.

Right at her heels, the Eye windmilled her arms, carefully stopping before reaching the edge of the curse. Taking a few steps back, she shrugged, then turned to walk away. "They really should win some kind of record for most stupidity in the shortest amount of time," she said as she used her rope to tie Phillip up, then patted his unconscious head. "Be back soon. Have to go grab a friend." With that, she smiled and then disappeared.

CHAPTER 4

A minute passed, and nothing happened. Not even the wind moved through the silent, thorny vines circling the Fairy Homelands. Another minute passed, and another.

By the end, May waited a full ten long, hugely boring minutes before slowly turning around to look.

The Eye was gone.

FINALLY!

"OOOOWWWWWW!" May shouted, releasing the scream she'd been holding in ever since she'd crashed into the ground. Standing up was the next order of business, but that wasn't quite so easy, not since both her arms had passed the invisible line of the sleeping curse and were now completely asleep. Numb, dangling arms made pushing oneself to one's feet a bit more difficult, after all.

Stupid magic.

May finally managed to twist to her knees, then push up to her feet without falling over as her arms, now free of the magic, began tingling painfully. She bit her lip to keep from shouting again (though really, who was going to hear her?) and stomped on the ground a few times until feeling finally returned to her hands and arms.

Now all she had to do was untie Phillip, then pull Jack out of the spell's field—without being able to get in far enough to touch him. At least the horribly evil girl had left her rope. May shook her head, then smacked her fist into her palm. Next time she saw that girl, there was some definite underhanded, sneaky-type face-kicking to be done.

May untied the prince, who groaned but didn't wake up. That wasn't a great sign, but at least he was alive. She quickly tied a loop into the rope, then spent the next very not-quick few minutes trying to throw it around Jack's feet. May managed to hook them a few times, but the rope kept sliding off as she pulled. Finally, when he was close enough, May just intertwined her hands, then threw them into the field to wrap around his feet, and dragged him in with numb arms.

Now that Jack was out, May turned her attention to the little golden fairy, but there was just no way. The fairy's flight and lighter weight had sent her way too far past the gate, and barring some kind of appearance by a cowboy with expert lassoing skills, the fairy would just have to wait until they figured out how to deal with the curse.

In the meantime that still left her with one sleeping friend, as no amount of shaking or screaming at Jack seemed to do anything. And May tried both. A lot. And then tried them again.

"Okay, I'm *not* kissing you!" she screamed finally. "I refuse to accept that kissing would take someone out of a coma! That is *not* legitimate medicine!"

Unfortunately, there was a distinct lack of doctors around to agree with her, something she often had a problem with. And the longer this went on, the less time they had to wake the fairies up.

Not to mention that sitting there alone at the outskirts of a completely silent city covered in enormous thorny vines was more than a bit creepy.

"Okay, you did this for me," May said to him as she bent down next to Jack. "I get that. And frankly I'm about two seconds away from going insane, trying to deal with this all alone. My grand— the Queen. She did this, all this, just to keep me from finding out which stupid fairy tale I'm from?! All this?! She's going to wipe out an entire city just to torture me? That's who she is?"

May grabbed Jack's hand and held it in hers without even noticing. "I . . . I just . . . I know I've said I'm okay, Jack, but I'm really not handling this. I mean, she's my . . . she was my family! All the family I had. All the family I *ever* had! I loved her, Jack. I really did. But I can't . . . I can't . . ."

A drop of water fell onto Jack's hand, and May realized her cheeks were wet. She sniffed hard and wiped at her eyes. "I . . . I need you guys to help. You're all I have right now. Remember that when you wake up, 'cause I don't want to hear about this for the rest of our lives, okay?" She poked a finger into his chest. "Let's . . . let's just hope it works. If it does, you have my permission to mock me for as long as you want. Just . . . just wake up, please?"

With that, she leaned over to kiss Jack.

CHAPTER 5

Jack woke up to find May's face just inches from his.

"AHHHH!" he yelled.

"AHHHH!" she yelled, pulling away.

"What were you doing?" Jack shouted at her.

The princess blushed heavily. "I definitely wasn't . . . I was . . . You were asleep!"

"I gathered that part," Jack said. For some reason his mouth seemed wet. Had he been drooling on himself? That's probably what May had been doing so close, laughing at him. Whatever. He certainly wasn't going to give her any more satisfaction about it now.

"I love waking up to nothing making sense," he said, wiping his mouth and shaking his head. "What happened?" He glanced around, then nodded at the still sleeping Phillip. "And why's the prince so lazy all of a sudden?"

Phillip groaned, and May blushed twice as hard. Jack looked at her curiously. "What's got you so red?"

She looked everywhere but at him. "I . . . didn't know you would just wake up on your own, certainly without anyone doing anything awkward and embarrassing!"

"Well, obviously I did," Jack said. "What happened?"

"It's a sleeping spell," May told him, gesturing out at the silver gate. "Some kind of curse. And we don't have much time to lift it, or—"

"Or what?" Phillip asked, pushing himself to a sitting position.

"Or everyone still asleep is going to die," May said quietly. "The Wicked Queen has dragons on their way."

"How . . . how did you know that?" Jack asked, suddenly wondering if girls really could read minds.

"The girl," Phillip said, then glanced around. "Where did she go? What did she tell you?"

"Girl?" Jack asked. "Wait, she was here too?"

"Too?" May said, raising an eyebrow.

"I, uh . . . Never mind," Jack said, trying to hide his discomfort and failing miserably. Still, he wasn't about to tell them that the girl had spoken to him in his dreams. One Eye was bad enough, but two? "So, um, who was this girl?"

"Pretty much what you'd expect with us," May said. "Seriously creepy, evil vibe, white circles on her armor thing—"

"Not circles," Phillip said, watching Jack a little too closely. "An Eye."

Jack raised an eyebrow, not liking the prince's tone. "Like the kind in your head?" Purposefully playing stupid was the quickest way to annoy the prince, Jack had discovered.

"Like the one who gave you his sword," Phillip said. "This would make two of them that have found us. Two Eyes."

Jack sighed. "Yeah, your math checks out. I get it. What did she tell you?"

"Well," May said, "it sounded like she had orders to set off whatever this sleeping spell is. But more than that, she wanted me . . . us . . . to go back with her, back to . . . the Wicked Queen." May paused and looked away, then seemed to push herself through the rest quickly. "She said that would keep us safe, but if we didn't go with her, we only had till sunset tomorrow. After that the dragons will be here to burn the Fairy Homelands to the ground."

"Burn to the ground?" Phillip repeated, his eyes going wide. "But there are thousands of fairies here. They would surely perish!"

"Hundreds of thousands," Jack said quietly.

"I think that's sort of the point," May added.

"It must be a bluff," the prince continued, but he didn't look too sure. "There cannot possibly be any more dragons around. The Western Kingdoms wiped them out after the Great War."

"Argue that with the girl," May said. "In the meantime we have to figure out how to unspell the spell."

"I don't think that's a word," Jack said.

May turned around to glare at him. "Really? *That's* what you're focusing on?"

"I believe the proper term is 'dispel,'" Phillip said.

"Either way, we better get going," Jack said. He started to move, then stopped and glanced around. "Um, *where* are we going again?"

"She said we wouldn't be able to figure the spell out without another fairy queen," May said, looking out over the sleeping fairies. "Maybe it's fairy magic. But if that's the case, how did she set it off? Can Eyes do magic?"

"No," Jack said.

"Of course they can," Phillip said. "Evil magic."

"They're not *all* evil—"

"Or so they would want you to think," Phillip said.

Jack glared at the prince. "Anyway, Phillip's bright, sunny optimism aside, Eyes can't do magic, not like this."

Phillip snorted. "Eyes can take the shapes of animals, turn invisible, change their appearance entirely to look like someone else—"

"That's all just illusion!" Jack shouted. "If they could wipe out a city full of the most powerful fairies in the world, you think the Queen would have had to take over half the world with a goblin army? They can't do anything even close to this!"

"Wow, someone's touchy," May said. "Getting back to the topic, though. We need a fairy queen, and the girl said that all eleven fairy queens were here."

"Eleven?" Phillip said. "I believe there are twelve." He cleared his throat, then began to recite, to Jack's horror. "Once thirteen, now just twelve, the queens of fairy in secret do dwell—"

"Oh please, *no*," Jack interrupted. "Don't tell me we've actually had to resort to nursery rhymes? Anyway, we do know one fairy queen who's *not* here, speaking of dragons."

"Malevolent?" Phillip said, a catch in his voice.

"It's not like she's got any kind of love for the other fairy queens," Jack pointed out. "Maybe this has something to do with her."

Suddenly a fire lit in Phillip's eyes. "Of course it does!"

"Whoa, someone's all of a sudden sure," Jack said, giving the prince a confused look.

"Do you remember the story I told you of my father's encounter with Malevolent?" Phillip said, his voice rising excitedly. "A baby princess was born to a king, and all the fairy queens had been invited to bestow blessings on the girl, all except Malevolent. She arrived anyway, and cursed the baby girl to die when her finger touched a spindle, only Merriweather was able to modify the curse to just put the girl to sleep."

"Sleeping Beauty, sure," May said, waving a hand for him to continue.

"Uh, do you mean sleeping baby?" Jack asked her.

"The fairy queens took the baby away, to keep it safe," Phillip continued. "Perhaps . . . perhaps they brought her here, and somehow the curse was set off by this Eye, and the magic was too powerful to be contained by just the princess?"

"That's a lot of 'somehow's and 'perhaps'es, but either way, what other option do we have?" Jack asked.

"We end up saying that far too often," May murmured.

"We will receive no help from Malevolent, especially if this is her spell," Phillip said. "She despises us almost as much as she despises her sisters."

"She didn't want to help us last time, either," Jack pointed out. "So we just force the issue again. If you have a better idea . . ."

"No, just a premonition of great danger," Phillip responded.

"So basically nothing unusual," May said.

Phillip smiled despite himself. "So back to the Piper, then on to Malevolent. I just—"

Jack found himself clapping a hand on Phillip's shoulder. "You're just afraid. It's okay. It happens to human beings occasionally. You've probably heard about it."

Phillip laughed, then brought the Piper's whistle to his lips. "If we are ready, then?"

Jack and May looked at each other, then nodded. The whistle shrieked in their ears, and again a whirlwind appeared, swirling around, making an uncomfortable amount of noise in the absolute silence of the Fairy Homelands. Finally, swirling mists pushed in all around them, and they found themselves back at the cave in front of the Piper's stump.

Except the Piper's stump was missing its Piper. Instead there was just a familiar-looking knife stabbed right through the old man's pipes.

Jack reached a trembling hand out and pulled the knife from the stump, the pipes sliding off it with no resistance.

"Isn't that . . . ?" May asked, then gasped.

"It's my grandfather's knife," Jack said, staring at the weapon. "The one we left in the Palace of the Snow Queen."

He looked back down at the stump, where four claw marks had gouged four lines almost as an afterthought.

"The Wolf King," Jack said quietly. "He's found us."

"I forgot how observant you three were," a deep voice growled.

Jack, May, and Phillip turned around to find the Wolf King in his animal form emerging from the mists, his teeth bared in a horrible smile.

"Tell me this, children," the wolf said. "Do your observational skills extend to counting? How many goblins, trolls, and ogres are behind me?"

At that, hundreds of monsters stepped out of the thick mists, each of them watching the three humans hungrily.

"I'm kicking that girl in the face SO HARD!" May shouted.

CHAPTER 6

S urrender," the wolf said, tilting his head slightly.

"I was about to suggest the same to you," Phillip said, his sword drawn and pointed at the wolf.

"The Queen wishes none of you hurt, if possible." The wolf's eyes gleamed despite the surrounding mist cutting off all available light. "Of course, if you resist, I could just tell her it *wasn't* possible, that I was forced to bite off an arm here or there. She's quite forgiving in such situations."

"I'm hungry, Wolf King!" one of the goblins yelled from the wolf's side. "Can't we at least eat one of them?"

The wolf frowned, and his head whipped out, bit down on the goblin's armor, and swung the screaming creature into the air and back into the monsters. Jack's stomach dropped as the noises coming from the crowd sounded as if the first goblin wasn't the only hungry one.

"Now, where were we?" the wolf asked.

Jack drew his sword out, the normal white glow flickering oddly in the fog. "You really want to do this?" he asked the wolf. "I seem to remember taking you down once or twice."

The wolf smiled at this. "Ah, the little fake Eye has grown a spine." He gestured to the goblins at his side. "You five. Take them."

The goblins let out a howl and advanced, each wielding a vicious-looking battle-ax.

Just as it had in the past, somehow time slowed down. Each goblin seemed to almost stop in place, while Phillip was virtually frozen as he pushed his way in front of May, despite her extremely slow protests. Jack half-smiled at that, then leapt forward, snapping the first goblin's ax out of its hands and into the air, kicking the second in the stomach, while grabbing the flying ax out of the air and smashing the third in the head with it.

The fourth and fifth goblins had just enough time to start to look frightened before Jack slammed their heads together, then whipped the first one's ax right at the smiling Wolf King's head . . .

When a black-gloved hand reached out and grabbed it, mere inches from the wolf's face.

"Not bad," Lian said, her smile the only thing he could see under her Eye cloak. "But not that great, either."

She disappeared, reappearing right in front of Jack before he even saw her move. She grinned right in his face, then slammed her fists into his stomach over and over, faster than he could follow. One last kick to his chest sent Jack flying backward to slam into the Piper's tree stump.

And just like that, time returned to normal and the girl was gone.

"JACK?!" May shouted in surprise while Phillip stared at the five goblin bodies that had fallen to the ground in front of them.

"Wasn't that interesting," the wolf said smugly. "You have gotten better, little fake Eye, but you're still nothing compared to the real thing."

"Brave words," Jack said, desperately sucking in air, "from a big bad wolf . . . who's hiding behind goblins and little girls. Why don't you . . . trot yourself over here and see how good I am?" Jack took a deep breath. "Maybe give me a minute or two first, though."

The wolf laughed like rocks tumbling against one another. "You humans always think pride is so important. You're faster than me, I'll grant you that. But how will your speed fare when you're overwhelmed by my army?" He nodded, and hundreds of goblins, trolls, and ogres surged forward, their hungry howls calling out into the night.

"The cave!" Phillip yelled, grabbing May and pulling her toward Jack.

"The one that all those children never came *out* of?!" Jack yelled.

"We do not have much choice!" Phillip said, rushing in. "We can make a stand from within!"

"A stand against all *that*?!" May shouted, grabbing Jack's arm as he pushed himself to his feet, almost yanking him off them again with the force of her pull. "Is there an aircraft carrier in there or something I don't know about?!"

Phillip didn't respond as he led them into the cave, Jack's sword still flickering oddly but giving them enough light to see by as they pushed their way in deeper. Behind them the monsters hesitated at the mouth of the cave, only to surge forward once again at the Wolf King's orders. Jack struck out with his sword at the walls, and the glowing blade bit into the stone, huge chunks of which fell to block the way.

Well, that was that. He'd given them a reprieve from the monsters by trapping them inside the cave. Perfect.

"Where are we going?" Jack asked as he squeezed his way between two pillars of rock. Everything was slippery from some unknown water source, and just keeping his footing was hard.

"Remember what the villagers in that town said," Phillip said, still pulling May deeper into the cave in an annoying way. "The Piper stole their children away into a cave, and the children never emerged. They must have gone *somewhere!*"

"Or been killed by the Piper," May said, yanking her arm out of Phillip's grasp as she stopped.

Jack passed her by and grabbed her arm too, almost carrying her farther in. "The wolf must have gotten him," Jack said as he pushed on, "but if he were in here, I'd take a murderous old musician over the monsters behind us, even with your tendency to fall for his music."

"If he can make me not afraid like that again, I'll take a little murderousness," May said, but kept moving forward.

The cave, however, didn't. First Phillip, then Jack and May, practically slammed into a solid rock wall just a few feet in front of the spot where May had stopped.

The light from Jack's sword lit the wall enough to show an intricate black outline drawn in charcoal on the wall, one of the most realistic-looking doors Jack had ever seen drawn on a cave wall. Which, admittedly, wasn't a huge group to begin with, but still.

"Open it!" May shouted.

"The drawing?" Phillip asked in surprise.

"Oh, I'm sorry, I didn't realize you were an idiot," May said. "It's *magic*, Phillip." She shook her head in disgust, then reached out to grab the doorknob.

Instead her hand just smacked against the flat rock.

"I hate to side with the prince," Jack said, "but that was seriously just amazing to watch."

"Perhaps there is a way to make it real?" Phillip asked.

"Perhaps there's a way to speed this up?!" May shouted as they began to hear goblin voices again. Apparently Jack's cave-in hadn't done as much slowing down as he'd hoped.

"There's only one way the Piper would open his cave-wall-door drawing," Jack said, shrugging as he pulled out the pipes the wolf had left as a message on the stump. "Anyone know how to play these?"

"I played clarinet in elementary school," May said, grabbing the pipes. "So, no. But I'll try anyway." She brought the pipes to her lips and blew.

Jack and Phillip both cringed at the resulting screech.

"I think they're broken," May said.

"Yeah, it's the pipes' fault," Jack said.

"Let me," Phillip said, taking the pipes from May's hand and blowing gently into them.

This time a simple but beautiful melody filled the small room, but the drawing didn't change at all.

"That was even worse!" Jack lied, grabbing for the pipes himself. "Seriously, how hard can this be?"

"They're just ahead!" a goblin yelled from behind them.

"PLAY!" May said, smacking the door over and over with her hand.

Jack put the pipes to his lips and gently blew on them. At first the instrument squeaked worse than May's attempt, but he quickly realized his error and managed to work out a simple little melody. Except, it wasn't simple. There was something in the pipes, something just aching to be let loose, to be released into the world and fill everyone's heads with its beautiful music—

A horrible scraping sound broke Jack's concentration, and

the rock just to the right of the drawing of the door in front of them pushed open. Behind it, a fat middle-aged man wearing the clothes of a six- or seven-year-old child glared at them.

"Can you stop with the horrible music, please?" he said, shaking his head. "If you wanted in, why didn't you just knock?"

CHAPTER 7

U m," May said, and glanced first at the middle-aged man, then at his clothes, and then at Jack and Phillip. "I'm not the only one seeing this, right?"

May's "um" just about summed it up, but their only options were creepy adult or death by monster. Jack paused, weighing both choices, then sighed.

Death by monster *would* be quicker, but he wouldn't be able to live with himself. Literally.

"May we come in?" Jack asked the man, who was bobbing his head in boredom.

"Why, of course," the man said, giving him an odd look. "Everyone's welcome in the Land of Never!"

May stopped. "Please tell me that's not what I think that is.

'Cause I'm *not* flying to the first, second, or third star on the right, I don't care who's behind us."

"Stars?" the man said with confusion. "No, I said it's the Land of Never! Here you *never* grow up, you *never* get old, never hungry, never bored . . ."

"Never wear age-appropriate clothing," Jack muttered.

"It's like a dream!" the man finished.

They glanced at the man, then at one another, and all three sighed. Crazy man it was.

Phillip pushed May in through the stone doorway, then followed Jack a second later, and the man pulled the stone shut just as the goblin voices began shouting excitedly on the other side. They'd gotten in just in time, it sounded like.

Jack turned to thank their savior, then lost his train of thought when he saw where they were.

"Oh my," Phillip said, as speechless as the prince ever seemed to get.

"We could just give up and stay here, you know," May said, her voice quiet.

Jack just nodded, not sure how serious she was, and not really wanting to find out. Because if she *were* serious? He had a sinking feeling he'd be perfectly willing to stay here for the rest of his life.

"Nice, huh?" the fat man said, smiling almost shyly.

"Nice" didn't quite sum up the river of chocolate that several enormously fat middle-aged men and women were drinking from. "Nice" didn't do justice to the rainbow that other chubby men and women slid down, landing with joyful shrieks in piles of fluffy white clouds. And "nice" definitely didn't fit the mountains of gold and silver coins that a few of the men and women were tossing up and letting hit them on the head.

"It's everything your heart desires," the man told them. "We have chocolate rivers, the dirt is made out of cookie crumbs, and it rains gumdrops."

"I hope you learned your lesson at the witch's house," May whispered to Jack.

"I really hope I didn't," he whispered back absently. "Phillip, have you ever heard of the Land of Never?"

"I have not," Phillip said, watching with disgust as a four-hundred-pound man jogged by, chasing what looked to be a swarm of cakes with tiny wings flying just out of his reach. The jogging, unfortunately, was causing tiny earthquakes of fat to ripple all around the man's overweight body.

"Me either," Jack said. "And I really don't like not knowing what I'm getting into."

"There's a fountain in the middle of town that shoots toys into the air, not water," the man said, skipping forward in front of them, clearly not listening to their conversation. "Our beds tell us stories as we fall asleep. And that's only if you *want* to sleep. . . . The sun never sets in the Land of Never if we don't want it to!"

"Kinda like a summer in the arctic," May suggested.

The man crinkled his nose. "You're weird!"

"*You're* weird!" she shouted.

"Shut up!" he told her, his fists balled up at his sides. "Don't make fun of me!"

"Then don't come at me with all that stupid!" she yelled back.

The man fumed, apparently trying to think of something to say in return, but finally just smiled. "Oh, well," he said. "It's hard to stay angry in the Land of Never. And you know the best part?"

"The ill-fitting clothing?" May asked.

"You never get any older!" the man said proudly. "You never grow up! We were all kids when we got here, and that was years and years ago, like thirty or forty! But we never aged a day!"

The man dropped a hand into the chocolate river, then pulled it out and sucked on his fingers as Jack slowly backed away from him, grabbing May and Phillip as he went.

"Um," Jack said. "Everyone else sees a chubby older guy in his forties, right?"

"You forgot 'insane' in that description," May said.

"Perhaps we should not remain here long," Phillip suggested, his hand resting on his sword. "If these people truly believe they are children, there may be some magic at work."

"Want some?" the man asked, holding up a hand covered in chocolate.

"I'm gonna go with 'never,'" May said. "So . . . the Piper brought you all here?"

"Yup!" the man said. "He saved us from having to grow up into mean old adults. Adults have responsibilities, he said, like paying their debts. Here there's no responsibility at all!"

"That's a big word for such a little kid," Jack told him.

"I'm pretty smart," the man confided.

"I can see that," Jack said, winking at the man. "And someone as smart as you probably knows all the ways in and out of the Land of Never, doesn't he?"

"Of course!" the man said, beaming. "I like to be the gate-keeper, and let in anyone who knocks!"

"Do . . . a lot of people knock?" May asked him.

"You're the first!" he told her proudly. "And I was there waiting!"

"That's just the most amazing story we've ever heard," May told him. "You're the bestest! But we can't stay. Where's another one of those doors? Preferably one that opens in the direction that we're going."

"The Eastern Coast," Phillip told him.

"That's where the pirates are from!" the man said.

"Pirates?" Jack asked. "There aren't any pirates, not anymore. Not since the mermen started terrorizing the oceans."

"Of course there are pirates, stupid!" the man told him, shaking his head as he somehow irritated Jack more and more with every word. "We fight them sometimes, whenever we're feeling adventurous! There's never any end to the things to do in the Land of Never!"

"That's just a superfun story," May said. "Now, where's that way out again?"

"Way out?" The man looked confused. "No, the gates only come *in*. Once you enter the Land of Never, you can *never* leave!"

CHAPTER 8

L et's try that again," May said, her voice lowering dangerously. "'Cause if I thought for a minute that there really
was no way out of here, I'd kick your behind back to age seven
for reals."

The man looked scared. "Stop being mean! I just told you,
you can't leave, so you might as well get used to it! Why would
you even want to?"

"Okay, we're done here," May said. "We don't have time for this."

"You have plenty of time for this!" the fat man told her. "You
can't leave!"

Jack and Phillip both had to grab May before she punched
him. "We'll just go out the way we came in." Jack grunted as he
restrained May.

"Can't!" the man said with a smug smile. "It's one-way. Some of the kids tried at first, but it never worked."

"Where *is* here?" Phillip asked. He glanced up at the sky above them. "Obviously we are not in the Piper's cave anymore."

"It was some kind of magic teleporting," the man said. "Lots of doors lead here, but none lead out. Well, unless our leader says you can go, of course."

"Your leader?" May asked. "Is he a seventy-year-old who thinks he's eighteen?"

"Don't be stupid, stupid," the man said with a sneer, forcing Jack and Phillip to grab her again. "King Pan is a boy, just like me. But unlike me, he's being held by big nasty pirates!" The man seemed to consider that for a second. "Hmm, maybe it's time to go rescue him!"

"Sounds like a plan," Jack said, still struggling to hold on to May. "We'll rescue your king from pirates, and he'll thank us by letting us out of the Land of Never."

"YAY!" the man yelled, then turned around. "Hey everybody! We're gonna go on an adventure to rescue King Pan from the pirates! Come on!"

All around them middle-aged adults popped out of the oddest places. Some were covered in chocolate from swimming in the river, their candy-filled stomachs rippling as they ran toward the group, squealing in joy. Two others rode up on rocking horses, the horses neighing loudly. One even dropped from the sky after flying in on a pair of wings attached to shoulder straps.

"Good idea, Icky!" the gatekeeper said. "We'll *fly* over to the pirate ship! Get more wings!"

"Yes sir!" The man with wings said, and flew off for more.

"Pirates!" one of the adults yelled.

"It will be an epic battle!" shouted a second.

"I like their monkey!" a third said.

"Monkeys are funny!" the first one said.

"I've literally never been more irritated in my entire life," May told Jack loudly.

"They're just kids," he said, then thought about what he'd said, and shuddered.

"Who are these older kids?" one of the adult women asked.

"We are here on an adventure," Phillip told the woman politely. Apparently even the prince's patience was perfect, as he seemed to have no trouble keeping his manners in the midst of all the creepiness.

His answer sent a wave of excitement splashing through the adults, and the questions doubled.

"What's the adventure?"

"Where are you going?"

"Where are you from?"

"Are you fighting any dragons?!"

"Are you fighting any pirate monkeys?!"

And then, worst of all, one of the adults began to sing. "Here we are, without a slip, off to attack a pirate ship!"

"Pirate ship! Pirate ship!" two others began singing along. "Off to attack a pirate ship!"

May looked at Jack, her eyes filled with horror.

"Join us now, don't be a dip, come along to the pirate ship!" the first one sang.

"Pirate ship! Pirate ship!" the rest of the adults chimed in. "Come along to the pirate ship!"

"OH NO YOU ARE *NOT*!" May exploded. "I cannot take another second of this! Stop singing!" She turned to the adults, who had gone absolutely quiet and were now all cowering pathetically in front of her. "YOU. ARE. ADULTS. You are *not* children anymore!"

The adults looked at one another, one or two beginning to cry. "What are you talking about?" one said. "We're still kids. Look at us. Look at our clothes!"

"This, all of this? It's not *real*!" May shouted. "You're living here, pretending you're still kids, acting like you're still kids, acting like time is standing still, but it's obviously not!"

"May, there is obviously some magic—" Phillip began, but she interrupted him.

"I don't even care, Phillip! It's time for these kids to grow up! They're sitting here living a dream, but . . . but it's not REAL. You can't stay a kid forever, and you have to move on. I don't care how happy your life is, if it's not real, then it's worthless!"

Jack sighed. This wasn't about the adults, as weird as they were. This was about May and her grandmother.

A tear rolled down May's face, soon followed by more, but that just made a few of the adults point and laugh. "Oh, you did NOT just do that!" May said, leaping for the nearest giggling adult.

Five minutes later Jack, Phillip, and May stood alone, the adults having run off in terror.

"Perhaps we should return to finding our way out by rescuing their king?" Phillip said, pointing at the beach just ahead.

Off in the bay the sun shone on a large wooden ship flying a black flag with a happy, smiling skull. From onboard a group of friendly pirates waved at them, gesturing for them to come over.

"Have I mentioned how messed up all this is?" May asked.

"A few times," Jack said. "Those aren't even *close* to pirates."

"It is just like the rest of this land," Phillip said, staring in confusion at the kid-friendly pirate ship. "It is life from a child's perspective."

"I don't care whose perspective they're from," May told him. "I just want a way out to the boat so King Whatever can let us back to the real world. Or, you know, the messed-up version we were just in."

"There's no boat or anything," Jack said, pointing at the shore. "And we obviously can't swim."

"Why not?" May asked.

Phillip and Jack both turned and stared in surprise. "Mermen?!" they said in unison.

"Didn't we cover this already?" May asked with a sigh. "Yes, we saw some creepy stuff in the river near Malevolent's castle, but that was it. And why would you think there are mermen here, anyway?"

"I don't think there are mermen here," Jack said, his voice cracking. He pointed down at the shore. "I think there are mer*maids*."

There, just off the beach, were three mermaids sunning themselves on rocks, the prettiest vicious killers Jack had ever seen.

CHAPTER 9

Do you think they saw us?" Jack asked, pulling the other two to the ground to hide.

Phillip stuck his head up, then poked it back down. "Yes," he said. "In fact, they are waving as energetically as the pirates."

"Kind of a *Bring on our dinner* wave?" Jack asked.

"More of a *Hello, friends*-type wave," Phillip said. "But we should not trust them for even a second. The stories former fishermen tell—"

"You guys are idiots," May said. "They're just people with fish tails! That's it. Now, let's go say hi with more talking and less waving. Maybe they know where we can find a boat."

"May, no!" Jack whispered, grabbing her, but the princess

yanked her arm out of his grasp and walked purposefully down toward the mermaids.

"Hello!" she yelled, waving back awkwardly.

"Hello, child of man!" the mermaids replied together, practically singing. Even their voices were pretty.

"Those are some pretty spectacular tails you've got there," May said, admiring them. "So shiny. You're all so beautiful!"

The mermaids looked between one another with a *How adorable* look, then turned back to May, shaking their heads in disbelief.

"You are too kind!" the blond one said.

"Really, much too sweet!" the redhead said.

"You are quite beautiful yourself, young lady!" the brunette said.

"We're trying to get ourselves out to the pirate ship there," May told them. "Any chance you know where there's a boat or something?"

"A boat?" the redhead said.

"No, there are no boats, not on shore. The pirates have one, of course. Would that help?" the brunette asked.

"Um, no," May said. She threw a wide-eyed look of crazy back at Jack and Phillip that showed her polite manners were quickly cracking. "No, we need to get out *there*, so we'd need a boat or something on *this* side."

"That's quite a problem!" the blonde said.

"And the pirate's boat really won't work?" the brunette asked.

"Yeah, this was a bad idea," May said, turning back to Jack and Phillip.

Jack quickly yanked her back up the beach, as if the additional two feet would make her safer. Not that these mermaids seemed particularly bloodthirsty, but still. This land really was far too perfect.

"Miss Human Girl?" the redhead said.

May sighed and turned back. "Yes, Miss Mermaid Woman?"

The redhead giggled. "You're so funny! I was just going to say, what about swimming out to the boat?"

The other two mermaids looked at the redhead like she was some kind of genius. Jack narrowed his eyes, wondering how they managed to feed themselves if they were this stupid. Or was it some sort of act, lulling humans into the water, then attacking?

"We could try that," May said. "But it's awfully far, and these two haven't ever swam before."

"Also, humans can't breathe as easily underwater as we can above," the redhead informed the other two, who seemed surprised by the news. The redhead sat back, proud of her own knowledge.

"Well, we could help them with that," the blonde said.

"Yes, with our tears!" the brunette said.

"But we'd have to cry, then!" the redhead said.

"For the sake of our human friends, we really should," the blonde said. "Now, ladies, let us think of something sad."

"Whaaaaaat is going on?" May whispered out of the corner of her mouth.

"I'm sort of comforted by the fact that I can't figure it out," Jack responded.

The mermaids went silent for a moment, their foreheads all creased with their effort to apparently be sad. But the moment quickly passed, and soon the three burst out in giggles. "I simply can't think of anything upsetting!" the brunette said.

"If I knew why they were doing this, I could totally give them something to be upset about," May whispered.

"Don't interrupt," Jack told her. "Their whole thought process seems fragile enough. Let's see where it's going."

"Oh, this is so sad that we can't think of anything sad!" the brunette said, then paused. Finally she gasped. "Oh! *That* is sad!"

And just like that, a single tear rolled down her cheek. She gently put a finger up to catch it, then dropped it into her palm. Each of the other two sniffed a bit, apparently at how sad it was that they couldn't cry, and both cried a single tear as well, while the brunette cried a second, apparently not able to stop.

May turned to Jack, her mouth hanging open. "I . . . I just . . . I just *hate* this place," she said, sounding surprised at her own feelings.

"You've mentioned that."

As soon as each had her tear, the mermaids' smiles instantly returned. "Now, humans, you will be able to breathe as easily as we do underwater!" the brunette said. "That way, if you can't swim, you can just walk over to the boat!"

"Um, how would your tears let us breathe underwater?" May asked.

The mermaids looked at one another in confusion. "That is their power," the blonde said. "Why would you ask such a thing? It's like asking why the sun giant drops his fireball into the ocean at the end of every day. It's magic!"

May dropped her face into her palms, apparently trying to cover her eyes from all the stupidity. "*No*, actually, it's science. But this is *so* not the time. I'm willing to try anything. How long will they last?"

"One day, no more," the brunette mermaid said mysteriously.

"Oh yeah? Why's that?" May asked.

The mermaids again looked uncomfortable. "Magic?" they finally said, almost questioningly.

Phillip stepped in front of May. "Do we really trust these mermaids?" he asked her and Jack quietly. "They seem far too eager to help."

"It's the Land of Never," Jack said, unsure himself. "They seem to be kid-friendly mermaids, so . . . maybe?"

"I like your confidence," May told Jack, walking over to one of the mermaids and gently picking up a somehow semi-solid tear. "So, what do we do with these? Put them in our eyes or something?"

The mermaids all looked at one another and laughed. "Of course not, silly!" the brunette said. "You swallow them!"

"'Cause that makes more sense," May said.

Phillip reached out and closed his hand over May's. "If you insist upon going through with this, Princess, I shall take the first one, just to see if it's safe."

"Yeah," Jack said. "Let Phillip go first. If he dies, then we'll figure something else out."

Phillip shook his head in disappointment at Jack, then took the tear from May's hand and quickly swallowed it. "Hmm. Salty," the prince said, making a face. "But how do I know if it worked?"

Jack pointed at the water with a smile. "Only one way to find out!"

Phillip just looked at him. "You are enjoying this a bit too much, I think."

"I think so too," Jack said. "Quit wasting time, though. Get to drowning already."

With that, Phillip slowly approached the water, watching the mermaids warily. When they didn't move, only smiled encouragingly, he lay down on the sand, leaned into the water, and dunked his head.

A minute passed.

"Do you think we should check on him?" Jack whispered to May, but just then Phillip jerked his head out of the water. Half-expecting the prince to suck in an enormous breath, Jack was a bit surprised to see him breathing normally.

"Quite right," Phillip said. "Astonishingly, I had no trouble filling my lungs beneath the water, at least not once I had the courage to take a breath. That took the most time, making myself breathe in."

"That's crazy!" May said. "And you didn't even cough up water!"

"I am not sure I breathed any in," Phillip said. "I do not pretend to understand the magic, but the water felt just like air to my mouth."

"My turn," May said, taking a second tear from one of the other mermaids and swallowing it. She immediately gagged, but jogged over to the water as well, lay down, and dunked her head in. A moment later she kicked her feet and yelled something, but whatever it was didn't make it out of the water intact.

"She's so easily impressed," Jack told the clapping mermaids, then reached over for the last remaining tear. . . . Wait, hadn't there been four? He must have miscounted. He took the tear, then swallowed it. The other two were right. The tears were almost unbearably salty. In fact, Jack almost heaved it back up, but managed to keep it down somehow. Just to test the magic, Jack knelt down next to May and dunked his head under the water too.

It did feel like water. His head still rose and fell from the little waves May was making, and he was definitely wet. But when Jack opened his mouth to breathe in, it felt no different to him than air.

"We're breathing underwater!" May said to him, and this time he heard her clearly. "This is *so* cool."

"Wow, I had no idea drowning you was all it took to get you back in a good mood!" Jack said, grinning at her.

"Yeah, 'cause why worry about the fact that we're stuck here if we can dunk our heads in water as long as we want?"

Jack laughed. "I only wish I could get stuck here a few more times just to enjoy it longer!"

"I think you might want to look up the meaning of the word 'stuck,'" May said, splashing him—or really just pushing water at him. Splashing didn't exactly work underwater.

"Hello, humans!" the redhead mermaid said beneath the waves from far too close a distance. "Are you having fun?"

"More than we should be," May told her as Jack unconsciously backed away from the mermaid's large fangs. He'd seen them earlier, but somehow being this close magnified them in his mind by about a thousand.

"I'm so glad!" the mermaid said. "And now, prepare to have even *more*! Your fellow children have just returned, ready to go to battle. It promises to be a grand adventure!"

Jack and May looked at each other, then slowly lifted their heads to find Phillip surrounded by giggling middle-aged adults covered in war paint and mismatched pieces of armor, pointing swords at the prince.

"I declare you older kids to all be pirate spies!" the man who'd opened the door for them shouted. "And what do we do with pirate spies?"

"Put them to death!" yelled the adults happily.

"Death by what?" the man yelled.

"Walking the plank!" the rest screamed.

"Take them to the pirate ship! They die as soon as King Pan is freed!"

The children began laughing and dancing all around them happily, until one of the larger men stomped over to May.

"Will you be our mother?" the man asked in a quiet, almost shy voice.

"And *there* we go," May said.

CHAPTER 10

Well, at least we know we won't drown if we walk the plank," Jack said over his shoulder to Phillip and May as the adults, all wearing Icky's wings, carried them—belongings and all—over the water toward the happiest-looking pirates Jack had ever seen. Not that he'd ever seen any, but by the definition of pirates being, you know, pillaging and plundering types, big friendly smiles didn't seem to fit.

"We'll have to sneak in!" shouted the man holding Jack. "Let's just hope the prisoners don't alert the pirates to our approach!"

"Yeah, we wouldn't want to ruin the surprise," Jack said as a pirate winked jauntily at him.

"I can see King Pan tied to the mainmast!" the adult holding May shouted.

"My warriors!" called a loud and clear voice from the pirate ship. "Free me that I might face this scourge of pirates with you!"

"Aye, aye, King Pan!" the adults all yelled, then turned and flew straight at the pirate ship.

"What happened to surprise!" Jack shouted in terror as they dove at a speed virtually guaranteeing death.

Fortunately, whatever magic held the wings aloft gave them some incredible stopping power, letting the adults all pull up at the last second and land gently on the pirate ship deck.

"Oh ho!" shouted a man in a long red coat, black curls spilling forth from beneath a red hat. "What have we here? More of King Pan's warriors?!" He pointed at the adults with a long sword, only there was no hand holding the sword, just a long, curved hook somehow connected to the sword's hilt.

"It's Captain Sword!" the adults shouted.

"You can't handle Captain Sword yourselves, my friends!" King Pan yelled. "Free me, and I shall duel him to the death!"

And then Jack got his first look at King Pan. Of all the inhabitants of the Land of Never, this was the first actual child he'd seen. The boy looked far too happy, with a smile that spread just about from ear to ear, revealing more teeth than anyone had a right to. He was dressed in different shades of green and had random feathers stuck in his hair, whether on purpose or from having just ended up there over the course of an adventurous day, Jack had no idea.

"Attack, my pirates!" Captain Sword yelled, and his friendly group of buccaneers launched a rather clumsy, pathetic attack at Pan's now apparently skilled adults, each of whom seemed to have no difficulty fighting off their pirate attacker. Pirate after pirate lost their duel, usually in some humiliating way, with Pan's adults smacking the pirates in the behinds with their swords, tying their shoes together, or even flying around the pirates in circles until the pirates grew too dizzy to stand up straight. All the while, King Pan narrated the battle as if he were watching it from a distance, not happily stuck in the middle.

"Pobsy, duck, you almost lost your head! Oh, Charlotte, I've never seen a pirate vanquished so quickly! You were just promoted to Field Captain General Lieutenant Princess! Gregory, behind you, BEHIND YOU!"

Contrary to the gripping commentary, Gregory was not, in fact, in any trouble, and while he handled his pirate, Charlotte and a few others made their way over to Pan to untie him.

Jack secretly hoped that freeing the obnoxious little kid would finally shut him up, but it seemed to make it worse. Grabbing a sword from one of his adults, Pan launched himself at Captain Sword, almost taking flight without wings, he moved so fast.

Captain Sword rather pathetically attempted a defense, but Pan just slapped the pirate's sword away, toying with him, teasing him with his sword until finally, almost mercifully, knocking him to the ship's floor.

"Tie our pirate prisoners up!" King Pan declared. "They'll walk the plank unless they lead us to their gold!"

"The mountains of gold back on shore just not cutting it anymore?" Jack asked.

Pan slowly turned to stare at the three of them, his look changing from surprise to something . . . scarier. "Well, look what we have here," Pan said, his voice dropping lower. "*Visitors.* Who might these old folks be?"

"Old?!" May said.

"Pirate spies, Your Majesty!" one of Pan's adults said.

"Then, they must know who *I* am!" King Pan said, smiling his creepy wide smile. "King Pan, the Slayer of the Deadly Sun Dial Crocodile! King Pan, the Premier and First Explorer of Skull Face! King Pan, the Only Boy to Ever Face the Fearsome Pirates of the Land of Never Bay and Live to Tell About It!"

"Must be a pain signing your name, huh?" May said.

The boy pulled a knife out of nowhere and tossed it between his hands. "*You* may just call me . . . King Pan!" He turned to the adults around him. "Well?"

Ragged cheers for King Pan sounded from the adults, and the boy nodded in satisfaction before turning back to Jack. "And you, my pirate spies, my Invaders of the Land of Never-Invade-My-Lands, if you do not bow before me this very instant, you shall suffer my displeasure. BY DYING!" Pan sneered. "And THEN I'll think of something TRULY horrible to do to you!"

Jack sighed. "Listen, I'd love to play out this whole little fantasy thing you've got going, 'cause it's adorable and all, but we really don't have time for this. Can you just show us how to get out of the Land of Never, and we'll leave you to your playtime?"

Gasps came from the adults. "You do *not* speak like that to Pan!" one shouted.

"*King* Pan," the boy said beneath his breath, his eyes locked on Jack's. "But you're right. No one speaks to me this way." The knife turned to point at Jack's heart. "I do believe you have just challenged me to a duel!"

"Nope, I really didn't," Jack said, holding up his hands in surrender. "Seriously, I don't want to hurt you. We're not going to duel."

"Challenge accepted!" King Pan said, laughing with a touch of the crazy as the children-adults separated, forming a circle around King Pan and Jack, Phillip, and May.

"Why don't you put the knife away before you hurt yourself?" Jack said gently, putting a hand out to reach for it.

Immediately the boy lunged, stabbing at Jack's hand. Jack quickly yanked his hand away, glaring right back at the boy now. "Oh, *really?*" he said to King Pan.

"Jack, I'm scared," May said, grinning at him. "I don't want the ten-year-old to hurt you!"

"I won't hurt him," King Pan said, smiling widely again, this time pointing all his teeth at May. "I'll just *kill* him. Don't worry, however. He won't suffer."

"How about we don't go that way," Jack said, not liking the look in the crazy kid's eyes. "Why don't we do a different kind of challenge?"

This seemed to confuse the boy. "Different than a duel to the death? What else could there be?"

Jack sighed again. "How about a challenge of wits?"

Pan brightened. "YES! We shall do exactly that. A challenge of wits. Agreed?"

"Uh, yes, I just suggested it, so agreed," Jack said. "Whoever loses has to do anything the winner says. Agreed?"

King Pan's eyes lit up like someone had poured lamp oil onto a candle in a fire. "Agreed! The challenge shall be that we each declare three rules. Then, restrained by those rules, we shall fight to the death!"

"Wait, that's not—"

"The first rule!" King Pan interrupted. He glanced slyly at his adult followers, then turned back to Jack. "The first rule is . . . in this duel, you will not have your right hand to use your sword. Instead, you'll have a HOOK!"

Jack rolled his eyes. "Wow, you've got a real thing for hooks, don't you?" He glanced down at his right hand, only to lose all sensation in his stomach.

At the end of his arm was a black iron hook.

"MY HAND!" Jack screamed, holding the hook in horror.

"Grab them!" King Pan yelled, and the adults locked their arms around Phillip and May as the other two surged forward at Jack's cry. "You agreed to the duel! You have only yourself to blame, pirate spy!"

Jack's mouth dropped open, and he just stared at the boy. How had Pan done such powerful magic? This was no ordinary kid! And seriously, what was with his fascination with hooks?!

King Pan turned to his silent followers. "Well?"

Another round of ragged cheering, and the boy's smile grew wider, if that were possible. "Now, your first rule for me?"

Jack gritted his teeth, staring at his missing hand, then at the boy in front of him. "My first rule is that I have my HAND BACK!"

"Ah, no canceling out other people's rules," Pan said, shaking his head with the same creepy grin. "As forgiving as I am, however, I will give you another chance to make your rule. But that is your only warning!"

"I . . . I want to consult with my . . . with my fellow pirate spies about my first rule," Jack said, still not able to get past the fact that *his hand was gone!*

"No," the boy said. "Permission denied. Unless . . . unless you want to use a rule?"

"Yes," Jack said quickly. "My first rule is that I get to talk to a friend before making any further rules."

"So be it!" King Pan declared, and Jack stepped over to May, shaking his new hook at the adults holding her back, until they let her go and retreated a small distance so as to not overhear. He whispered something to her, gesturing at his bag with his hook hand, then returned to the center of the circle.

"Now, on to my second rule!" the boy declared. "For this duel you shall . . . BE BLIND!"

Instantly, all the light emptied out of the world like water pouring out of a glass. Jack gave an anguished cry, and threw his nonhook hand up, feeling around for something to orient himself, but the mocking laughter seemed to come from all around him.

"NO!" May yelled. "Pan, we forfeit! Put him back to normal!"

"No backing out!" King Pan shouted joyfully, his voice coming from somewhere to Jack's side. "Now, your second rule?"

"My . . . second rule," Jack said, his heart racing. Was he really going to be giving up his life for some kid's game?! "My second rule is that this duel *isn't* to the death!"

"Rule forfeited!" King Pan declared happily. "As I said, you cannot contradict a previous rule of the duel, and therefore you give up your second rule."

"Please, Pan, let him give up!" May shouted, her voice from somewhere behind Jack.

"Giving up is for quitters!" King Pan declared. "Now, my final rule?" Jack could practically hear him smile as widely as was humanly—or whatever he was—possible. "My final rule . . . is that you shall be totally and completely paralyzed, unable to move."

Immediately, Jack's entire body froze, and he toppled over

onto his face, his body as stiff as a board, and just as motionless.

Well, *that* was going to make it hard to win.

"NO!" May yelled.

From the other side Jack could hear Phillip struggling against the adults as more and more piled onto the prince. But unfortunately, hearing was all he could do at this point, and that wasn't much help to anyone.

"And now," King Pan said from just above his head. "What is *your* final rule?"

Jack tried desperately to say something, anything, but his mouth wouldn't move any more than the rest of his body. He couldn't even blink to spell it out in code.

"No final rule?" the boy said gleefully. "Why, you're forfeiting two rules in a row! I have to say, you're awfully confident in your ability to win this battle of wits!"

"He doesn't forfeit his final rule!" May said. "He told me what it was going to be!"

King Pan paused. "What? What do you mean?"

"During his first rule!" May shouted. "He told me what his final rule would be!"

King Pan sounded confused. "But, but you cannot prove what he did or did not say."

"Yes, I can," May said. "Look." Jack could hear her rummaging through his bag, and pulling out just what he'd told her to. "See? This is a Story Book. It accurately describes whatever is told to it. And Jack told me and the Book what he wanted his last rule to be."

"LIES!" King Pan shouted.

"TRUTHS!" May shouted right back, and Jack heard her flipping pages before giving a triumphant cry. "HA! See? Wanna read it out loud for the literacy-impaired middle-aged children out here?"

"'Jack spoke to May in a whisper,'" King Pan read painfully slowly. "'"This is crazy. What he says comes true," Jack said to her. "And look at that creepy little smile. You know the little monster's gonna play dirty."'"

Here, King Pan stopped. "MONSTER?"

"Keep reading, you little monster," May told him.

"'"Now, if he does play dirty, and for some reason I can't give my last rule," Jack told May and his Story Book, "here it is, and if he doesn't believe it, just show him the Story Book. It'll prove this is my last rule."'"

King Pan took a deep breath and finished reading. "'"My last rule," Jack said, "is that King Pan has to *lose* the duel of wits."'"

CHAPTER 11

Light flooded over Jack, and all his limbs relaxed all at once. He pushed himself unsteadily to his feet, then smiled at the not-so-smug boy sitting in front of him.

"But . . . but I can't lose," Pan said, throwing his hands up impotently. "Not Emperor Pan the First, Benevolent Ruler and Most Handsome Boy in All the Land."

"Don't worry," Jack said. "As Emperor Jack the First, Pretty Irritated Ruler but Not Too Bad a Guy Honestly, I won't have you executed. BUT." Jack picked Pan up by his shirt and looked him straight in the eye. "BUT you do need to follow through on your deal. You do as *I* say now. To start, you're going to end whatever magic is keeping these adults here. They're no longer kids. They need to grow up . . . or at least realize that they did, like, forty years ago."

"But no one has to grow up in the Land of Never!" Pan whined.

"Well, okay, then we can go to my second option," Jack told him. "In that case, I exile you forev—"

"FINE!" Pan shouted. "I'll end all my spells!"

The boy didn't make a move, but suddenly Jack heard gasps all around him.

"I'm . . . I'm old!" one of the adults shouted.

"You *are* old!" another said. "Wait, so am I!"

"And fat!" a third said. "How did we get like this?! I thought we could eat sweets all day and never change!"

"You idiots. You think even magic can make that possible?" Pan asked them crankily. "You're all stupid stupidheads that I didn't have fun with anyway!"

Jack glanced at the boy, starting to reprimand him, then noticed that the adults weren't the only thing that had changed. Whereas he'd been holding a human boy just moments before, now he held a half-goat, half-human creature.

"Gah!" Jack yelled, dropping Pan to the ground.

"Ow!" Pan said, rubbing his behind. "What!"

"Oh wow, he's a . . . whatever those things are!" May said, pointing and snapping her fingers over and over as she tried to remember.

"A satyr," Phillip said quietly. "Mischievous, yet usually harmless, as they are mostly too preoccupied seeking their own pleasure to cause any real trouble."

"I wasn't going to hurt anyone!" Pan yelled.

"Except ME!" Jack said, poking himself hard in the chest. A little too hard, to be honest, but the point had to be made. "ME you were going to *kill!*"

"Oh, you're fine, you big crybaby," Pan said. "Now, didn't you say something about having to go?"

"I want my mother!" one of the men said.

"Me too! I want to go home!" said one of the women.

"NO!" Pan yelled. "You'll all ruin everything! I need you to stay here and play with me!"

"I think it's about time they went home to their parents," Jack told him. "Let them go."

"NO!" Pan shouted. "NO, NO, NO, NO, NO! You can't just leave me like this!"

"You lost," May pointed out. "You have to do what Jack says now."

Pan glared at her, then back at Jack, his eyes filled with fire and hate. "Fine. Go! All of you, go!" He waved his hands, and one by one the kids seemed to fold in on themselves like paper folding in half, disappearing into thin air.

"I don't even care!" Pan continued, stamping his feet and waving his arms dramatically." Just leave me here all alone! You'll beg me to let you back into the Land of Never, but I won't! The Land of Never *never* wants you back!"

"Yeah, they'll probably be okay with that," Jack told him. "And you better have sent them back to their real homes. No tricks."

"You're so suspicious!" Pan told him indignantly. "You won. I am honor bound to do what you say. Now you go too. I'll send you away, just GO."

Jack held up a hand. "Not just yet. First, we need you to end a magic spell for us."

Now Pan looked at him suspiciously. "What *kind* of spell?"

"The kind that puts an entire city of fairy queens to sleep," May told him.

Pan laughed loudly. "Next you'll tell me to do away with the Wicked Queen! Seriously, get out of my lands."

"The princess is not joking," Phillip said. "We need you to dispel a curse—"

"You think a satyr can do that kind of magic?" Pan shouted. "If I could, you think I'd need to *trick* those kids into thinking they'd never aged? All we can do is illusion and some minor transportation spells; you'd learn those too if you had to walk around on these legs. But any spell that can take out a fairy queen is going to need someone equally as powerful, and there are *very* few of those people left."

"Give us names," Jack said.

"The Wicked Queen," Pan said, counting on his fingers. "And . . . that's it. Otherwise you'll need a fairy queen or an Ifrit or something."

"I vote 'pass' on the Ifrit," May said, raising her hand.

"Looks like its Malevolent after all," Jack said, glancing over at Phillip, who winced at her name. It'd been three months since the evil fairy queen had caused the prince so much pain, but the memory didn't go away as easily as the wounds had under her magic.

Pan's look went from indignant to curious. "Why would you ever want Malevolent's help?"

"None of your business," May told him.

Pan brightened immediately. "But that sounds like an adventure!" He leapt to his feet, landing as a human boy once more. "And there's no one as heroic and adventuresome as Prince Pan the Pantheist!"

"I'm pretty sure that doesn't mean what you think it means," May told him.

"It SHOULD," Pan told her.

"You're not coming," Jack said. "Just send us to her castle."

Pan laughed again. "She's not there. No one is. No one's heard from her in months!"

"So we'll find her," Jack said, quickly growing irritated with the creature, and he'd started pretty irritated already.

"She's hiding from the Wolf King," Pan said with a sneer. "If *he* can't find her, then you're less than out of luck. You've got zero luck. You've got *negative* zero luck!"

"Sounds about right," May said.

"So find us another fairy queen, there have to be more," Jack said. "Give us a name and a location, and we'll leave."

"If something took out the Fairy Homelands, there *are* no more," Pan said. "Twelve queens, minus Malevolent the Exiled, and you've got eleven, all living on high in their magical land, not letting anyone in who can't hold a tune." He kicked at the deck of the ship. "Stupid musical magic."

Jack's heart sunk. "They can't have all been there. One or two *must* have—"

"Well, there's the one who gave it all up, of course," Pan said.

"But she's a special case. And if you want *her* name, you'll have to beat me in another—"

Before he could finish, May leaped forward and punched him in the face. Pan fell backward to sit down hard on the deck of the pirate ship, completely stunned. Finally he looked up.

"Fair enough," he said. "Her name is Mariella, but no one calls her that, not anymore. Not since she fell in love with the Sea King and gave up her fairyness to be with him." Pan frowned theatrically. "Now she's the called the Sea Witch by the merfolk. Terribly tragic story. The Sea King didn't love her in return, despite the fact that she'd turned herself into a mermaid for him."

"Are you sure that's how the story goes?" May asked with a frown.

"Yes, stupid girl," Pan said, rubbing his cheek where she'd hit him. "The fairy queen became a mermaid. It's the first time anyone ever actively chose to go fish."

May snorted, while from behind them someone stirred against the ship's cabin.

"What's that ye be sayin'?" the pirate captain, Captain Sword, asked. Jack had almost forgotten the pirate crew was still tied up.

Pan sighed. "Our game is over. Go home. These people ruined it all for you. I'll apologize for them, since they seem to be completely without manners."

"What's that about the Sea Witch and the Sea King again?" Captain Sword asked, pushing himself to his feet. Now that Pan's magic had worn off, the man looked both older and hairier. A beard ran down almost to his waist, with streaks of darkish blue throughout. His clothes, once regal and red, now were entirely black, covered in a black coat. On top of his head sat a three-sided hat, and at his waist was a wicked-looking sword.

"Oh, be quiet already!" Pan shouted, not even looking at the man.

The pirate growled, then flexed his arms, and the ropes tied around him burst, freeing him. Not a second later, the former Captain Sword held a real sword in his now restored hand to Pan's throat.

"Who . . . who are you?" Pan screeched.

The pirate roared, and slammed Pan against the side of the boat. "I'm yer death if ye don't answer me question! And yer death be named Captain Bluebeard! Now, where can I find the Sea King?!"

Jack and Phillip both gasped. Captain Bluebeard, the man so wanted by kingdoms without number that he had to dye his beard blue to disguise his true identity? The pirate so evil he married, then killed *dozens* of women, just for their dowries? The creature so horrendous even the sea itself was said to reject him?

If it were possible, Pan's eyes grew even wider. "I . . . I know you! You're the pri—"

"NOT ANYMORE!" Captain Bluebeard roared, and picked Pan up bodily with one hand. "Ye've run out of time, little man! I'd make ye walk the plank, but it won't be easy walkin' with no legs to do it with!"

"Wait, let's talk about this!" Jack shouted. "We need him still!"

With no warning at all the pirate's other hand flew out and smashed Jack in the face, sending him spinning around to crash into the railing that extended around the side of the boat. Jack hit the railing hard, doubling over it to look out over the water.

And there, staring up at him, were the three mermaids who'd given them their tears earlier.

Except now all traces of friendliness were gone. Now they just looked hungry.

"Grab him!" the brunette hissed.

The redheaded mermaid exploded out of the water high enough to grab Jack's shirt with both hands. She pulled him up and over the ship's rail, then they both fell back to the water, disappearing under the waves.

CHAPTER 12

C aptain!" a pirate yelled. "The boy!"

"Jack!" May shouted, and ran for the side . . . only for Phillip to stop her.

"Mermaid tear," the prince mouthed, and May nodded.

"Jack!" May shouted again. "Oh, I am so upset that you're overboard. I just hope that you can survive!" She winked at Phillip, who was looking at her oddly. She shrugged in response. Whatever was going on, it might not hurt to have someone who could do some rescuing if the situation called for it.

"Ah, one less of ye to worry about," Bluebeard said without a trace of a smile. "Tie up the other two, lads, and then we'll set about learnin' what we need to know from this Pan!"

Weighted fishing nets appeared out of nowhere, falling

straight at them. The weighted sides of the net slammed down onto the deck, crashing May and Phillip down to the wooden planks, Phillip landing beneath May.

Through the holes in the net, May watched booted feet walk away with a screaming Pan, while other booted feet ran around, following the captain's orders. And then an extremely non-booted foot stopped right in front of May's face. That foot was so non-booted, in fact, it was just bone.

"It's *supposed* to be a peg leg," May said, shaking her head. "Your whole stupid magical world can't get anything right, can it?"

The pirate with the bone foot bent down and looked at May with what appeared to be his one good eye. "The man I took this from weren't usin' it, lovey. Why use a peg when I can get meself the whole foot?"

"'Cause feet don't work that way!" she yelled. "Where are the ligaments, the muscles, the tendons! You can't walk on bones! There's nothing holding them together. The bones would all just fall apart!"

He smiled, showing off a mouth with only two teeth, and those on opposite sides. "Intimidatin', though, ain't it?" The one eye rolled over Phillip and May, and the smile dropped. "The captain wants me to be a'questionin' you two. I assume your friend, the one who just disappeared 'low the waves, won't be doin' much talkin'. . . not if he be a'drowned."

"He wasn't much of a friend," May said. "Right, Phillip?"

"Ah," the prince said, and too late May realized that she'd never heard him lie before. "Um," he continued, but stopped as May elbowed him hard. "We are on an urgent mission," Phillip said finally. "If you let us go, you will have our thanks."

"I'll have yer thanks?" Bone Foot said. "What would I be wantin' those for? Thanks ain't no currency I never heard of! Now, get to explainin' why you be needin' a fairy queen!"

"It's a long story," May told him. "We need a dress for the ball and can't find any in our size. Is there someone else around we could talk to, someone who's not using a bunch of disconnected bones as a foot?"

"Perhaps the captain?" Phillip said.

"No one's speakin' to anyones till I'm ready for ye to be," the pirate said, poking at May with a bone hand. Really, a bone hand too? Yeah, there was no *way* that could work. "And I'm not bein' done with ye yet. Now, how did ye end up in the Land of Never?"

"How do you think?" May yelled. "One of the little kid adults let us in! Did you not notice that Pan hated us just as much as you? Also, I refuse to accept that you can point with bones not connected by anything!"

A few more of the smelliest, dirtiest, and beardiest men May had ever seen approached the net. Those men with eyes glared meanly at them. Those missing eyes just eye-patched them, but equally as meanly.

"Maybe ye were fightin' the Pan and maybe ye weren't," the pirate with the skeleton limbs said, raising an eyebrow as he poked May in the leg. "Where's yer proof?"

She kicked back hard, but ended up hitting Phillip instead.

"They're allies o' the Pan!" a pirate yelled from beyond May's vision.

"They're all goat people too, more than likely!" another yelled.

"Let's cut 'em up and see!" a third yelled, this one brandishing a nasty-looking curved knife.

"QUIET, you bilge rat-eatin' swine!" roared a voice, and the pirates instantly went silent. The group split apart, revealing Captain Bluebeard, now extremely Pan-less.

"Cap'n Bluebeard, sir," Bone Foot said, respectfully lowering his head. "They claim to have no nothin' with the Pan, Cap'n. That said, we ain't been seeing proof as of yet."

"Does they now, Skinny," Captain Bluebeard declared, his

eyes twinkling as he lay one hand on the hilt of the sword at his waist. "And yet, the Pan just claimed that he knows who these children be, just as he knows of me. Says they're important types to some important-type person. How would he have been goin' about gettin' such information about two children without any alliance with 'em?"

"As a prince, I cannot lie, Captain," Phillip said. "You may take me at my word. We are just as much victims of Pan as your crew was."

The crew gasped, and May slapped her forehead. The prince sometimes wasn't the most worldly of . . . well, anyone.

"A prince?" Bluebeard said, a smirk growing in his beard like some kind of fungus. "Some mighta believed it not bein' in their best interest to tell a bunch of pirates such as me crew that ye be royalty, and therefore in the care o' rich parents that might be a'payin' to see that head still attached to that neck of yours."

"PHILLIP," May shouted, pushing the now-shocked prince backward before he could say anything to make things worse. "LET ME HANDLE THIS. Listen, Captain Pirate Guy. We're on a deadline here, so save the ransom threats for later, okay? You can do whatever you want to Pan. I might even help you. But you heard us say we needed the help of a fairy queen, and we do, urgently. Right now it sounds like the only one is underwater, right where you stuck our other friend." May tried to look sad, faking grief over Jack's fake death, but his absence did worry her. How long did it take to swim back to the surface? Was he okay down there? Or was he planning some elaborately stupid rescue that would get them all killed?

The last one. Of course.

"Ye be in luck, then, girl," the captain said, his eyes twinkling dangerously. "It just so happens that I be lookin' for something down beneath the waves as well. So maybe there be some sort of agreement we could come to?"

"Agreement?" May asked, her eyes narrowing suspiciously. "Like what kind of agreement? If you need money, we can get it . . . eventually. His castle isn't exactly close, but . . ."

"Oh, no money," Bluebeard said, leaning down to look her right in the eye. "No, I want something much more valuable from ye two. I want the Sea Witch too. And you're gonna bring her to me."

CHAPTER 13

Two mermaids dragged Jack farther underwater as the last one watched to see if there was someone following them, probably to keep anyone from sharing their meal.

"Let me go!" Jack yelled, and just like before it was as if he were speaking in air, not underwater. The mermaids' tears were really something . . . not that there seemed to be any danger of the mermaids crying now. Unless they were sad from their stomachaches after eating him whole.

"Oh, stop struggling," the blonde said as she dragged him down. "One merperson is as strong as three of you people."

"Or four of *you*, specifically," the brunette said from his other arm, shaking her head in disgust.

"I get it," Jack said. "You're going to try to kill me with

subtle insults. I'm not stupid. I caught that one. I see what you did there."

"We've got a real genius on our hands, sisters," the redheaded mermaid said from above them. "How ever will we outthink him?"

Jack glared up at her. "Listen, last time I talked to you three, you were all two oars short of having any oars, so I don't want to hear it."

One of the mermaids holding him smacked him hard in the back of the head with her tail. "That was Pan's illusion, you idiot," the blonde said as they approached the seafloor. "You really believed we were that stupid?"

Jack looked at her, and decided not to answer.

Her eyes narrowed. "I really wish we *were* going to eat you, just for that."

Jack suddenly felt some hope again. "Wait, you're not going to?"

"Use smaller words, Sisters," the redheaded mermaid said. "This one's slower than the Southern Current."

The other two mermaids laughed a bit at that, which irritated Jack. "I bet that's the fastest current in the world," he told them as they dropped him to the seafloor.

"It moves backward," the blonde told him, sitting herself on a rock to one side of him while the brunette and the redhead settled themselves around him as well. "Which seems about right in your case."

"But we didn't bring you down here to point out how unintelligent you are," the brunette said. "That was more just a special treat. We need your help."

"And *this* is how you ask for it?!" Jack shouted.

"Let's eat him," the blonde said. "I don't care if it does mean war, it's not worth talking to this land monkey anymore."

"Aren't all monkeys land monkeys?" Jack asked.

"That's it, he's mine!" the blonde said as she grabbed him and yanked him backward. Fortunately, her two sisters pulled them apart and calmed her down.

"Maybe *you* should just play what we call the quiet game," the redheaded mermaid told Jack after everyone had calmed down. Jack started to speak, then just nodded. This wasn't the first time he'd had this effect on people.

"Pan brought us here almost forty years ago," the brunette mermaid told him. "He needed . . . actors for his adventures with the children. He found us and that pirate ship above."

"We were begging Bluebeard to stay away from our father, the Sea King," the redhead said.

"Your father?" Jack asked. "You're mermaid princesses?"

"He's talking! He's talking! I'm gonna eat him!" the blonde shouted.

"YES," the brunette said, answering Jack's question while keeping a close eye on her sister. "But try to stay with me. Bluebeard wants something, something our father wants to keep away from him at any cost. And when I say 'any cost,' I mean my father would be willing to wipe out your entire species to keep this thing away from Bluebeard."

"Wipe us out?" Jack said. "But we're already staying out of the ocean . . . right now being an exception. How could he hurt us?"

"You don't want to know," the brunette said, shivering. "He's done magical experiments with sharks that would give you nightmares."

"Either way, that's something you won't have to worry about, as long as you keep Bluebeard away from our lands," the redhead said. "This isn't a threat, it's a warning. We don't want humanity destroyed any more than you do. You're cute, like little talking pets to us."

Jack narrowed his eyes, then shrugged. "Yeah, fair enough, we are pretty cute. So what's this thing that the pirate's looking for? And how do I keep him away from it?"

The mermaids looked at one another. "It's not some*thing* so much as some*one*," the redhead said. "Specifically, our sister."

"He wants a mermaid?" Jack said, eyebrows rising in surprise.

"Just be quiet and listen," the redhead said. "Years ago . . . at this point, almost fifty years . . . our sister fell in love with a human."

Jack raised an eyebrow. "A human? But isn't she half-fish?"

"Aren't you half-monkey?"

"Being quiet now."

"My sister loved this man so much, she decided to become human to be with him," the mermaid continued. "Of course, that took magic, which in our world only the Sea King knew how to do. That all changed when a fairy queen fell in love with our father and became a mermaid herself. That's actually where our sister got the stupid idea. What she didn't really think through was that it didn't work for the fairy queen, and it wasn't going to work for her."

"I don't know, it seems like a sweet gesture," Jack said, May's smile coming into his head out of nowhere.

"A sweet gesture?" the mermaid shouted. "Giving up everything you are for some man you don't really even know?"

"Well, see, you make it sound all *bad* when you say it like that."

"Again, be *quiet*. Anyway, my sister began visiting this fairy queen, whom most merfolk began to call the Sea Witch, given that she would perform small acts of magic if you did her favors. After my father rejected her, the Sea Witch pushed most merfolk away, my sister being the sole exception." The mermaid paused. "See? She abandoned her old life for love, and had it blow up in her face!"

"Speaking of Sea Witches, this one sounds fascinating," Jack said as subtly as he could. "Any idea where she is now?"

"You don't want to know," the mermaid said. "Anyway, our sister learned some magic from her. Fairy queen magic is musical, and my sister always had a talent for singing. So she learned enough magic to give herself legs, then went looking for her human." The mermaid sighed. "Needless to say, my father wasn't thrilled. In fact, he was so not thrilled with a human stealing away his youngest daughter that he went up after her, took her back, and closed off our world to humans forever."

"That seems a bit extreme," Jack pointed out.

"Welcome to my father," the mermaid said. "Either way, this pirate, Bluebeard, seems to have been employed to find our sister for this human. But after many, many failures, our sister sent us to go find Bluebeard. She wanted us to deliver a message, but just as we finally found him, Pan found us all, and here we are."

"What's the message?" Jack asked.

"Are you Bluebeard?" the mermaid asked him.

"Fair enough."

"The only message Bluebeard needs to hear is this: *Stay away*," the mermaid said. "He's got some new plan involving the Sea Witch, but I can tell you right now it will only lead to bad things. I tell you this for the sake of your entire species. My father is powerful enough to go to war with all of humanity, and you really don't want that happening. So whatever you do, do not come after my sister, the Sea Witch, or anything else underwater. Do you hear me?"

Jack put his hand on hers, looked straight into her eyes, and gave her his most sincere expression. "Loud and clear," he said, wondering if she could see how fast he planned on breaking every single one of her rules.

CHAPTER 14

The pirate ship seemed bigger now than when May had seen it from shore. Maybe that was part of Pan's magic too. The satyr didn't seem too magical to May right now, tied up to a chair in what looked to be Captain Bluebeard's cabin.

"I was playin' yer game for nigh on forty years, Pan," the captain said, his eyes gleaming dangerously as he stalked around the terrified creature. "And that means ye be owin' me forty years o' me life back, d'ye understand? Or should I be carvin' those forty years outta yer *own* life?"

"Mmmmph!" Pan said, the gag in his mouth keeping him from saying anything.

"Tell me what I be askin', goat boy," the captain said.

"Mmmmmph!"

"He doesn't seem to be cooperatin'!" Captain Bluebeard shouted.

"That can't be smart fer his health, Cap'n," Skinny pointed out.

"That it can*not*, Skinny." With that, despite Pan's screaming, Captain Bluebeard kicked his chair backward, crashing the satyr to the floor. "Where do I be findin' the Sea Witch?" Bluebeard asked quietly, sounding that much more dangerous for it.

Pan just stared back silently, his eyes wide.

"Okay, enough," May said, and took the gag out of Pan's mouth. "We're not treating him like this anymore."

"FORTY YEARS this creature wasted of mine!" Bluebeard roared, blowing May's hair back with the strength of his bellowing. "FORTY YEARS! I'll be treatin' him in whatever manner I be wishin'!"

"You want my help?" May said, pushing Bluebeard backward. "Then you'll ask him NICELY! Otherwise I'm jumping over the side along with my friend."

"Princess," Phillip warned, but May just reached out and pinched the prince's lips closed.

"Well?" May said, raising one eyebrow.

Bluebeard slammed a fist down hard enough to split his own

table, then sighed. "Pan, where be the Sea Witch. Show me on me map. Now."

Pan immediately grabbed the map and pointed to a spot just six or seven inches away from a random shoreline, one with a roundish castle on it. "There, she's there! That's where their capital city is! There! Please, I've told you what you want to know—"

Bluebeard grabbed Pan with one hand and ripped him out of the chair with the other. "SEND US THERE!" he roared. "Send ALL of us, and this entire ship, to that spot or I will rend you limb from gaunt limb!"

Pan squeaked his agreement, and suddenly everything began to wrench away, as if someone were pulling apart two pieces of glued paper, then reversing until they fell back into place. Nothing looked that different, but the view out a cabin window of the water looked the same whether you were looking at a bay in the Land of Never or the middle of the ocean.

And then something occurred to May as her entire body went deathly cold. They'd just left the Land of Never, and Jack with it.

"Send us back!" May screamed, grabbing Pan out of Bluebeard's hand and slamming him against the wall. "SEND US BACK NOW!"

Bluebeard pulled Pan away from her. "Ye'll rot in the brig for a few decades. See how ye like it!" he said, throwing the satyr to one of his pirates. "And if ye try any magic on me crew, I'll cut off yer shadow and feed it to ya!"

Pan nodded silently over and over as two pirates carried him away.

"NO!" May screamed again. "JACK! We have to go back!"

"Oh, yer drowned friend?" Bluebeard said calmly, all traces of his rage now replaced with a friendly ease. "I wouldn't be a'worryin' about him if I were ye."

"I will worry you in the face if you don't bring us back right now!" May screamed.

Phillip drew his sword and leapt at the pirate, but out of nowhere someone grabbed the back of Phillip's shirt, dragged him to a halt, then stuck a flickering, glowing sword right to Bluebeard's throat.

"No need to go back," Jack said, his soaking clothes dripping on the floor. "We're all here, aren't we, Captain?"

Bluebeard stared down at the glowing sword at his neck. "I didn't realize we had the pleasure of one of the Wicked Queen's Eyes on board me ship," he said, giving Jack a steady stare.

"You still don't," Jack said. "We're leaving. We have to get halfway across the ocean to find the Sea Witch. May, Phillip, there are probably about a dozen pirates trying to get through the door I just locked behind me. I'm gonna suggest we find another way out. Like maybe the window."

"Even those who've sampled the mermaids' tears might wish to take a moment before jumpin' into merman-infested waters," Bluebeard suggested, his eyes still on Jack.

"Merman-infested waters?" Jack said. "Where *are* we?"

"Directly over the capital city of the mermen," Bluebeard mentioned. "There be safer places to go for a pleasure swim."

"Wait," May said. "You knew we could breathe underwater?"

"Ye think we didn't see you all at the shore, makin' fools o' yerselves in the water?" Bluebeard laughed. "Just because I wasn't in me right head, under that fool Pan's control, doesn't mean I wasn't payin' attention!"

"You seem a lot less enraged now too," May pointed out suspiciously. "You were just faking all that crazy?"

"Fakin'? No," the captain said, giving her a careful stare. "But don't be misunderestimatin' Captain Bluebeard anytime soon, lassie. I don't be who ye think I be!"

"You be someone without a good grasp on yer grammar, is who I think ye be," May pointed out.

"Am I?" Captain Bluebeard asked softly, his pirate accent

dropping away completely. "Whatever would make you believe such a thing, my lady?"

Phillip stepped between them. "Enough. We know where the Sea Witch is now. What would you have us do, Captain?"

"Have us do?" Jack said. "We're getting the Sea Witch and leaving. End of story."

"Put away that cursed sword of yers before I feed it to you, Little Eye," Bluebeard said with a wide smile. "These two made a deal with me."

"Oh, please don't tell me," Jack said, shaking his head. "You want her too?"

"How did you know?" May asked, raising an eyebrow. "He said he'd get us to the Sea Witch if we bring her back here. Though there are still quite a few parts of this deal that are pretty unclear. Like, how do we find her, and why are we bringing her back?"

"All good questions," Bluebeard said. "And all have easy answers! The Sea Witch is known to have a lair outside the city. And as fer why do I want her?" Bluebeard said, pushing Jack's sword away from him. "'Tis a job she can help me with, nothing more. But a job that will see me rich beyond me wildest dreams."

"Some would think all this might make the Sea King angry," Jack said, just as quietly.

"That's my issue, Little Eye," Bluebeard said, his voice lowering dangerously. "I can handle His Majesty just fine."

Jack paused again, then nodded. "In that case, I'm on board," Jack said, then glanced down at the ship. "You know, both literally and . . . oh, forget it. We'll find the Sea Witch, bring her here so she can help you, then have her take us back to the Homelands. Sounds like a plan." Again, he hoped Bluebeard wouldn't see through him. All they had to do was find the Sea Witch, then run, avoiding the whole pirate-merman fiasco just waiting to happen.

Bluebeard grinned widely. "And just in case ye be plannin' on breaking yer deal with me—say, just findin' the Sea Witch, then runnin'—my nets will be waitin' fer you." He pushed his face up to Jack's, forty years of bad breath blowing in Jack's face. "And me pirates . . . they get hungry when they fish."

Jack blinked a few times at the man's breath while May made a disgusted face right next to him. "Thankfully, we'd never even consider breaking our deal," Jack told him.

"Perfect!" Bluebeard yelled. "We'll wait till the sun giant puts his fireball out, and then get you three in the water and findin'

the Sea Witch! But before ye go, ye three might want to be doin'
somethin' about those legs o' yers." He stopped, then brightened.
"Maybe Pan will come in handy after all!"

"Oh, that doesn't sound good in any way," May said.

"Things never do," Jack said.

CHAPTER 15

They had a few hours before nightfall, and after the events of the last day, sleep seemed like a good plan, if an unlikely one. May, as she had for the last three months, tossed and turned, which kept Jack awake worrying about her.

At least, awake long enough for sleep to arrive, smack him around a little, then knock him out completely.

"Well, look who's making some progress," said a girl in a dark blue cloak as Jack woke up beneath a familiar-looking oak tree. Lian sat in the branches, absently balancing the pointy tip of her sword on one finger, barely paying any attention to it.

Jack glanced up at her, then shook his head. "I wish we were. If only we could figure out how to get out of the Land of Never.

You know what? Have the Wolf King bring his army in. I think we're ready to give up."

"You're playing a dangerous game, going after the Sea Witch," Lian told him, either seeing through his bluff or completely ignoring it. "And for what, the help of a pirate? I've heard nothing but good things about Bluebeard, after all. All those wives, dead. But I'm sure you know what you're doing."

"Listen," Jack said. "I appreciate your advice, mostly because I know you have our best interests at heart. And I can't say this hasn't been fun, because I get confused with double negatives, but I really have somewhere else—really, *anywhere else*—to be right now, so I'll be seeing you." He turned and walked away.

Only to find that a minute later, he did see her, as the oak tree reappeared right in front of him. He sighed, wondering if that could get any more annoying.

"Taking on the Sea King?" Lian asked him, still in the branches. "In his element, beneath the waves? Even my Queen fears him there. You're stupider than I gave you credit for."

"I'm stupider than a LOT of people give me credit for!" Jack shouted back. "Now stop trying to find out my plans!"

Lian laughed, then hopped down weightlessly from the tree.

"Where do you think we are, Jack? You really think you can hide things from me in here?"

"What's that supposed to mean?"

"It means we're in your dreams, you idiot," she said, shaking her head in disgust. "And where do you think your dreams live? Think about it, even if it hurts. If I'm in your head, I have access to everything else in here, what little there might be. See that city over there?" She pointed at the city in the distance. "It's obviously not really a city, but there's a reason you've got such big walls around it. That represents all your secrets. All your dreams." She smiled mockingly. "All your feelings for a certain princess—"

"GET OUT of my head!" Jack shouted at her, then drew his sword and leapt straight at her.

Lian didn't even bother moving. Instead she just grabbed his sword out of midair and held it in place, despite Jack struggling with all his strength against her. "I've already been through the city, Jack," she said. "It's been a learning experience. You really don't think much of dear old dad, do you?"

Jack just growled in frustration and kicked out, but Lian caught his leg with her own foot, and knocked it away. "That's not all I saw in there, Jack," she said, still smiling. "There are memories you have that you probably don't even know about, memories locked away so deep that you probably never even knew they were missing."

"I like that you think I believe anything you say," Jack said quietly, still pushing as hard as he could on the sword she held in place.

Lian laughed, then abruptly dropped his sword, sending Jack tumbling forward. She elbowed him as he fell past, knocking him to the dirt, then sat down on his back as soon as he'd landed, pinning him to the ground. "I'm sure you don't. And you're right, what missing memories could I possibly be talking about? I'm sure you remember that injury you had when you were younger, why your parents sent you to live with your grandfather, what happened to your father. You *do* remember all those things, right?"

Jack tried to roll away or push himself up, but somehow the girl seemed to have gained about a thousand pounds, and he couldn't push her off. "I've lived with my grandfather all my life," he spat. "And I was *never* hurt as a child. Nice try, though."

Lian sighed. "I'm just trying to help you here, Jack. Don't you get it? You're on the *wrong side*. Your good guys? The Charmed One? Who do you think *messed* with your memories in the first place? And why would he do that, Jack? Why would an Eye want to make sure you don't remember certain things about who you are, where you're from? When did he do it? Did he know you, back when he was still alive? Why would he not want you to remember your father? Your mother?"

"GET OFF ME!" Jack shouted, and doubled his efforts, but nothing would even sway the girl.

"This dreamland, it's not real," Lian told him. "You basically can do whatever you want in here, which makes it perfect for training to be an Eye. That's why the Charmed One met you here . . . only, you wouldn't listen to him. Which was smart, I'll give you that. Doubt whatever anyone says until you find the truth out for yourself. It's one of the first precepts of being an Eye."

Abruptly the weight on Jack's back lifted, and he rolled over to find Lian in the tree's branches once more. Jack pushed himself to his feet, glaring at the girl. "If he can train me to beat you, I'm all for it. Bring him back."

"Oh, he can't return while I'm around, I've made sure of that," Lian said with a shrug. "You don't need him lying to you while I'm trying to spread a little truth."

"Didn't you just say I shouldn't believe what anyone tells me?" Jack hissed.

"See, you're learning already!" Lian said, applauding him. "You'll find out eventually. You'll see who's telling the truth and who's lying to you. And then tell me you're on the right side of all this."

She smiled widely just as everything began wavering. He was waking up.

"Good luck with lying to the pirates, Jack!" Lian shouted, waving good-bye. "They're known for chopping off the heads of anyone who betrays them, so that might be a problem!"

And just like that, Lian and the tree were gone, and Jack opened his eyes to see the princess leaning over him.

"Yeah, I couldn't sleep either," May said, still tapping his shoulder.

"Um, right," Jack said. "What's wrong. Nightmares?"

"In a way," She said, her face unreadable. "Jack, I think I should turn myself in. You know, to the Wicked . . . to my grandmother."

CHAPTER 16

They left Phillip to sleep, then walked up some rickety stairs to the main deck. Since they weren't moving, or sailing, or whatever the word was, the pirates didn't have much to do, so they just clustered in small groups, staying quiet so as to not attract any unwanted merman attention. Most just chatted quietly, but one group clustered around Skinny, playing a disturbing game using his finger bones instead of actual dice.

Stopping at the ship's railing, far enough away from the pirates for some privacy, May and Jack watched the sun slowly tumble into the ocean, the heat already sizzling the water.

"I'll never get used to that," May said, her eyes reflecting the orange and purple sky.

"Then we're all thankful the sun giant does his job despite

your discomfort," Jack said as the ship gently bobbed up and down.

"Tomorrow night, Jack," May said. "We've already wasted one day, and the dragons will be there tomorrow night. And then it's all over."

"You think that was wasted?" Jack said, raising an eyebrow. "Did you not *see* how badly I destroyed Pan in that contest of wits?"

"You're amazing," May said, glaring at him. "Can't you ever be serious?"

Jack paused, then sighed. "You're sort of serious enough for all three of us, May. I . . . I guess I've just been trying to take your mind off things."

"Nice try, but the world won't let that happen," May said. "But if I gave myself up . . . if I turned myself in, maybe my grandmother . . . maybe she'd—"

"Stop calling her that," Jack said, pushing away from the railing to look straight at her. "Don't call her that anymore, okay? Because there is NOTHING of her in you, do you hear me? NOTHING."

"You don't know that," May said, looking back out at the ocean. "I'm so . . . so angry, all the time. Angry at her, angry at me, at *us* for letting her back out into the world. I just . . . I don't know how to make things better."

"You're doing that right now," Jack told her. "You're making things better by saving the Fairy Homelands. By finding out who you are. By doing exactly what she doesn't want you to do. Don't you get it? The fact that she's trying so hard to keep us from finding that out, that must mean something! There must be a reason!"

"Yeah, I'm sure I'll find out and live happily ever after."

"Happily ever what?"

"It means that I'll be happy forever, 'cause that's how fairy—uh, kids stories end," May said, the wind blowing her hair. "Except they don't, do they? Obviously not."

"Uh, no," Jack said, giving her a confused look. "How could anyone possibly be happy forever? You really think you're never going to stub your toe, or get sick, or fight with your friend? No one lives happily never after."

"*Ever* after."

"Whatever. I've never heard of anything so stupid. Talk about a kid's story."

"So what's the point, then, if we can't be happy? Why are we doing any of this?"

"Oh, there's definitely happiness," Jack said, turning his back on the ocean and looking at her. "But it's just about moments, not ever-afters." He grinned. "Like when you're right in the middle of the worst adventure imaginable, but for a minute, it's just about sitting on a boat in the middle of the ocean with your friends, with no one trying to kill you in any kind of horrifying way. You have to appreciate these moments when they happen, 'cause obviously we don't get many of them."

May glanced at him, and started to smile in return, for the first time in a while.

So of course someone had to come along to ruin it all. "*That* is a beautiful sunset!" Phillip said.

"Drink it in, Your Highness," Jack said, glaring at the prince. "It might be the last one you ever see."

"Oh, I have faith that we can handle the mermen," Phillip said, smiling at him.

"Sure. Let's pretend that's what I meant."

"We were just talking about why we're doing this," May told the prince.

"That is easy," Phillip said, stepping between them with a wide smile. "We do this because it is right! I can see how you might think this responsibility, this adventure we are on, that it is too big for us, or that we would be better off just giving the

Queen what she wants, that it would save lives. But neither of those things are true."

"You heard that?" May asked, but Phillip held up a hand.

"Considering that we do not know who or where you come from, we cannot say that handing you over to the Wicked Queen would not make things worse, correct?" Phillip said. "Not to mention, the Queen had more than sufficient reason to wipe out the Fairy Homelands because of their power and their alliance with the humans. Coincidence or no, we are not the only reason she is doing this."

"But what if she'd stop?" May said. "What if by giving myself up, she—"

"Or what if we put a stop to her plans and keep you free?" Phillip said, the wind blowing his hair as well. "What if we three embrace the road destiny has laid before us, and accomplish what we have set out to do, stealing victory from those who would do us harm, and finally learning the truth of your history, Princess?"

"I'm hearing a lot of what-ifs in there," Jack said.

"Of course, for we have not yet finished this quest," Phillip said. "But we shall, and when we do, and stand triumphant beside Merriweather and her sisters as they fight back against the Queen's armies, you shall realize I am right. For we three will be heroes! And nothing can stop the noble of heart, no matter how evil might try!"

"It must be pretty nice in your world, huh, Phillip?" Jack asked. "All flowers and rainbows?"

"No matter our past," Phillip said, ignoring Jack, "no matter what mistakes we have made, we can do nothing more than try to live well in the present and strive to make the future a better place. And we are doing that very thing now. We had the noblest of intentions when rescuing your grandmother, Princess, and still do now, but the difference is, we know who our enemies are, and that they want us stopped. That should be reason enough for confidence, even joyful enthusiasm, for our task at hand!"

"You're right, Phillip!" May said, slamming a hand down on the railing. "Let's go jump in the ocean and try not to drown, just to annoy my grandmother!"

Phillip laughed, and May hugged him, shaking her head, while Jack sighed, glancing over his shoulder at the pirates behind them . . . and then at the sword on his own back.

Did they really know who their enemies were?

CHAPTER 17

It sure looks wet," May said, scrunching up her nose. The three of them sat on the ship's railing, this time surrounded by pirates, three of which were holding Pan tightly. In front of them a grim, grinning Bluebeard waited impatiently.

"Aye, wet, and colder than ye can imagine," Bluebeard said, his voice quieter than normal, more of a dull roar than the usual bellow. "Ye'll most likely be miserable and chilled to yer very bones. Such is the pirate's life."

"Oh yeah?" May said. "I don't see any of *you* going in."

"Hope that ye don't," Bluebeard said. "If I set foot in the water, expect that things are pretty much as bad as they get."

"Leaving on a positive note, I like it," Jack said. "Can we get on with this? I can barely see."

The sun giant had extinguished his fireball about an hour ago, and the light of the moon only did so much. There were no torches lit on the ship, so no prying merman eyes would see them and come to investigate, but that did make bumping into huge wooden planks a bit more of a constant than Jack would have liked.

"Ye heard the Little Eye, Pan," Bluebeard growled. "Do yer thing. And one hint that yer performin' different magic than I tell ye, and ye'll be a head shorter than ye are now."

"I get it already," Pan said. "I do this, and you set me free. I don't, and I . . . Well, let's just move on. I'm doing it." He closed his eyes, wiggled his tail a bit, then opened them. "And, done."

"Nothing happened," Jack said, then looked at the wide eyes of the pirates in front of him.

"Perhaps take a look at yer lower regions, Little Eye," Bluebeard said.

Jack looked down to find a slippery bright green fish tail growing out of his waist, and gasped . . . only to have the tail immediately disappear, revealing his legs once more.

"Well, *that* was impressive for half a second or so," he said.

"At least you got one," May said. "Mine never even changed. And wow, Phillip's is still there. What's going on?"

"You're all stupid," Pan said. "My magic requires happiness, so says the satyr code. If you don't think happy thoughts, it goes away."

"But you used magic on Bluebeard for forty years, and he doesn't seem like the happiest guy for it," Jack said. "How'd it work on him?"

Bluebeard gritted his teeth. "Pan offered me and me crew our fondest wish if we went with him, then magicked us into believin' we were gettin' it. It's our fault fer believin' his lies at the start."

"They weren't lies," Pan sniffed. "It's not my fault you hate fun. If it helps you three, I can use magic so you'll think you're happy."

"NOPE," May said. "We'll do this ourselves. I'm not letting you magic me therapy."

"This seems like a bad idea, May," Jack said. "I don't know if you've met me, but being constantly happy isn't really where my talents lie."

"Phillip's still half-fish, Jack," she said. "He's doing it. You really think *you* can't fake happy for a few hours?"

"Ignorance is bliss in the prince's case," Jack said.

"Like you can't pull off a little stupid." May snorted. "Ready? Pan, let's try this again."

This time all three got tails, though May's faded in and out for a minute. She scrunched up her eyes and began to repeat something quietly to herself, and the tail soon firmed up.

And then Jack realized that he was neglecting his own happy thoughts, as his tail began to fade as well. Immediately he began to think about all the things that could make him happy. Going home . . . Well, not really. His grandfather would just want him out on another adventure. Any thoughts of family just went to his father, and that made the tail almost disappear entirely. Saving the fairy queens and finding out who May was, that was a good thought, but for some reason his tail still wavered.

Stupid magic! Why couldn't there just be a world without magic or princes or wicked queens or any of this?

Instantly Jack's tail turned completely solid.

Pan wiggled his tail again, and now they were wearing appropriately merfolk-ish shirts.

"Get in already, ye mound of whimpering sots!" Bluebeard said. "All ye have to do is hold on to the anchor chain as it lowers. It'll take ye straight to the ocean floor. We should be over the Sea Witch's lair by now, if my navigatin' is correct." He winked. "And it obviously is."

The three climbed over the railing and grabbed ahold of the anchor. May moved to the bottom, the only one of the three with any swimming experience, but that also meant she was the first to hit the water as the anchor lowered, which it did with an alarming speed.

"GAH!" May shouted as her tail broke the surface. "SO COLD! *Burning* with cold! You ladies are gonna love this!"

Jack and Phillip looked at each other as the anchor continued its descent, sending May completely underwater. "She makes such a compelling case," Jack said.

Phillip smiled, then silently screamed as he hit the water as well. Jack sighed, hating them both, then winced as the ocean rose up to meet him.

The chill bolted through his body like lightning, freezing his blood as his heart tripped over its own pacing. He'd never been so cold in his entire life, but there was no turning back now. This was it. They were all in.

Beneath the waves the water pushed back and forth rhythmically, despite the anchor's weight. The three of them held tightly to the chain, frantically breathing in and out, hoping for any degree of warmth they could find.

"Whoever's idea this was needs to *pay*!" May yelled. Again,

Jack expected bubbles of air to escape as she talked, but none emerged. Magic was strange.

"If payment involves getting out of the water and anything to do with fire, I'm all for it," Jack said.

As the anchor continued down, May gasped. "Was that a fin out there?"

"Where?" Phillip said, pulling himself down the chain to pass May. "I shall protect you, Princess! Stay behind me!"

"It was just a fish," Jack said, though he had to push past a lump of terror in his throat to speak at all. "A *big* fish, but still. Everyone, calm down."

"Oh great, sharks, even better," May said, climbing up the anchor chain a bit.

"Sharks?" Phillip asked.

"Huge fish with tons of teeth," May said, shuddering a bit. "You'll love them."

"Either way, we're going to have to deal with the mermen eventually," Jack said, biting down to keep his teeth from chattering, though from the cold or the terror, he didn't know. "If we stick to the plan, we should be okay."

"And since when have our plans ever worked?" May asked, her voice getting a bit shrill.

"Have faith, Princess," Phillip said, though he didn't sound much better than she did.

"Yeah, Princess," Jack said. "We're bound to get lucky one of these times."

CHAPTER 18

As it turned out, the lair of the Sea Witch wasn't really that far from the anchor, which was good. The farther they progressed, the deeper the water got, and that much water for some reason didn't agree with the moonlight. The light must have just gotten bored or lazy and given up before coming all the way down to the bottom. Fortunately, just as the last bit of moonlight gave up, an eerie glow from below appeared, giving them enough light to see by.

"Look," Phillip said, his fishtail swaying gracefully as he pointed down at the glow. "Fallen stars."

Jack followed his gesture to find a scattering of fallen stars, each one only a bit larger than his hand, glowing just as they had in the night sky. "They always seem to fall into the ocean," he agreed. "They must just land here and gradually die, losing their glow."

"Okay, seriously?" May said. "No. That's a starfish."

"A fish?" Jack asked, swimming closer. "It doesn't look like any fish I've ever seen."

"A *star*fish!" May said, gritting her teeth. "Look, I'll show you—"

Phillip quickly followed her and pulled her back away from the star. "Beware, Princess," he told her gently. "We do not know what dangers the stars may hold."

"It's *not* a star!" May shouted. "It's just the same shape!"

"It's glowing, May," Jack pointed out, trying not to get her going. "Just like a star. You have to admit it makes sense."

"But it *doesn't*!" May said, almost pleadingly. "It's a fish, or something like a fish, I don't really know! It's maybe not really a fish, it's something else, but still a fish! An animal! Kinda! Like coral! I know it's not supposed to glow, but there aren't supposed to be mermen either, and I'm all right with that, but I will *not* say those are fallen stars!"

"You know, this really isn't important," Jack said, gently turning May away from the fallen stars. "Let's just move on, shall we? Whatever the stars—sorry, fish—whatever they are, they're giving us enough light to see by, right?"

May just looked at him sadly. "Well, yeah, I guess."

"Well then," he said with a smile. "We'll just leave it at that. We must be about to the Sea Witch's lair."

"It is right there, in fact," Phillip said, nodding in the direction they were going. "Just at the edge of those fallen stars."

"THEY'RE NOT—"

"Remember, happy thoughts!" Jack said, noticing May's fish tail fading in and out as she grew more frustrated. "Let's get on with things. The faster we find the Sea Witch, the faster we don't run into any mermen."

As they all began to swim off, May steadily avoiding looking at the fallen stars, repeating something happy quietly to herself, Phillip fell in beside Jack.

"Do you find it odd that we have yet to *see* a merman?" the prince asked him quietly.

"I find it fantastic more than odd, actually," Jack said, gritting his teeth and thinking of his own happy thought over and over. "Maybe our plan is actually working for a change. Ever think of that?"

"How likely is that?" Phillip countered. "Do you remember traveling to Malevolent's castle, the trip by the river?"

"Vaguely," Jack said, rolling his eyes.

"Try to recall it," Phillip said, clearly missing the sarcasm. "We never approached within ten feet of that river, yet mermen watched us the entire way." He glanced all around them. "It worries me that we have yet to see one."

"The ocean's a big place," Jack said, awkwardly turning himself in all directions, but all he could see was empty water and glowing stars. "Maybe there were more in the river because they know that's where humans live? Either way, I don't see any here."

"The question is, can *they* see *us*?" Phillip said solemnly. "I will keep my sword ready, all the same."

Jack shook his head. "We can't use swords, you know that. Not unless it's absolutely necessary. If they are falling for our disguises, pulling our swords off our backs will completely give it away. Mermen use tridents, not swords. Unless they attack, our weapons stay hidden."

Phillip sighed. "I never liked this plan."

"Blame Bluebeard," Jack said, half-smiling. "If he'd just thrown us into a dungeon like everyone else we met, none of this would have happened."

The ground in front of them was littered with grotesque, stunted plants, two lines of them bordering a path of glittering rocks that led toward a dead-looking cave. As Jack and Phillip caught up to May, Phillip shook his head. "As obviously happy as I am, this seems a bit unnatural for the home of a fairy queen, my friends," he said. "We should be cautious."

"The stones are kinda nice," Jack said, pointing down at the path leading to the cave.

"I think those are eyeballs," May said, swallowing hard.

"Of course they are," Jack said, then pushed some bile back down into his throat.

His tail wavered again, and Jack immediately began imagining a world without eyeballs or Sea Witches or any of this, fixing the tail in place immediately.

"Well, I guess we should go in and see if she's home," May said, but no one moved. A minute passed, then two, the bent plants swaying with the current.

"Maybe she's not even there," Jack said. Right now, that was an even happier thought than any of his daydreaming about non-magical worlds that didn't exist.

"Then we should go in and see if we can find out where she went," May said.

No one moved for another minute.

"We always seem to get in over our heads," May said, breaking the silence. "Why do we ever think we can *do* this stuff?"

"It all sounds so much easier in theory," Jack said. "But we really need to just do this already. Phillip?" He gave the prince a push forward. Phillip yelped and shot a dirty look Jack's way, but turned back toward the cave and began to slowly swim toward it. Jack moved to follow him, with May right behind.

As they swam forward, they created little ripples that sent the deformed plants lining the path into ugly little dances, almost convulsions, as they passed. The strange thing was, the dancing continued after the water settled back to the ground. Probably just the water's current.

As they got closer to the cave, it looked no more inviting than the path of eyeballs and bent plants. And it wasn't as if the plants were uniform; there wasn't even any sort of beauty in symmetry. No, instead they were each a different size, even a different color, which was odd. In fact, some of the plants were a dark gray, a color Jack never would have associated with anything plantlike. Still, it was hardly a leap to think the fairy queen's magic had affected the local plant life.

The eyes, Jack just ignored completely.

No matter how much Jack would have wished it otherwise, he and Phillip did finally reach the mouth of the cave. Inside, shadows seemed to swirl and bubble, a nauseating effect aided by the eerie glow of what few fallen stars were still around. Despite that glow, the going would be tough without more light.

"I know what I said," Jack whispered to Phillip, "but I think I have to use my sword."

Phillip frowned. "I dislike relying on such an evil object just for light," he said. "However, we appear to have little choice in the matter."

Jack sighed. "It can't be a good sign that no matter what we do, we have 'little choice.'"

Phillip nodded back up toward the boat. "We could always turn back."

Jack sighed. "Wouldn't it be nice if we could."

The prince clapped Jack on the shoulder. "You are a decent fellow, Jack," Phillip declared softly. "If this is to be our death, it has been a pleasure to fight at your side."

"I'm sure it has," Jack said, then took a deep breath and pulled out his sword. Instantly the entire area lit up with a ghostly white glow as the translucent sword's inner liquid lit on fire, though again, it flickered oddly. What was causing that?

Under the light of the sword, the plants by the path began

to wither and shake, and the eyes between them shone like small suns, but other than that, the light didn't seem to attract any unwanted attention. At least, not that was revealing itself.

"Looks like you might have been right about using our swords," Jack said to Phillip, carefully searching for any sign of mermen. "I hate to be optimistic here, but I think we got away with the light."

"Small victories are still victories," Phillip told him as May swam over to them.

"Why," she said, "is there another kind?"

"I wouldn't get your hopes up," Jack said, bringing the sword around to shine it into the cave.

Phillip watched the sword, his expression unpleasant. "I swear, Jack, if you had heard the stories I had about the Eyes . . ."

"Not all of them were bad, right?" May said. "I mean, the one who talks to you in your dreams sounds okay, right, Jack?"

"The Eye *speaks* to you? In your dreams?!" the prince asked, dark suspicions flashing all over his face by the light of the sword.

"Uh, whoops," May said, looking around at anything but Jack. "This probably isn't the time to discuss—"

"You never told me," Phillip said, still focusing on Jack.

"This really isn't the time, Phillip," Jack agreed, trying to get around the prince but not able to maneuver himself with the agility May had. "We're already making enough noise. We need to get in and out before we bring an entire army of merfolk down on us!"

"Then why are you causing your sword to glow so brightly?!" Phillip demanded.

Jack started to yell back, then realized the prince was right. Why *was* the sword glowing so brightly? And getting even brighter with every second?

"Oh *no*," Jack said quietly.

"Oh *yes!*" said a remarkably familiar voice from all around him. "Probably shouldn't have used the sword, Jack," Lian said. "Not when someone's been messing around in your head."

Jack quickly pushed the sword back toward its sheath, but just as he raised it over his head, the light exploded like three sun giants rolling their fireballs right into each other.

CHAPTER 19

Whoops!" Lian's voice said from everywhere and nowhere. "Well, that can't be good! I bet that could be seen for miles and miles! Hope no merfolk saw it!"

"What did you do!" May shouted, her eyes wide with surprise and anger.

"*I* didn't do anything!" Jack yelled, shoving the sword into his sheath, were it went dark as usual. Perfect timing. "The girl—the Eye—she messed with it somehow. I heard her, talking in my head, laughing."

Phillip grabbed Jack by shirt vest and threw him against the wall. Back on land, the jolt would have hurt, but under the water, Jack barely felt the hit. "The female Eye is talking to you in your head?!" the prince shouted, veins popping out all unroyally across his face. "If she is in your mind, she knows all our plans! And if she knows, then so does the Wicked Queen!"

"I haven't told her anything!" Jack shouted back.

"Stop it, Phillip!" May said, trying to pull the prince off of Jack. "Jack wouldn't betray us!"

"Oh?" Phillip said. "Because the Wicked Queen claimed either he or I would betray you, and I know that *I* could never do such a thing." Phillip turned his gaze back to Jack. "How long has the Eye been talking to you, Jack? How long has she had access to our plans?"

"I've seen her . . . twice in my dreams, and only heard her just the once when I haven't been asleep," Jack told him, his huge irritation at being manhandled by Phillip unfortunately offset by the guilty suspicion that the prince might be right.

"Twice in your dreams?!" Phillip said. "You have been compromised by an Eye!"

"PHILLIP!" May said, yanking backward on the prince's shoulders hard enough to pull him away from Jack. "He didn't do anything wrong!"

"Give up the *sword*, Jack," Phillip said, trying to pull himself out of May's grasp without hurting her. "That evil thing holds more power over you than you know. You have to destroy it, if it has not gotten to you already!"

"It hasn't gotten to him!" May said exasperatedly. "It's just a stupid sword! Jack's the exact same idiot as he was before he found it!"

"The sword isn't trying to turn me to evil, Phillip!" Jack said, realizing he'd probably be saying the exact same thing if it actually were. "The previous owner of this sword . . . He was on our side, believe me! He fought the Queen."

"Or so he told you," Phillip said quietly.

"Not helping!" May shouted.

"Believe me, he did!" Jack shouted. "If I told you who he was, you'd know!"

"Yeah, you–" May started, then stopped. "Wait. You know who he was?"

Jack winced. "Um, sort of."

"You never told me that," she said, her suspicious look beginning to match that of Phillip's.

"It didn't matter!" Jack said, desperately clutching at anything that'd keep the knight's secret from May. "Just trust me, he's on our side!"

"Our side?" Phillip said. "That is practically their motto. They make you believe they are your friends, then cut your throat in your sleep. And *that* is if they like you. I heard stories of a man who spoke out against the Queen without realizing an Eye was present. The next day his fingers were found nailed to his front door." Phillip gritted his teeth. "*Only* his fingers, Jack. The rest of him was never found . . . at least not that was identifiable."

"Okay, *ugh*, first of all," May said, before turning back to Jack. "Just tell him who the Eye was and end this, Jack. If that's what it takes, what does it matter?"

"It might matter to you," Jack said softly.

"What, me?" she asked, her face falling. "I mean, I guess they all have something to do with me, considering . . . but just tell him. It can't be that bad. I . . . remember that she . . . she said he was Snow White's late husband."

Jack sighed deeply. "I hate to disappoint you, May, but it usually *is* that bad. He was Snow White's late husband, yes. This sword came from the only Eye ever to turn against the Wicked Queen—"

"The Charmed One?" Phillip blurted out. "But you found the sword within that giant!"

"So?" Jack said, avoiding May's confused look.

"But stories say the Charmed One perished at the hands of the Wicked Queen," Phillip explained. "In her castle, after he helped the rebels break in. The Queen killed him with his own sword for his betrayal, and as a final strike at Snow White before she fled."

May jumped as if struck, bending over slightly. "She . . . The Wicked Queen killed him?"

Phillip finally realized that he had said too much, and shut his mouth much too late.

"Just . . . just finish the story, Phillip," May told him.

The prince sighed. "The Charmed One betrayed the Wicked Queen because he loved Snow White. The two fell in love and married, and the Wicked Queen killed him for it."

"Long story short," Jack said, "the Charmed One wasn't evil, and neither is his sword. And he was the one trying to . . . I think to train me in my dreams, until—"

"Until?" Phillip asked.

"Well, until the girl got into my head. Ever since, the Charmed One's been kinda, um, missing."

"Jack," May said, letting go of Phillip. "None of that is good. Why didn't you tell us about her?"

"Yes, why didn't you tell them?" came Lian's smug voice from all around him.

Jack growled in frustration. "Because it's none of your business! Neither of you have to deal with this. It's . . . it's all up to me, all right?!"

"Oh wow," May said, backing away. "Jack, maybe that thing *has* gotten to you."

"It HASN'T!" Jack shouted. "Now, I don't care what you two do. I'm going to find the Sea Witch before we get eaten alive by mermen!"

With that, he flipped around and swam into the cave, not knowing or caring if the other two were following him.

Somehow, swimming was harder than before, so Jack glanced down, only to find two legs. His fishtail was gone, along with any chance of happy thoughts. Well, fantastic.

Not trusting the sword enough to use it with Lian in his head, Jack had more and more trouble seeing as the tunnel grew darker, though eventually a subtle glow began wafting off the creepy plants on the ocean floor, giving him just enough light to see by. Eventually the tunnel began to widen out into an open area, this one filled with crevices, hidey-holes, and other tucked-away areas completely filled with all manner of bottles, jars, and nets.

Hanging upside down from the ceiling, a throne made of some sort of reddish material filled with holes dominated the room, while directly underneath it a bubbling pool of glowing liquid miraculously somehow stayed put in a rock cauldron, not mixing with the water at all.

"No one's here," said May from behind him as she and Phillip slowly swam into the room.

Out of nowhere, Jack suddenly heard humming, just as a bolt of white lightning as bright as the sun sizzled through the water and exploded against the wall behind them, blowing a hole right into the rock. All three of them whirled around to find a small army of mermen staring at them, lined up like soldiers. And in front of the soldiers stood one of the most beautiful mermaids Jack had ever seen, long red hair swaying in the water, lightning playing between her fingers as she hummed, her tail a shimmering shade of green.

"Humans?" the mermaid said, sounding surprised as the lightning disappeared. "It's been quite a while since I've seen your type down here. What's the word for your young? A 'school'?"

"That's fish," May said quietly.

The mermaid smiled. "Ah, yes," she said. "A school is where your young are educated. But a school of fish? Why would you call it such?"

"Why play with them, Meghan?" a merman to the woman's right said quietly, this one wearing a metal helmet in the shape of a shark's mouth, a visual that didn't particularly match the bright blue, almost feathery tail that started at his waist.

"I am not playing," Meghan said, throwing Blue Tail a smile. "I've always been fascinated by humans, that's all."

This seemed to annoy Blue Tail. "And how did that end?"

Meghan's eyes narrowed, and she shook her head. "You promised you would never bring that up again."

"You're right, I'm sorry," Blue Tail said. "But enough with these creatures. We followed them here. This was obviously their goal. They seek to steal from the fabled Sea Witch, apparently." He smiled at this, though the smile didn't reach his eyes.

"How are you breathing underwater, humans?" the mermaid asked. "Creatures as young as you shouldn't know magic that complex."

"Um, someone helped us with that," Jack said, not sure how much to share just yet. "Either way, we're not here to hurt you, so—"

"Hurt *us*?" Blue Tail almost whispered. His tail twitched and he shot forward, stopping just inches from Jack's face. "And how exactly could you do that?"

All of the frustration of the last few minutes exploded in Jack's chest, and abruptly the entire world slowed down. Instantly Blue Tail, Meghan, the rest of the mermen, everything froze almost to a complete halt. Jack, his eyes completely empty, took his now black sword off his back and raised it to the merman's neck, then released everything to speed up once more.

"Let's be honest," Jack said to the surprised Blue Tail. "I wouldn't be able to get you all. But I could get a few, maybe even most. And my two friends? They're a lot faster than me. So maybe just *listen* to us for a second?"

"You're an *Eye*," the mermaid said, lightning now playing over her fingers again. Jack couldn't tell if she said it with respect, fear, or hatred . . . or some fun combination of all three.

"Not exactly," Jack responded. "Unless, you know, that helps?"

Meghan smiled. "Only in that it tells me clearly which of you is the most dangerous. You're right, Mako, we need to stop playing around." She raised her hand, and a tornado of water exploded toward Jack, a lightning bolt crashing in the center of the tornado.

Instantly Jack slowed time once more, and brought the sword up to block, but the blast was too fast. The sword barely managed to deflect the lightning, while the brunt of the water tornado sent Jack flying back against the nearby cave wall.

"Kill the others," the mermaid declared calmly. "I'll take the Eye."

"We must be quick," Blue Tail said. "If the Wicked Queen

dares send her Eyes to the Sea Witch's lair, then the King should hear about this."

"Stop calling it a lair," Meghan said. "It is my escape. Nothing more."

"YOU'RE the Sea Witch?" May blurted out.

"Do not call me that," Meghan said, turning her lightning-crackling hands toward May.

"But we need your help! The Fairy Homelands—"

May abruptly went silent as the mermaid hummed quickly, and seaweed wrapped itself around May's mouth. The mermaid floated closer, glaring at her. "If you value your life, you will never mention those fairies again," she said.

"I've changed my mind," Blue Tail said, looking a bit more thoughtfully at the three of them. "We may indeed learn something from these children." He turned to look at Jack. "For instance, how one so young might hold such power, yet not have any idea how to use it."

"You're just bitter," Jack said, sucking in water to fill his lungs, "'cause I . . . was faster than you and . . . your pretty blue girly tail."

Blue Tail smiled dangerously, then said one word: "Frenzy."

Instantly the entire group of mermen attacked, shooting off in every direction. Jack focused, blocking the first few hits, but there were too many merman, all moving just a bit slower than he did, and eventually a few blows made it through his defense. Moments later Jack, Phillip, and May were separated, each one bound with ropes of braided seaweed, then dragged before Blue Tail and Meghan.

The Sea Witch frowned. "This is a mistake, Mako. You're knowingly bringing an Eye into the castle of the King of the World?"

"I'm curious why the Wicked Queen would send obviously untrained soldiers into our realm," Blue Tail said, then glanced at Meghan. "Whether or not it brings up bad memories."

The Sea Witch sighed, then abruptly nodded, a small smile playing on her face. "I do love you, Mako, but sometimes you can be so very irritating," she said, and turned away.

"Bring them," Blue Tail said to his fellow mermen. The three humans were each grabbed by two mermen, then roughly dragged by their now revealed feet after the swimming creatures, off apparently to meet the king of the entire world.

CHAPTER 20

Word must have spread quickly about the capture of the humans, as mermen and mermaids lined their route all the way from the lair of the Sea Witch, almost as if they were watching a parade, the most silent parade in history. Not one word, not one noise escaped from any of the merfolk. Some looked angry, some looked satisfied, but most just looked afraid. More than one refused to even look in their direction.

"Something's off about all of this," Jack whispered to Phillip, who was being carried next to him. May, on the other side of Phillip, glared at the merfolk mobs, seaweed still covering her mouth.

"They are frightened," Phillip replied, his eyes running over the merpeople. "Not only are we invading their realm, but you are an Eye. There is nowhere, land or sea, that has not been terrorized by the Eyes."

"Phillip, would you shut up?" Jack whispered. "I'm *not* an Eye! It's . . . it's complicated."

"What's complicated?" Blue Tail asked Jack quietly from behind him. "Your mission? The more you tell us, the better things will go for you."

Jack tried to look back at Blue Tail, but the mermen holding him just yanked him forward. "Tempting," he said. "I mean, I do like you guys, and I feel really close to you now. Like we're best friends. We just have this instant bond. And I think you feel the same. Am I right?"

Neither merman answered.

"Oh stop, you're embarrassing me," Jack said. "But here's the thing. There's no mission. I'm not an Eye. We're just here to find a fairy—"

Suddenly Jack's mouth was filled with seaweed and he couldn't speak.

"What did I say about that?" the Sea Witch told him. She glanced at Blue Tail. "Eyes are known to lie, Mako. Best not listen to him."

"How can we decide what are lies and what is truth if he cannot speak?" Blue Tail said, reaching forward to pull the seaweed from Jack's mouth.

"The King will know," the Sea Witch said, gliding between Jack and Blue Tail. "The King knows all, does he not? He shall rip the truth from the Eye. Maybe if you're good, you can have whatever's left to use for target practice."

Blue Tail smiled. "As you wish, Meghan." He reached past her as her eyebrows raised in suspicion. But instead of removing the seaweed, Blue Tail gestured, and the procession began moving once again. "And you are correct," Blue Tail continued. "This is a matter for the King. He will get to the truth of all this."

The Sea Witch's eyes narrowed, but she patted his shoulder affectionately and swam to the head of the column.

"She seems anxious," one of the mermen holding Jack's arms said to Blue Tail, this one with the lower half of a dolphin. "Is everything still going swimmingly between the two of you?"

"Of course," Blue Tail said, then threw a glance at Jack. "At least, it was before this uncomfortable reminder of her past. But now's not the time to speak of such things." Blue Tail kicked his bright, feathery tail and swept ahead of Jack, patting him on his head as he passed, much like a human petting a dog. It was hardly a comforting gesture.

As they continued, Jack noticed a path of something red begin beneath his feet, something that almost resembled tree bark . . . or the throne back in the Sea Witch's lair. Whatever it was didn't look comfortable, so for once Jack was glad not to have to walk. The path grew and filled in as they walked, even as more and more merfolk began lining it. "If I may, what type of material is this, sir?" Phillip asked one of the mermen holding his arms. Even when facing an army of vicious, predatory merman, the prince's manners stayed perfect.

"Coral," replied the merman, a shimmery yellow-tailed monster wearing a spiked blowfish helmet made of gold.

"It has a certain remarkability to it. I have never seen anything quite like it," Phillip replied.

The merman grunted in reply, but Jack noticed he smiled a bit proudly, if just a bit. Maybe having manners didn't hurt with people . . . even fish people.

Other roads of coral now blended into the one they used, and the combined road became much more ornate, with elaborate archways and starfish shining on what seemed to be some kind of writing, maybe directions or a street sign. Jack noticed that the writing on the sign pointing back the way they'd come had a picture of an open mouth absolutely filled with teeth.

Apparently there were warnings about going into the lair of the Sea Witch.

Just then, Phillip gasped in surprise, and Jack looked up to see a glowing golden spire appear on the horizon. As they continued on, more of what looked to be a twisting and spiraling castle appeared, almost as if it had grown straight out of the ground.

"The Palace of the King of the World," Phillip's golden merman told them proudly. "As alive as any of us. The coral shaped it themselves."

"Mmph . . . mephive?" Jack said into the seaweed, forgetting no one could understand him.

"Looks as if that is the case," Phillip responded, still staring at the castle. Jack glanced at him. He couldn't have understood him . . . could he?

"Mpn phho muphermpn mphe?" he asked.

Phillip turned to look at him. "Why would I not be able to? But now is not the time for riddles, Jack. We need a plan."

"You need to keep quiet, young one," the golden merman said, but it seemed less threatening than an effort to keep them all out of trouble. Either way, Phillip went silent, and Jack turned back to gawking at the seemingly living castle they were being carried into.

The palace had no doors, no locks, obviously no moat. Mermen and mermaids swam freely in and out, something Jack had never seen on the surface. Was there no concern for the King's safety? Where were the guards?

As they continued in, they passed doorways without doors, some leading to hallways but others leading to what looked like huge piles of gold, jewels, and treasure.

"That is a treasure to rival any I have seen on land," Phillip said. "But is there no fear of theft?"

The golden merman grinned. "What could the King of the World possibly have to fear? All of his subjects both respect and adore him. Nothing beneath the sea even approaches his power, and that goes double for anything in that suffocating void you call air. The King prefers to let all his subjects share in what he has—so long as none of it goes anywhere."

"Fugu, maybe a *bit* less sharing with the prisoners?" Blue Tail murmured as he swam back toward them. The golden merman, Fugu, blushed and quickly shut his mouth.

"Anyway, we're here," Blue Tail continued, stopping the company in front of a large archway, beyond which lay a shadowed room. "Leave the monkey-leggers with me. They're no danger, not this close to the king."

Jack tensed, readying himself. If he could grab his sword from where Blue Tail had slung it over his back, they might have a chance. The mermen on either side of him released his arms, and Jack focused hard, waiting for time to slow. . . .

Except it didn't. The world didn't slow down at all. If anything, it seemed to speed up, as instantly Blue Tail appeared right in front of him, a smile covering his face.

"Got that out of your system, did you?" he said, then pulled the seaweed off of Jack's and May's faces. "You'd think I was hatched just this past week, as gullible as you believe me to be." At that, he reached over his shoulder and removed Jack's sword.

Only to hand it right back to Jack.

"JACK!" May yelled. "NOW! SWORD HIM! SWORD HIM IN HIS FACE!"

But Jack just replaced the sword on his back, eyeing Blue Tail carefully. "It wouldn't do any good," he told May, not taking his eyes off Blue Tail. "We may just be in trouble here."

"You may just, at that," Blue Tail said, still smiling as he gestured for Jack, Phillip, and May to go into the shadowed room where the King of the World awaited them.

CHAPTER 21

There was no throne in the throne room. In fact, there were no seats of any kind . . . nor anything else. From what little Jack could see in the shadows, there was nothing in the room beyond the walls encircling them and a dark ceiling that seemed to let light in from different spots every time he looked.

Jack took a step closer to May and Phillip, both for protection and just to not feel so alone in the vast room. "Well," May whispered, "it's wet, I'll give it that."

A shiver ran up Jack's spine, and he quickly looked around as the other two crowded even closer. They were all feeling it, whatever *it* was.

"Is someone watching us?" May asked, shivering with a chill not from the water's temperature.

"The walls," Phillip said, nodding to his side, and Jack glanced up. Was he saying there was someone there?

And then a large green eye swiveled around to stare right at Jack. The walls weren't stone or coral. They were fish. The biggest fish Jack had ever seen.

"No wonder the King has no need for guards," Phillip said. "One of those creatures could swallow the three of us whole."

"That's a pleasant thought," May said, threading her arm through Phillip's.

Jack forced a laugh, staring at May's arm in Phillip's. "These things are smaller than giants, Phillip. Don't tell me you're *afraid!*"

Phillip threw Jack a slightly dazed look. "Of course not, Jack," he said. "This is what I have been trained for. You are all quite safe in my care here."

"Not all of us," Jack said, giving May a dirty look that she never noticed. "And how, exactly, do you expect to save us if those creatures attack?"

"The whales?" May asked. "You know they don't eat humans, right?"

"They haven't in a century," a deep voice rumbled from above them. "But perhaps they haven't lost the taste for your kind just yet."

All three of them looked up, but all they could see was the shifting light of the moving "whales," if that's what they were called.

"Who speaks?" Phillip demanded, pushing May behind him and stepping forward.

And just like that, Phillip was gone, a lone bubble popping in the spot where he'd stood a moment before.

"PHILLIP!" May screamed, and she immediately disappeared as well.

Jack whirled around, his sword drawn, but the sword's glow seemed to struggle against the shadows . . . struggled and lost as it slowly flickered out. He glanced at it in shock, then pushed it back into its scabbard and turned to the archway . . .

Only to watch the walls push together, collapsing the archway into nothingness. Great.

"Do not leave yet, little human," the deep voice rumbled again behind him, this time at Jack's level. "It's you I wish to speak to, *Eye*."

Jack whipped around, but saw nothing but a lazy flicking of a triangular tail.

"I'm no Eye," Jack said, his gaze flying around the room, just catching a glimpse here or there of the tail, or the glow of yellow eyes. "And we mean you no harm."

"You could no more harm me than you could stop the tide," the voice growled from above him again. "Your Queen had a hard time believing that, at first. Or did she not tell you about the others she sent?"

"She . . . Others?" Jack said, still frantically looking for the King.

"I'm actually a bit surprised that she sent you three into my realm so . . . blatantly," the voice said, always behind Jack. "Before, she had the common sense to at least completely turn your brothers and sisters into merfolk before sending them down to spy on my people. Not you, though. I cannot begin to fathom what she hoped to accomplish."

"She didn't send us," Jack said quickly. "I'm *not* an Eye. I just—"

"Perhaps she hopes I will destroy you," the voice said behind him, now just a foot or two from Jack. "Perhaps you are no longer of use to her, and she wishes me to do her dirty work."

Jack slowly turned, and found himself staring at a merman easily twelve feet long from the tip of his tail to the top of his head. The King's bottom half was a sleek white and gray finned fish of some kind, but the human half of the King looked no less lethal, nor did the golden trident he held casually in his hand.

"Perhaps if I destroy you and do her a favor, she will finally leave my people be," the king said, appearing to consider the idea.

"She doesn't even know I'm here," Jack said, throwing his hands up in surrender. "Really, we only came to find a—"

The trident glowed brightly, and lightning began playing around its tines. Faster than Jack could see, the king reversed his trident and launched it in Jack's direction.

It hit Jack with the force of a crashing wave, catching him by his shirt in one of the razor-sharp tines, plowing into the coral floor and pinning him there.

"All I asked was for your kind to leave ours alone, Eye," the king said, his eyes flashing with lightning matching that of his trident. "A half century ago our kind traded freely, but then . . ." The King's face contorted in rage. "But then your people took my *daughter*, Eye!" His voice rose as he grew angrier, and here and there the whales jumped in fright. "Your kind took her from me! I had to go onto land MYSELF to take her back! It was all I could do not to wipe that pathetic little kingdom out completely, but for the love of my daughter, I let that . . . that *prince* and his people live. But never again has a human been allowed in the water. Never again! Yet now you are here." He swam down and looked Jack right in the eye. "You three, you will tell me everything you know about the Queen's plans. Or I will feed you to the sharks. *All* of the sharks, at once."

Jack swallowed hard. "And if we tell you?"

"Then I shall merely lock you away until you starve to death," the King said, yanking his trident out of the ground, freeing Jack. "You have one hour to decide."

And with that, Jack disappeared in a bubble burst as well.

CHAPTER 22

Well that was stupid," May said as she reappeared. Then she realized she was talking to herself, and repeated the same thought in her head. And then she realized that maybe she'd be better off spending her time looking around rather than making snarky comments in her head.

Then she decided that there was nothing better than making snarky comments in her head, but still . . . looking around was probably smart.

"Hello?" May said to the darkness surrounding her, darkness not really that unlike the throne room she'd just been disappeared from.

The familiar-looking darkness didn't answer her, which was irritating. That meant that Phillip, at least, had been disappeared somewhere else, not in hearing range. What was even more irritating was that Jack might still be back in the throne room, and who knew if he was okay? Jack was just so useless on his own! Honestly, without her around he'd probably been eaten by another giant. Or worse. Yeah, probably worse.

"Hello?" May said again, tired of the annoying darkness. She felt around the floor beneath her, and decided it was probably coral. She was still swimming, so at least she hadn't been magicked right out of the ocean. Not that returning to land would have been such a bad thing. At this point she might have even welcomed it, Sea Witch or no. Not without Jack and Phillip, but still.

Anyway, what was the Sea Witch's deal? They'd just tried to talk to her, and she went and freaked out at the tiniest mention of fairies. It was rude, first of all, but there were a lot of second of alls.

"This whole *place* is rude," May said as she slid her feet carefully over the coral, moving slowly in the darkness. "If by 'rude' I mean stupid. And I *do*. Jerks." And they were jerks. After all, they were the ones who couldn't even get their own stories right. The Sea Witch wasn't the one who turned into a mermaid in the story. It was the mermaid who turned human! Which, granted, sounded like it had happened, but hadn't everything turned out okay in that story? Or was that the cartoon version, not the original? Had anyone even *read* the original?! May hadn't ever been allowed to read fairy tales, for reasons that were now becoming a little bit more obvious.

Her right foot tapped a wall, and she pushed her hands up against it. Coral again. At least it wasn't a whale, which was a plus, given that whales could probably swallow a bus whole, not to mention her. Of course, Jack was probably still back in the whale room, with whoever it was, the King of the Seven Seas. If that boy did something dumb like get hurt, she really was just gonna have to kill him.

The coral wall seemed to be curving around, so May followed it until she felt an indentation, something that reminded her uncomfortably of bars in a jail cell. She frowned; this whole thing seemed a little too familiar, reminding her of Malevolent's cells. Granted, she had regrown most of her sarcasm, but there probably weren't a whole lot of imps living underwater anyway.

"Way to go, Jack," she said, yanking on the bars. "How am I supposed to rescue you when I'm all locked up?"

"Perhaps I can help," said a voice from the other side of the bars.

May squinted, trying to see who or what was talking, but

unless who or what was solid darkness, she was at a loss. "Maybe you can," May said tentatively. "But I'm gonna need to hear any conditions up front. You know, like if you help me escape, then you get to eat me, that sort of thing."

The voice sighed. "I have no desire to eat you. I need to know why you're looking for the Sea Witch."

May forced a laugh. "See, I was just throwing that *eating* thing out as a wild possibility, and now you're talking as if eating me isn't a wild possibility at all, more like a household-dog- or cat-tame possibility." Why was her eyesight taking so long to adjust? Talking to this person blind wasn't helping her comfort level at all. "And why do *you* care about why I care about the Sea Witch?"

A familiar-looking mermaid with red hair and a shimmering green tail floated up to the bars. "Because she was very special to me," Meghan said.

May gasped, then realized something wasn't making sense. Well, more than usual. "Wait, I thought *you* were the Sea Witch."

Meghan sighed. "I never really believed the myths that humans were less intelligent than merfolk, but perhaps there is some truth there. I am *not* the Sea Witch. At least, not in the way you mean. You're referring to . . ." She paused. "You're referring to a fairy queen."

"YES, that's her, that's the one we want!" May shouted. "Where is she, so I can call *her* the Sea Witch and she can help us?"

"I'm afraid she's not able to help anyone," Meghan said. "The Sea Witch is dead."

"Dead?" May said, hope floating away from her like bubbles rising to the surface. "No . . . NO. No, no, no. She can't be dead. She's not dead. We *need* her! She's the only one who can help her people. There's a spell, a curse! And she needs to go home, to go back to her homeland and fix it!"

"I'm very sorry," Meghan said. "She was . . . quite important to me as well. I still grieve her absence to this day, almost fifty years later."

"Great, you go ahead and grieve her," May said, flopping herself to the coral floor as quickly as the water would let her. "It's a good time for it. There are about to be a hundred thousand fairies in need of some grieving by this time tomorrow."

"She was my mentor," Meghan said, apparently having heard none of what May had said. "A friend to me when no one else was. She understood what I was going through, as neither of us felt as if we belonged among our own people. Her kind treated her horribly, could never understand her love for a merman, my father. And once she left, they resolved never to speak to her again. So she gave up her old life to become something new."

May started to say something about how that was a long way to go to impress a man, but kept her mouth shut, figuring now was maybe not the best time.

"My father soon rejected her," Meghan continued. "He was as blind as her kind had been. He couldn't understand. I was her only friend here, a kindred soul. She taught me that there is magic in music, and gave me the power to do what she had done, even if she didn't realize it."

It took a second, but the mermaid's words gradually filtered through May's dark daydreams of dragons flying toward the Fairy Homelands. "Wait . . . who's your father?"

"The Sea King," Meghan said, her back still turned.

"You're the princess?" May asked. "The one who turned human to be with your prince?"

It was like a jolt of electricity hit Meghan right in the back. "What . . . what do you know of that?"

"Some of your sisters told my friend," May said. "They said Bluebeard's looking for you. He's the one who brought us here, to find the Sea Witch. He said he needed the Sea Witch to help him on a job. Sounds like you're the job. Maybe your prince sent him here to find you again?"

"You're lying," Meghan said, pushing her face up to the bars to stare May in the face. For some reason May had assumed Meghan would be older, given that she'd supposedly turned human, like, fifty years ago, but aside from the yellow eyes and sharp fangs, the woman pushing her face against the bars didn't look more than her early thirties, tops.

"Uh . . . okay, whatever you say," May told her, taking a step back. The mermaid's voice might have been gentle, but those eyes . . . It felt like the look a lion gave children watching it in a zoo. Only this time, May was on the wrong side of the bars. "Listen, we're all a little on the sketchy side with the whole Blue-beard thing. I get it, he's creepy, but you said something about the Sea Witch giving you power—"

"She didn't give me anything; she taught me how to sing," Meghan said absently. "I was one of the few she'd ever met who could match her voice, and therefore could use the magic of the fairy queens. Why? Why would he come, after so long?"

"Oh, he's been trapped for, like, forty years," May told her. "Along with your sisters. Long story. But this could be perfect! With your Sea Witch magic, you could help us save the Fairy

Homelands AND do whatever it is that Bluebeard needs to get you back to your prince! Then everyone's happy, or tragic, or whatever it is you're trying to be by giving everything up for your human boyfriend!"

"The fairies don't deserve my help, not after how they treated my friend," Meghan said. "And as for . . . Bluebeard, I . . . It's been so many years, I—"

"I could take you to the ship," May said quietly. "You know, so you can talk to him about your prince, and see what's what. But if I do that, I'm going to need *your* help."

"Are you trying to bargain with me?" Meghan said, her eyes narrowing. "I could just leave you here. My father intends to starve you, or feed you to the sharks."

"Gah," May said. "And wow, by the way. 'Cause we didn't do anything but show up here. That's really sweet of him. But you realize if either of those two delightful options actually happens, I won't be able to take you to Bluebeard, which I'll do *if* you free my friends, and help us end a curse on the fairy queens. Honestly, you may be the only person in this entire world who could!"

"Curse?" Meghan said absently, not really paying much attention.

"It's a long and kinda complicated story that I really don't want to get into with you right now, but to sum up, the fairies and fairy queens are all about to die, and our only chance of saving them is to bring a fairy queen back with us. We couldn't find any others, except that supposedly the Sea Witch is—*was* one, and—"

"Just stop for a moment," Meghan said, turning away again. "This isn't just about love, or bitterness, or any of that."

"So what's the issue?" May said impatiently. "And if we could move this along, that'd be amazing. We're really not doing well on time here."

"When I turned myself human," Meghan said slowly, "my father blamed the Sea Witch. After he followed me to shore and took me back here, he put the Sea Witch on trial."

"So?" May said. "It's not like she did anything. You did all the magic yourself, right?"

Meghan nodded. "But my father didn't care. Instead he found her guilty . . . then executed her." She looked up at May, her eyes reddish, though any tears were hidden in the water. "It is my fault the Sea Witch is dead, human. Because I used her magic, I killed her!"

CHAPTER 23

Jack bubbled into existence just in time for something hard to slam into him, sending him smashing into what felt like vertical pillars of coral.

All the water whooshed from Jack's lungs, and he glanced up to see . . . nothing, since it was completely dark.

"Buh?" Jack said when he could breathe.

"Jack?" a certain familiar prince said.

"Phillip?!" Jack shouted. "What was *that* for?!"

"I was attempting to break free of this cell!" Phillip said. "Why would you choose to appear directly in front of me?!"

"You're right," Jack said, shaking his head. "I'll know better than to do that next time." He glanced around, barely able to make out the prince, but nothing else. "You're sure we're in a cell?"

"Yes. My eyesight has adjusted, and I explored a bit before you showed up. Unfortunately, the coral is strong, so I weakened it as much as I could by picking away at it, then—"

"Then kicked off the wall, right into me," Jack finished. "Great plan, up until the part where you almost knocked me out. Where's May?"

Phillip gasped. "The princess was taken as well?! Jack, you were supposed to protect her once I was removed from the situation!"

"How could I have been so stupid, not to realize that?" Jack said. "Seriously, put that genius mind of yours on a better way of getting out of here than hitting the bars really hard, 'cause it's just wasted analyzing all my mistakes. I can't wait to see what you come up with!"

"Perhaps your sword?" Phillip said.

Jack stopped, blushing hard, glad the prince couldn't see him. But after a quick reach to his back and finding no sword, Jack thankfully switched back to sarcasm. "Oh, *fantastic* idea! It'd help if they hadn't taken it from me!"

"It would appear that we are trapped here, then."

"Either that," Jack said, sitting down on the coral floor, "or fed to sharks. We'll know either way in an hour."

"An hour?" Phillip said, punching his hand. "We do not have much time to escape and rescue the princess, then."

"Let's hope your escaping skills are as good as your grasp of time measurements," Jack told him, feeling around on the ground. Somehow the coral floor grew right into the walls, as there wasn't even a seam.

"Perhaps we could get help," Phillip suggested as he picked away at the bars. "Perhaps we could find this mermaid princess, the one her mermaid sisters mentioned."

"Oh, I'm sure she's coming along at any second," Jack told him. "I bet she'll randomly show up here and poke her head in these bars to chat. 'Cause that's *so* likely to happen." He rolled his eyes. "Your grasp of reality frightens me sometimes."

"Speaking of reality," Phillip said, his tone darkening, "I believe it is time to explain to me how the Eye speaks to you in your dreams." Jack just grunted, so the prince continued. "Stories say that the Eyes typically kill the strong but infect the minds of the weak-willed in order to better control the populace."

"Do those stories have a twist ending?" Jack asked, his anger rising. "Seriously, I love when they end all crazy."

"One story that I have heard begins with a small puppy—"

"Okay, ENOUGH!" Jack said, standing up and confronting what

he first assumed to be Phillip but turned out to be the wall just to the right of the prince. Adjusting on the fly, Jack turned his anger away from the innocent coral and back to Phillip. "I'm *not* weak-willed, I'm not being controlled, and I'm not turning into an *Eye*, Phillip!"

Phillip sighed. "Unfortunately, that is what I would expect someone being controlled to say. I cannot take the chance, not with the princess's safety. This new Eye, the girl . . . she affected you. Perhaps you are even now leading her to us."

"Like that would ever happen!" Jack shouted. "That girl has no idea where we are!"

"Oh, hey you two, what's going on?" said the last person in the world Jack could have ever wanted to speak up at that moment.

Abruptly a glowing white sword lit the water.

And then, so did a second sword.

On the other side of the bars floated a mermaid with a red fishtail and dark brown hair. And in each hand was the sword of an Eye.

"You two really should have worked on your disguises a little better," mermaid Lian said, looking them up and down. "I can't tell you how little I believe you're mermen."

Jack growled in frustration, then whirled around, punching with all his might through the bars, straight at Lian.

His fist stopped less than an inch from her nose, but the mermaid never moved.

"Oooh, so close!" she said with a smile, then drove the flat of Jack's own sword down on his hand. He yanked his hand back, throbbing to the very bone, but he wasn't going to give Lian the satisfaction of knowing it hurt.

"It's okay, I already know," she told him, and he growled again. This couldn't be happening!

"Why are you here?" Phillip asked her. "We are trapped, what more could you want? Do you wish to gloat?"

"Oh, nothing so classless," the mermaid said, her tail flicking gently in the water, somehow keeping the rest of her body almost entirely still despite the flow of the water. "I'm actually here to let you two out."

Both Phillip and Jack raised an eyebrow, and the mermaid laughed. "Oh, don't look so surprised. I didn't say I was going to *help* you, just let you out."

"And why would you do that, then?" Jack asked as he glared at her with all the hatred in the world, hoping she felt every last ounce.

"Well, first I'm going to take the three of you back to land," she told him, counting it off on her fingers. "Then I'm going to deliver you all to my Queen."

"That's not going to happen!" Jack told her in a deep, intimidating voice. "Well, maybe the first one. Okay, so one of those things is going to happen, but it won't be the second one—"

"Be still," Phillip told him, his focus on the mermaid.

"Wow, you'll just let anyone control you, won't you?" Lian said to Jack. "Me, the princey prince here . . . Does May order you around too?"

"*No one* controls me," Jack told her.

"Except the Eyes," Phillip said.

"And anyone else you happen to meet," the mermaid sniffed. "Anyway, you need to get back to land, so let's get going." She paused. "Oh, and third, if you'd let me get to it, is that we're going to kill the Sea King's daughter."

As Jack and Phillip just stared at her, stunned, Lian slapped her fin on the ground impatiently. "Seriously, I don't have all day, and that's a long list! Are you ready to go or what?"

CHAPTER 24

O h, wow," May said, staring at Meghan, who wouldn't look at her. "But it wasn't your fault. It was your father."

"He couldn't believe it!" Meghan shouted, still not looking. "I told him exactly what happened, that I had performed the magic, not her. But he wouldn't accept that I had done such things! And for that she paid with her life."

"Well, that's completely tragic," May said, "but apart from all that, I'm not really seeing where all the beating up on yourself comes in."

Meghan turned, her eyes burning a deep yellow. "Consequences are consequences, whether we expect them or not. And I must live with the fact that I caused her death." She shook her head slowly. "I cannot see . . . my human prince. I have moved on. Anything I felt for him, it's passed."

May sighed. "Listen," she said in her most sympathetic voice. "I feel for you, I really do. But it's time to put on your big-girl pants and get over yourself."

Meghan looked up, her eyes wide. "I'm sorry?"

"You should be!" May shouted, the fake sympathy pretty much forgotten. "Honestly? I couldn't care any less about all this tragic prince-mermaid love. I just want to save thousands of fairies before they get burned by dragon fire. But I can see how your problems are much more important than their lives."

"That is none of my concern," Meghan said, and turned away again.

"You know, I would have asked the Sea Witch," May said quietly, "but she isn't exactly around to help me now, is she. *Why* is that again?"

And there it was, a guilt card ten miles high by an infinite miles long. Meghan, meanwhile, slowly turned to look at her, appearing to have some trouble forming words, she was so in shock, and May didn't blame her. If May had been Meghan, she would have hit her May self over and over with her bright green tail. But May wasn't Meghan, she was May. And May had things to take care of. The last thing she was going to do was just leave those fairies to die, all because she'd released the Wicked Queen back into the world.

"You're right," Meghan said quietly.

"I'm what?" May said, a bit distracted by her own guilt.

Meghan shook her head. "You're right. If not for me, the Sea Witch would be here now to choose whether to return to her people and save them all. Perhaps this was her chance to reconnect with her family. And maybe I . . . could begin to make up for what I did to her."

"Yes, you could," May said, "and I like where you're going with this. But maybe let's not forget who's really at fault here. Namely, your father, the crazy guy with the trident."

Instantly Meghan's hands flew through the coral bars and grabbed May by her shirt, then yanked her hard against the coral. The mermaid pulled her own head to the bars, and with fangs bared and eyes blazing, she stared right into May's soul. "You will NOT say such things about the King of the World!"

May nodded quickly, the water suddenly dropping in temperature about fifty degrees. And that was a drop of fifty degrees Celsius, which she really had no idea how to convert, but she knew meant it was way colder.

"If you so much as raise your voice about my father again, I will abandon those fairies to whatever deity they worship," Meghan told May softly, then slowly let lose her grip on May's shirt and dropped her back to the seafloor.

"Right," May said, her pulse racing a marathon. "Nothing but compliments for your dad from here on. So, speaking of that other thing, how about you just magic me and my friends straight on to the Fairy Homelands, then?"

"No magic," Meghan said, glancing around. "My father would know. That is why the Sea Witch had her lair so far from his palace. But even that is not safe, not with him on guard against your little friend, the Eye. No, we must get closer to land. That's where I did my own magic the first time, just to be sure he didn't find out."

"Which he obviously never did, so *that* plan is foolproof," May said.

"It wasn't the magic that alerted him, girl," Meghan said, bending over to pick up an overly large piece of coral. "It was a young merman who followed me out of concern, then told my father for the same reason." She sighed, fitting the coral between the bars of the cell. "He's not going to be happy about this either."

Things started to fall into place. "That Mako guy?"

Meghan nodded. "It was a long time ago, and I know he had good intentions. . . . I've come to forgive him now. But it was years before I could even look at him, and years past that before I could develop feelings for him."

"Maybe less of the soap, and more of the opera," May said. "We'll get you back up to Bluebeard, who can take us to land, where you can sing us to the Fairy Homelands, and everyone's happy!"

"Bluebeard is waiting for you, correct?" Meghan asked. May nodded, and Meghan continued. "If my father learned that Bluebeard was even on the seas again, let alone this close—whether I intended to return to the human world or not—it would mean war, and terrible deaths on both sides." She glared at May. "NO ONE must know about this. Do you understand me?" With that, she braced the coral, then pushed as hard as she could.

The coral bars exploded apart, and Meghan knocked the remaining bits out of the way as May watched in awe. Each of those coral bars had felt like solid rock to May. How strong *were* the merpeople?

"So, keeping a low profile is definitely on the plus side," May said. "But there are two small leggish problems with that."

She kicked up with her legs, and wiggled them at Meghan as she pointed at them.

"Stop that," Meghan said with a little disgusted look. "It's a bit *unseemly*."

May stopped immediately, raising a questioning eyebrow. "But you . . . Your prince had legs."

"I tried not to look," Meghan sniffed. "Regardless, we can cover your shame with a formal dress."

"You have dresses long enough to cover your tails?" May asked. It seemed odd at first, but why wouldn't they? It's not like their feet needed to touch the ground for any reason. Really, the dresses could be—

Meghan handed her a bundle tied in seaweed. "This one is around forty fins long."

May stared at the bundle in much the same way Meghan had stared at her kicking legs. "Uh, right. So where are we going?"

"To the Sea Witch's old home, in the palace."

"I thought you said—"

Meghan sighed loudly. "She performed her *magic* in her cave. You really think a civilized person would live in such a dank, colorless place?"

May started to say something about how she thought all fish

lived in caves, then decided it might be better to actually shut up for a second. Meghan watched her warily, then continued.

"We need the Sea Witch's songbooks if I am to find the magic you say we'll need. After we find them, we will go free your other human friends. We do not have much time. When an hour has passed and my father realizes you have escaped, he won't stop until he's flayed the skin from your bones like human fishermen cruelly do to marine life."

May swallowed hard. "You all were a lot cuter in the cartoon, you know."

CHAPTER 25

Almost faster than Jack could follow, Lian sliced a hole in the coral bars using both swords, circling them in opposite directions. As soon as the coral bars fell into the cell, the swords disappeared into sheaths on her back just as quickly. "Ready, ladies?" she asked, gesturing politely for them to exit.

First Phillip, then Jack, slowly swam out of the cell as Lian waited impatiently. As soon as Jack's feet floated to the floor, he looked at Phillip, who nodded.

Immediately they both threw themselves at the Eye.

Just as fast, she slammed both boys into each other, then flipped around, grabbed their arms and yanked them up behind their backs.

"Well, that was impressive," she said, pushing up hard as both

Jack and Phillip groaned in pain. "Here's the thing," she said. "I don't have time to beat you two up every other minute. So I'll just say this: I can always tell my Queen I couldn't find you, then leave you to the Sea King. And that is going to be one unhappy father when he finds out humans killed his daughter."

"We will not help you just to save ourselves!" Phillip shouted.

"We could at least consider the idea," Jack hissed at the prince.

Lian laughed. "If it helps, Your Princeness, you'd also be saving your darling May. Do you really want to sentence her to death, or is it better that she stay alive with a grandmother who loves her?"

"The Wicked Queen is not capable of such emotions," Phillip said as he struggled against Lian, who barely seemed to notice.

"I'll admit she can be a bit . . . heartless," Lian said, then giggled. "Sorry, inside joke. So you're saying you're okay with leaving May here to be eaten by sharks, then."

"NO!" Phillip shouted through gritted teeth. "I shall do as you say. But the moment you—"

"Sure, sure," Lian said, then looked to Jack. "What about you, genius? You willing to throw away your life, or your princess's, just to spite me?"

Jack just looked at her for a moment. "You do make it sound

tempting, but no. You're right. I can wait for a better time to take you down."

Lian raised an eyebrow but nodded. "That's close enough to a yes. Well, then, let's get to killing mermaids! First, to the Sea Witch's old place."

The tunnels they found themselves swimming through dove and rose at random, sometimes spiraling around before emptying out into other passageways. Lian didn't seem to have any problem with directions, as she never even hesitated when picking a new tunnel.

Even the tunnel that led right to a dead end.

"Whoops!" Jack said with a wide smile. "Looks like someone's lost!"

Lian just rolled her eyes and pointed up. "Try not to be so stupid," she said. "It's hard, but give it a real effort. You don't have to just think in four directions when you're underwater." With that, she kicked off, shooting right into what looked like the ceiling, but instead slipped into a crevice just big enough for a human or merman to slip through.

This tunnel, if you could call it that, wasn't really much more than a vent in the rock, narrowing as it went. If Jack hadn't seen Lian slip through ahead of him, he'd have doubted if he could make it through. Still, his shoulders scraped harshly against the rock at times, and the tight quarters began making Jack nervous for some reason, as if the walls had been waiting for just the right moment to collapse, and now was that time. Knowing his luck, it wasn't out of the realm of possibility.

Just when Jack thought he couldn't take any more of this, that he had to get out of the tunnel *now*, Lian grabbed his arms and pulled him up into a room glowing with yellow light.

Not yellow light. Golden light. Gold. Gold, gold, gold, everywhere.

"One of the Sea King's treasure rooms," she said, pointing at the incalculable treasures all around them. Piles of gold coins large enough to dive into filled most of the room, barely held back from overflowing into the vent they'd just crawled through.

But it wasn't just gold. There were vases full of red opals, blue rubies, and orange sapphires. A statue made entirely of a black rock that seemed to suck the light out of the room around it. Priceless books. Well, the books hadn't stood up too well to the water, but the rest was still impressive.

"Spoils of war from attacking humans," Lian said. "When the Sea King first declared that no human was allowed in or on the water again, most didn't believe him. So mermen sank ship after ship until the message got through."

"I can't tell you how much I'm enjoying everyone's stories today," Jack said, "but aren't we in a hurry to get out of here? Maybe save your uplifting history lessons for your next victims."

"*Someone's* cranky!" Lian said indignantly. "Anyway, we have to go slow. Any alarm here will warn the Sea King, and that will mean we all end up fish food."

"I can handle slow," Jack said.

Lian winked at him irritatingly, then led them to a wall on the opposite side, and another horrifyingly tiny vent. She pushed, pulled, and inched her way in, scraping off a few scales on her fake tail as she went. Jack looked at Phillip with a sick look, then followed her in.

What felt like five of the worst years of his life later, Jack pulled himself out into a new room, this one with coral bars all around the open walls.

"Um, I think we took a wrong turn somewhere," Jack told Lian, who put a finger up to her lips.

"No talking," she whispered. "They shouldn't be hungry—I think they were just fed—but let's not give them any excuse."

"Them?" Jack said, then felt a wave of water brush against his back. Jack slowly turned around to see row upon row of jagged, rough teeth swimming right over him.

"Man-eating sharks," Lian said as another of the twenty-foot-long fish swam directly below them, its black eyes dead as some sort of undead monster. "Well, merman-eating sharks. All of the ones in here have attacked merfolk at one point or another. The merpeople don't kill them, since the sharks are just doing what comes naturally, so they lock them away for safety reasons."

"What do they feed them?" Jack asked as one of the creatures swam by with something red and unpleasant hanging out of its mouth.

"Usually fish," Lian said, swimming away slowly. "But if you didn't tell the Sea King what he wanted to know, you'd find out what else pretty quick."

Every inch of Jack wanted to swim away as fast as he could, but Lian kept barely moving, each of her strokes displacing almost no water whatsoever. Jack tried to match that, but anytime a shadow fell over him, he couldn't help himself, he had to kick away as fast as he could.

"Jack!" Phillip shouted, then yanked Jack down as one of the creatures swam right through the spot Jack had been in, its tooth-filled mouth open wide in anticipation. "That one had been watching you," the prince told him. "I think we should exit this area as fast as possible."

Up ahead Lian pushed herself into yet another crevice, and Jack was never so happy to see one. The monstrous creatures were far too large to fit into such a small space, but why was she taking so long to go in?!

"Any time you're ready!" Jack said, his voice rising as his panic did. The creature that had narrowly missed him had already circled around for a second pass, and his dead black eyes locked on Jack's.

The mermaid finally disappeared into the crevice, but it was too late. If Jack tried to get in now, the creature could bite him in half as he wriggled up inside the vent.

"GO, Jack, I will protect you," Phillip said, pushing Jack up to the opening.

"From THAT?!" Jack asked.

"GO!"

Jack quickly yanked himself up and desperately pulled himself in, but it was slow going; the vent was just too narrow. Below him he could almost feel the creature approaching, closing in, its mouth wide open . . .

And then Phillip punched the creature right in the nose.

The shark reared up, then swam right past the prince, its dead black eyes looking almost surprised. But surprise wasn't going to work more than once. Jack moved as fast as he could, finally giving the prince enough room to start in as well.

"HURRY!" Phillip hissed as Jack made his way up. Fortunately, the crevice opened just ahead into a new room, so Jack quickly pulled himself out of the way. He glanced down into the vent, but saw only darkness.

"Phillip?" Jack asked.

And then a hand popped out, almost stopping Jack's heart, until he realized it was still attached to an arm. Jack quickly pulled Phillip up and out, and the prince seemed whole enough.

Well, except for the huge hole ripped in his pants' leg.

"Let us never do that again," Phillip said, his eyes wild.

"Shh," Lian said, smacking the prince in the back of the head. She swam slowly forward, listening to voices from the other room.

"Let's not forget, we need to get Jack and Phillip before we go!" said May, and Jack suddenly felt a world of tension drain out of him, just knowing that May was alive, okay, and feeling good enough to be complaining pretty much as usual.

"We will," said another voice, one that sounded like the mermaid from the Sea Witch's lair. "But first we must find the Sea Witch's songbooks!"

Lian's eyes narrowed, and she inched forward.

"So you keep looking, and I'll go get the boys," May said, and her voice got louder as she spoke, as if she were swimming closer.

"Aha!" the mermaid said. "I think I found them! And by the way, that direction leads to the shark pens. Stay with me if you want to be safe."

"Ah," Lian said as she swam out into the other room. "But what if you're the one in danger?" With that, she drew both her swords and flew out of Jack's view.

Two women screamed, and a third voice, a masculine one, shouted, all before Jack could even move. And then one of the women went silent, and the entire room exploded with light.

CHAPTER 26

Less than ten minutes earlier, May had swum slowly through what felt like a crowd of hundreds of merpeople, the end of her dress trailing about thirty feet behind her. Apparently formal dresses on mermaids weren't quite the common thing that Meghan had presented them to be, considering *everyone* was staring.

"Isn't it a little late at night for all these people?" May whispered, a smile frozen on her face as she faked a friendly queen of England wave at the onlookers.

"Merfolk sleep throughout the day," Meghan answered quietly. "We are not slaves to your light cycles as you land folk are."

"That's exactly what we call them too, light cycles," May said. "Nice one." She glanced around at the crowds, all of which seemed to have stopped whatever they were doing to watch them. "Maybe next time you do this, pick a slightly less conspicuous outfit?"

"Oh yes, I'll happily pick between all the fin-hiding disguises I typically have on hand," Meghan said. "Just swim with confidence. They will assume you are from some lesser merfolk kingdom, here for a royal visit. They're probably more impressed by the expense of the gown than by you."

"Right," May said. "I've always known I was less impressive than what I was wearing."

"That's a beautiful dress!" one little mermaid girl called to her.

"I made it myself!" May said, her fake smile cracking a bit. "Now run—uh, swim along. Nothing to see here." The little girl smiled shyly, then flippered back to what May assumed was her mother. The mother was staring too, but with less believing in her eyes. Uh-oh.

"Maybe try for less attention, not more?" Meghan said. "The palace is just ahead. We should be out of the public eye in just a moment, so try to keep things under control, please."

"Ah, control," said a familiar merman's voice from behind them. "So easily lost, right, Princess?"

Meghan froze, causing May to swim right into her. They both flipped around (slowly in May's case, considering her thirty-foot dress) to find Captain Mako smiling at them, his hands clasped behind his back.

"You haven't introduced me to your friend, Meghan," he said, then turned his gaze to May. "Though I must say, she looks familiar. Please, give me a hint where I've seen her. I could use a leg up here." He smiled. "Silly me, using a human expression like that. I can't imagine why!"

Meghan's eyes narrowed. "What are you doing here, Mako?"

He swam a bit closer. "I was actually looking for you, and here you are. And with such a lovely mermaid beside you . . . wearing one of *your* dresses, if I'm not mistaken?"

"You *cannot* tell my father," Meghan said, her voice low and dangerous. "Please, I must do something for this human."

"*Must* you?" Mako asked, his voice lowering as well. "And what might that be, if I can ask?"

Meghan winced. "There are things that I did in the past that I haven't yet made up for, and—"

"The human prince," Mako whispered, his tone dropping even further in temperature. "Is that what this is? They're here to bring you back to your human?"

"No!" Meghan said. "How could you even think such things, after all this time?"

"Because we're speaking with a human girl not two fins from us!" Mako whispered more forcefully. "What else am I to think?!"

"It has nothing to do with him!" Meghan said, her low voice rising as well. "They needed the help of the Sea Witch—"

"Who is dead," Mako said. "End of story, it sounds like."

"*I* can help them," Meghan said. "And if you have any feelings for me whatsoever, you'll get out of my way and let me do just that!"

"But why humans?!" Mako asked. "I can't help but think—"

"Oh yes you can!" Meghan said. "You *can* think, but you don't! This doesn't have anything to do with that human!"

"It really doesn't, so maybe we should move on now?" May said. If there were a slow-conversation Olympics, these two would have been standing on the podium with medals around their necks a half hour ago.

Both of them glared at her.

"She is right, there's no time for this," Meghan said. "And people are starting to notice. I need to do this. I can do it with your help or without it, but I *will* do it. Which will it be?"

"I'm coming, of course," Mako said, "if just to ensure your safety."

"Oh yeah, the defenseless human in a mile-long dress can be

pretty dangerous," May pointed out, and this time ignored their glares. "Seriously, clock's ticking."

Meghan turned and swam into an upper floor of the palace, and Mako followed her, leaving May alone with far too many merpeople still staring. She gave them the queen wave one more time, then swam as fast as she could after them, twisting into and out of dark hallways until she almost plowed into Meghan, hunched over a moss-covered rock in the middle of a dark, sparsely furnished coral cave.

"Help me move this," she told Mako, who muttered to himself a bit but followed her orders.

"Let's not forget, we need to go get Jack and Phillip before we go!" May said as they muscled the rock out of the way.

"We will," Meghan said, pushing herself into a hole left beneath the moss-covered rock. "But first we must find the Sea Witch's songbooks!"

Meghan pushed herself in deeper until just her tail stuck out, as Mako watched both her and May with some suspicion.

"So you keep looking, and I'll go get the boys," May said, swimming away from Mako. The merman captain was a little too annoyed for her taste, and that look didn't seem to be headed toward happy anytime soon.

"Aha!" Meghan said, wriggling out of the hole holding several thin stone tablets. "I think I found them! And by the way, that direction leads to the shark pens. Stay with me if you want to be safe."

"Ah," said a voice from the direction May had been heading in. "But what if you're the one in danger?"

With that, the darkness lit up as two glowing swords both struck out, heading straight for Meghan.

May and Meghan both screamed in surprise, while Mako shouted something that May couldn't understand, as a mermaid, a glowing sword in each hand, backhanded one sword into Mako's face and threw the other right at Meghan's heart.

Meghan's eyes lit up like the sun as she began to hum, and lightning exploded from her hands directly at the sword. . . .

Which did nothing to stop its forward momentum.

What did stop the sword's momentum, however, was Mako's hand as he grabbed the blade in his palm. The pain from both the Eye's attack and the sword's cut were clear, but neither showed on the merman's face as he tossed the glowing sword back behind May, then turned to face the Eye.

"Oh, come on," the Eye said, looking annoyed. "You've got no chance here, fish-man. You versus me? You're slower than your tide!"

"Then it's good he's got help," said a familiar voice, and relief washed through May like a flash flood as she realized it was Jack. He slowly swam into view, the sword Mako had just thrown in his hand and Phillip at his side.

"Ready to try this again?" Jack asked the girl.

She smiled. "More than you know!" the Eye said, and just like that, everything fell into chaos.

CHAPTER 27

Jack moved to attack, but before he made it even a foot, he crashed backward, Lian's tail slamming into his chest faster than he could see. Bouncing off him, the Eye crashed into Mako, sending the merman tumbling into Phillip, while a stray lightning bolt from Meghan almost hit May before Lian smashed the mermaid into the coral wall hard enough to knock her still.

All this happened before Jack could even move again.

As Jack slowly pushed himself up from the ground, gasping for water, Lian picked up Jack's sword again and waved it around a bit. "I hadn't ever held the sword of another Eye before meeting you," she said. "The Charmed One must have been pretty powerful! He's done things to this sword, changed it somehow. I'm impressed!"

"You're gonna be . . . a lot more . . . impressed in a second," Jack said, still on the ground.

Mako shouted some sort of war cry and attacked again, ducking under Lian's sword as she swung it at him, only to find her tail hitting him right in his face. Phillip managed to avoid getting hit this time, moving to stand in front of May . . . or at least he tried. Lian grabbed his arm as he passed by and spun him around to throw him into a humming Meghan, knocking another bolt of electricity into the coral wall, this time exploding an enormous hole in it straight to the water outside.

Jack groaned loudly and pushed himself to his feet as best he could.

"You might just want to stay down," Lian said, not even looking at him or breathing hard.

Mako roared and attacked once more, and this time Lian sighed as her sword went back into its sheath and she blocked every one of his attacks with just one hand. "Seriously," she told him, effortlessly moving faster with every blow, "any time you want to stop this would be fine."

One last block, and she smashed him in the face with the hilt of Jack's sword, then turned to find Jack plowing right into her . . . or at least that was the idea. Instead Lian was suddenly two feet to the side, and Jack slammed into the coral wall.

Uh-oh.

"Uh-oh is right, Jack," she with the smile. "That *almost* had a shot at working. Kinda like your whole try at saving all those fairies for your little princess. How's that going for you, by the way?"

Jack took a deep breath, forcing himself to focus . . . only something else seemed to take over instead. His eyes went black, and time seemed to slow down, as it had in the past. Without thinking, he grabbed a piece of broken coral from the wall and whipped it at the spot where Lian was standing, then leapt to her side just as quickly.

Lian dodged the coral, throwing herself into Jack's path. Jack's momentum slammed her into the wall right next to Phillip, and in the fraction of a second when she was dazed, Jack grabbed his sword from her hand and held it to her throat as the color drained back into his eyes.

How had he just done that?!

"Oh, that's *fun*," Lian said, blinking. Her sword leapt off her back and slashed Jack's out of the way, freeing Lian. "Looks like someone else took over there for a second, huh?" She swam just out of Jack's reach, watching him closely. "I've always wondered how good the Charmed One really was. Maybe now's my chance to find out?"

And then Lian attacked.

Every time Jack struck at her with his sword, she easily parried it, then slapped Jack with the flat of the sword. Over and over this happened, each time humiliating Jack, if not hurting him. Whatever had helped him before, when time had slowed down, wasn't doing much now, and Jack quickly grew angrier and angrier. Finally, roaring in frustration, Jack launched his sword out—and at the last minute reversed it, driving the hilt as hard as he could right into Lian's face.

The Eye pulled back at the last moment, and Jack's attack barely missed her nose. "Oh, well done!" she said, almost looking surprised. "But maybe it's time to stop messing around."

With that, faster than Jack could see, the Eye slammed him against the coral wall. Before Jack could even blink, Lian was there, grabbing his shirt and crashing him into the opposite wall.

"Fun, huh?" she said, then launched a flurry of punches into Jack's stomach more times than Jack could count in the span of a second.

"Is it fun to play at being an Eye, Jack?" Lian asked. "Was it fun thinking you were outwitting my Queen? How about showing off to your little friends with one of our sacred swords? That must have been so *entertaining* for you!"

Jack tried to focus through the pain, and launched out with his sword, but Lian just snorted, not even bothering to move. Instead she clapped her palms on the blade, yanked it from Jack's hands, and slammed the hilt back into Jack's chest.

"You don't get it, do you?" she said, slapping Jack in the face with her tail, then slamming him down into the floor. "You can't save them. You can't even save yourself! You play at being some kind of hero, but you're *not*. You have no idea who you really are, and you *never* will!"

His chest heavy, and with sparkles bursting in front of his eyes as he struggled to breathe, Jack looked up to see Lian drop his sword right in front of him, almost tauntingly. "I'd take that away from you if I thought you could do anything with it," she said. "But as much as I'd love to keep having fun here, I don't have any more time for this. I need to make sure the mermaid princess dies first."

"Good luck with that," Captain Mako said from the hole in the coral wall. He grinned, pointing outside. "Half my army is on their way here right now, just seconds away. The sharks will feast well tonight!"

Lian sighed, then knocked the hilt of her sword into Mako's head—only for him to lock both arms around her waist and pull them both over backward, right out the hole in the wall.

"NO!" Lian shouted as she disappeared out the hole.

"MEGHAN, GO!" Mako shouted, and they were both gone.

"GO, GO, GO!" Jack shouted, pushing himself up. "We need to get out of here!"

May and Phillip both quickly pushed themselves up, then helped Meghan to a standing-floating-whatever position.

"The songbooks!" the mermaid said, grabbing for them. "I need them to figure out the correct music to take us to the Fairy Homelands!"

"Take them and let's go!" May shouted, looking out the hole in the wall. "Right now there are about a thousand mermen swimming this way, and I'm pretty sure they're not gonna be thrilled to see humans!"

"My father can't know about this!" Meghan said, almost pleading with them.

"Perhaps it is too late for that," Phillip pointed out. "Now we must flee if we hope to keep our lives. Will you come with us?"

Meghan glanced from Phillip to May to Jack, and sighed. "I . . . I will do this. For Mariella. I'll go."

"Good," May said, grabbing her hand. "We've got one shot at this, and that's only if we can make it to the pirate ship."

"To Bluebeard's ship," Meghan said, then shook her head. "No, this must be done. Hold on to me, children. I'm a faster swimmer than all of you."

The three of them grabbed hold of her arms, and Meghan exploded out of the hole, shooting like a backward-falling star up toward the sky. Looking up into the rush of water was too hard, so Jack glanced down, and saw that May hadn't been too far off with her guess a few seconds earlier. Below him, merfolk civilians swam as quickly as they could out of the way of hundreds of mermen, all armed with tridents.

And just above all those soldiers was a mermaid girl, swimming away from an unconscious Captain Mako and straight for Jack as fast as she could, an extremely annoyed look on her face.

There was no chance. Lian would reach them first, just before the soldiers did. There was no way they could reach the relative safety of the pirate ship. Meghan just wasn't fast enough, not carrying the rest of them. Lian wasn't as quick a swimmer as the mermen, but she was an Eye, and that made her beyond fast enough.

There was just no chance that they were going to escape.

And all Jack could feel was disappointment. This was his

fault, after all. Somehow Lian had followed him. The Wicked Queen knew where they were, and what they were doing, because of him. Not to mention that it was his fault the Queen was free in the first place.

Why couldn't he be good enough? Why couldn't he do even this little thing for May? Why couldn't he be a hero?!

He couldn't mess this up, not now. He couldn't just *fail* again!

"You're not serious," said Lian's voice in his head. "Tell me you're not serious!"

Jack just nodded to himself, silently hoping that, whatever happened to him, he'd take Lian down with him.

"You can't be this stupid, Jack!" Lian said in his head, while below she glared furiously at him, getting closer every second. "They're going to get caught anyway!"

"No, they won't," Jack whispered to himself. "I'll make sure of it for once."

"NO!" Lian shouted.

"Yes," Jack said, then turned to look up at Phillip, Meghan, and his princess one more time. He watched May for a moment, watched as her hair covered her face from the water flow, watched how tightly she held on to Meghan . . . and in his head he said good-bye.

Then Jack let go of the mermaid.

And just like that, May glanced down and saw him. Her eyes went wide and she yelled something, but by that point she was much too far away.

Jack just shook his head, then smiled at her, putting all the apologies he could into that one smile.

Then he sighed, flipped over, and swam down toward the approaching horde of mermen, as well as an extremely angry Eye, his sword glowing bright as the sun.

CHAPTER 28

May's eyes were shut tight, water pulling at her from all sides. It was like getting yanked along behind a boat after falling over on water skis, only the boat wouldn't stop, and the skis were a half-woman, half-fish apprentice fairy queen.

And then, for some reason, the mermaid seemed to jump forward slightly, as if she'd gotten a burst of speed out of nowhere. Maybe they were close to where they were going? May opened her eyes but couldn't see anything above them as the water plowed into her face, so she glanced down instead.

Just in time to see Jack falling back to the ocean floor.

"NO!" she screamed. "NO, JACK, WHAT ARE YOU DOING!"

Jack just smiled, then turned and swam down into the army of mermen, his sword lighting his way.

"NO!" May screamed again, and let go of Meghan as well . . .

Only to have some idiot grab her hand.

"Princess!" Phillip said, dragging her along by her arm. "Do not let go!"

May frantically tried to pull her wrist out of the prince's grip, but he was too strong. "Let me go!" she screamed. "Jack! He needs my help!"

"Jack made his choice!" Phillip said. "If the fairy queens are to survive, we must escape!"

"NO!" May yelled, still fighting against Phillip. "JACK! COME BACK!"

"Trust that he knows what he is doing!" Phillip shouted at her.

"I *don't* trust him!" May screamed, her eyes wild as she fought against the prince. "He makes stupid choices when I'm not around! He's going to get himself killed. Let me GO! JACK!"

Just as she screamed, Jack plowed into Lian, his sword striking hers, both glowing hot like the sun.

"NO!" she screamed again.

And then a brilliant light exploded up at them, blinding May completely. Something rumbled ominously, and when May's vision cleared, she saw that the mermen were still on their way, and Lian was gone . . . but Jack's unconscious body was sinking right into the army of mermen.

"JACK!" May screamed as the mermen below began attacking, throwing their tridents up, cutting through the water from all directions. One trident grazed Meghan's tail, and she shouted in surprise and pain, stopping just long enough for the mermen to close the gap even more.

The mermen seemed to be on all sides of them, throwing tridents or just swimming toward them with the three-pronged spears.

"There!" Meghan shouted, and pointed up. May followed her finger to see something huge blocking out the moonlight, like an enormous cloud cutting through the ocean.

The sea grew darker and darker, the only light coming from below them as May and Phillip readied themselves to fight, as much good as that'd do them.

Behind her, Phillip shouted, kicking at a merman who'd grabbed his foot. Next to him Meghan ordered the soldiers away, but they ignored her, concentrating on taking May and Phillip back dead or alive.

This was it. They weren't going to make it.

And then, like magic, a trident flew *toward* the mermen,

slicing through the water from somewhere above them. It struck one in his arm, and the creature let out a horrible shriek. More tridents flew down from above, a few connected by large nets that surrounded and enclosed groups of mermen, weighting them down and dragging them to the bottom of the ocean.

Even as May gaped in surprise, a net came flying down at her from above. It caught her, Phillip, and Meghan inside it, then immediately shoved them together and began pulling them all toward the surface with astonishing speed.

Mermen around them tried grabbing for the net, but more tridents from above kept them at bay, even while other nets filled with mermen dropped past them. May noticed for the first time that the tridents from the surface weren't the golden color of the mermen's. They were a dull metallic gray.

And then May, Phillip, and Meghan exploded out of the water, and the sounds of waves, rigging, and yelling filled May's ears. She pushed Phillip out of her way, just to get a look . . . and there was Bluebeard, hanging from the rigging of the ship as his pirates aimed tridents at the mermen below.

Bluebeard let out a roaring laugh. "Ah, I love when me plans come together so easily!"

CHAPTER 29

Wooden planks came rushing up toward May as the net holding her, Phillip, and Meghan crashed to the deck of the pirate ship. All around them pirates began cheering, led by their captain.

"LET ME OUT!" May shouted, struggling to free herself. Skinny and a few other pirates obediently cut her lose, and she immediately made a leap for the railing on the side of the ship. She climbed up over it, then leaned forward to dive back in—

Only to come to an abrupt halt in midair, hanging out over the ocean.

"Now, where do ye think yer goin', little princess?" a voice said quietly, and Bluebeard pulled her back on board the ship.

"I'm going back in!" May screamed at him. "Jack's still down there. I have to go get him! Someone needs to rescue him!"

"The Little Eye is still below?" Bluebeard said, actually seeming a bit surprised, but that was momentary. "We'll mourn the lad after we celebrate!" With that, he dropped May to the deck and turned around to grin stupidly at Meghan.

Meghan, however, did not grin stupidly back.

"Maarten," she said, then stood up on two human legs. "Looks like the spell still works."

"You . . . you haven't aged a day, my love," Bluebeard said without a trace of his pirate accent, his voice full of emotion. "You're still as beautiful as the setting sun and twice as radiant."

She sighed. "Maarten, no. No, you can't say that to me. Not anymore. Not this many years later."

Bluebeard stepped forward, confusion pouring over his face. "Years? It's felt like *lifetimes*, Meghan. I've searched for you. I haven't ever stopped."

"Yet you never did the one thing that'd let you find me, did you?" Meghan said, looking away. "You never . . . You sent these children to find the Sea Witch, but instead they brought me, and you . . . you couldn't even . . . It doesn't matter. Too much time has passed." She turned and walked toward the ship's cabin, then paused and deliberately switched direction to go belowdecks.

"Let me know when we get to shore, please. I must study the Sea Witch's songbooks to figure out how to get to the Fairy Homelands."

Bluebeard . . . Maarten . . . watched her go, and the light seemed to fade from his eyes as she stepped away. "But . . . ," he said to no one in particular. "But I . . ."

"What is happening, Captain Bluebeard?" Phillip asked. "I thought you had just been hired to—"

"A disguise," Bluebeard said quietly. "An effort to avoid an all-out war on the Sea King's part. I made up this identity, started horrible stories about myself, all to keep my kingdom safe, as no one would know where I was. But Meghan knew. She knew I searched for her, but I needed the Sea Witch. She could have fixed all this."

"Women. Fickle as the very sea herself, eh, Captain?" Skinny said, but a look from Bluebeard shut him up immediately.

May just glared at both of them. "Do you not GET that my friend is still down there?!" She ran back to the side of the boat and pointed. "We aren't going *anywhere* until we go get him!"

"May," Phillip said, stepping in front of her. "Jack made his choice. He sacrificed himself so that we could save the Fairy Homelands and find out who you are. If we try to rescue him, his sacrifice will have been in vain, and we may fail in both quests. That is not what he would want."

"You think I care what he wants?" May said softly. "You and he . . . you're all I have left. And there's no way I'm losing either one of you, not because of me. NEVER because of me." She sighed. "Now, are you coming or not? 'Cause I'm going either way."

"Don't be stupid, girl," Maarten said, shaking his head. "You'll be killed and accomplish nothing. No, to face down the mermen, you'd need—"

"I'd need people used to dealing with them," May finished, glancing around at the pirates holding tridents. "You mentioned something about you and your crew going underwater before, Bluebeard, that things had to be pretty bad for that to happen. Well, things are pretty much as bad as they can get right now."

Maarten gave her a careful look. "Yes, perhaps they are. There are ways we could help, but they're dangerous to both me and my ship, not to mention putting us all under the Sea King's power. We could lose everything. How important is this boy to you?"

She glared up at him. "I'll still be looking for him forty years later."

Maarten nodded, then looked down at the deck. A moment

passed, and he looked back up, the emotion gone but the twinkle back in his eye. "Get on yer feet, ye lazy scum!" Bluebeard roared. "We got a man overboard and we're goin' down to get 'im! Move it, lads. We're a'sinkin' the ship!"

May blinked. "Wait a second. You're what now?"

"You wanted us to save your little friend, didn't you, Princess?" Bluebeard said, yelling at pirates seemingly at random to do this or tie down that. "Well, we need to get down to him to be doin' that, don't we?"

"I . . . I guess," May said as she and Phillip moved out of the way of the pirates running everywhere.

"One thing," Bluebeard said to her, leaning over, and again it seemed to be Maarten talking. "If I do this for you, Princess, then I will need something in return."

"Help me rescue him, and I will do whatever you want," she said.

Maarten stared down at her. "You must agree that at some point in the future, I will ask for something of yours and you will give it to me. It doesn't matter what that is, or when I—"

"Done," May interrupted, shaking his hand.

The pirate looked at her curiously. "You are willing to give up anything for him?"

"Wouldn't you give up anything for her?" May asked, nodding belowdecks to where Meghan had gone. This was for Jack. Nothing else mattered.

Maarten sighed, then nodded. "Perhaps I'll find a way to show her that as well." A second later, his eyes twinkling again, Bluebeard roared to life. "Send her below the waves, boys!"

Sinking the ship looked a lot like the opposite of what May figured they'd be doing to start sailing. The ship itself was about as long as a football field, or some other really long thing, given that May honestly could never remember how long football fields were. A hundred yards? That was like three hundred feet, wasn't it? The boat did seem long, but she was over five feet tall herself, and so that'd be like sixty of her end to end. Only sixty? Or was that a lot of herselves? Stupid analogies. The boat was *big*, that should cover it.

Besides its bigness, it had four masts with all kinds of sails and ropes tying them together in some elaborate spiderweb of confusion. The pirates scurrying over the web, however, looked exactly not like spiders, given their beards, peg or other assorted legs, and general screaming of obscenities as they yanked at seemingly random ropes, pulling one here, yanking one there. They couldn't really push on the ropes. That's not how ropes worked.

But whatever pulling they were doing was working, as the sails were coming down, leaving behind a set of masts that looked like empty tree branches in the winter.

"Bottle it, you bilge rats!" Bluebeard shouted. Skinny pushed May and Phillip to the center of the boat as a monkey with an eye patch saluted Bluebeard, growled out an "Aye, sir!" and climbed the center mast with a bottle on its back.

"Did that monkey just talk?" May whispered to Skinny.

"Can't confirm nor deny such things, peaches," Skinny told her. "Wouldn't want the little bugger to get hunted down, after all, as a talkin' ani-malmal."

"I'm gonna take your other hand if you call me that again," May whispered back.

"Aye, pumpkin," Skinny said. "Now, if I could gets the lot of you toward the center of the ship, we're about to get bottled in, and ye don't want to get in the way of any dangerousness, if ye catch me meaning."

"I got exactly none of what you just said," May said. "What's going on?"

The monkey reached the top of the mast, aimed the bottle up above it, and then banged it down hard on the mast. The monkey began chanting something in . . . Well, it sounded like monkey, to be honest. There was a lot of high-pitched shrieking, grunts, and general monkey noises.

And just like that, the bottle began growing. In fact, it exploded in size, rapidly becoming large enough for the entire ship to fit into its opening.

The bottle's opening narrowly slooped right over the boat, then smacked into the water with a loud splash. The bottle bobbed for a second as the boat magically centered itself exactly in it. Then water began slowly filling the bottle, and the whole thing began to sink into the ocean, pulling the boat down with it, leaving just enough air in the bottle for them to breathe.

It was a ship in a bottle, just . . . wronger.

"Well, this isn't possible," May said, crossing her arms. "Seriously, no. The air in the bottle would make us float."

"Part o' the magic," Skinny said reverently as the monkey climbed back down and stuck out his tongue at May.

She pointed at him and gave him a dirty look. "You just made my list, little man," she said as the entire ship sank beneath the waves.

CHAPTER 30

What did you *do*?!" an enraged voice shouted.

Jack's entire body screamed in pain to the point that even opening his eyes hurt. Still, he cracked them just enough to see. Only apparently his eyes weren't behaving like they normally did.

Everything was swimming like he was underwater still. One second he could see Lian, her face flushed with rage below her hood as she screamed at him. But then the scene waved out, and a different scene floated up.

"What did you do?" a girl's voice said—a familiar, if much younger, voice.

"I lost the pail," said a boy's voice sadly, just as young, and just as familiar.

Jack rubbed his eyes, and Lian was back, still screaming at him.

"You threw everything away! Do you realize how pathetic that is?!"

"I did what had to be done," he told her, pushing himself to his feet, only there was nothing to push on. Everything felt too uneven, too much like liquid to get any kind of purchase. Again the young boy and girl floated up, and he watched as they looked into a well on top of a hill.

"It's gone," the boy said with a pathetic frown. "There's no way we can reach it."

"You're gonna be in so much trouble!" the girl told him, laughing.

The boy seemed to realize this, and an evil look came over his face. "I'm gonna tell them that *you* lost it!"

The girl stopped laughing abruptly. "What? You're lying!"

"So?" the boy said, grinning at her. "I'm telling on you!" With that, the boy turned and ran toward the edge of the hill they were standing on.

"NO. Don't!" the girl yelled, running after him.

"I'm telling! You can't stop me!"

The girl screamed in frustration, then pushed the boy hard in the back.

The boy yelped in surprise, and then tumbled over the edge, right down the hill.

"Oh no!" the girl yelled, looking around in every direction. She swallowed hard, took a deep breath, and dove after the boy.

"STOP THAT!" Lian screamed, and the scene of the boy and girl exploded in all directions, drifting away like smoke in a breeze. "You don't get to see that, not anymore!"

Now that the other image had disappeared, Jack found himself sitting in some kind of walled city, empty buildings all around. And then he realized what that meant.

This was the city in his dreams. How had he ended up here? And hadn't Lian said this was where something had been locked away? What did it all mean?

"What was that? Who were they?" Jack asked, shaking his head in confusion.

"You don't get to know that," Lian spat, then kicked him in the side. "You LOST that privilege when you threw away everything you could have been, like some idiot!"

"Who are you to tell me anything?" Jack growled at the girl. "You don't belong here!"

"Oh really?" she asked, then picked him up and slammed him against the brick wall behind him. "You don't get it, do you! You haven't learned a thing! The Charmed One didn't teach you, so I'm going to, if I have to kill you to do it!"

"You're just mad because I *beat* you," Jack shouted, grinning widely at her. "If I hadn't held you back, you would have captured them. I *won*!"

"NO!" Lian shouted, slamming a fist into the wall hard enough to break it. "You *lost*, but you're too stupid to see that! You sacrificed yourself for nothing! You turned *heroic*!" She said the word like it left a foul taste in her mouth. "Don't you get it, Jack? What needs to happen for you to understand that YOU ARE NOT THE HERO IN THIS STORY!"

With that, Lian dropped Jack to the ground hard, but for some reason her words stung more than the impact. "Shut up!" he yelled. "You don't know what happened! I . . . I couldn't—"

"You couldn't *what*?" she demanded.

"I couldn't . . . I couldn't save her!" Jack said, pushing to his feet and taking a step toward the girl, his anger pushing the pain away. "I told May her grandmother was Snow White, but I was wrong, and look what happened! I freed the Wicked Queen, and it was MY FAULT. And now I can't even save a whole city full of innocent creatures, let alone the one person in this entire world who doesn't treat me like scum because of my father! I failed, okay?! I failed in every possible way! I couldn't beat you, I couldn't beat the Sea King, I couldn't do anything. There was no way. You were faster than me, smarter than me. Every single thing I tried, you saw coming. I couldn't run, I couldn't hide, I couldn't outwit you."

Lian laughed mockingly. "Why would you ever think you could?!"

"Shut up," Jack said quietly. "You have no idea what you're talking about."

"You think you're so talented now, Jack?" she asked. "You think you're some kind of magical hero, someone who can move faster than people can see and knock arrows out of the air? Well guess what, Jack! There are only about a *hundred* Eyes who can do exactly what you can do, only they can do it faster, better, and a thousand other things besides! You don't have their experience *or* their training. All you have is your *head*." She shook her own head disgustedly. "But even that you seem willing to throw away the first chance you get!"

Lian gestured, and a window opened in the brick wall. On the other side Jack's body was being dragged behind Mako toward the Sea King.

"You think you can defeat the Sea King with your sword,

Jack?" Lian asked him. "How'd that work for you the first time? Why do you think my Queen hasn't ever attacked the Sea King?! Because she's scared of him! He's too powerful down here. She can't defeat him. So she waits for her opportunity, Jack. Because she's clever, and wise, and always ready to take advantage of weakness. And she saw weakness here, Jack. Weakness on your part. Weakness on the Sea King's. And she's already set things into motion, thanks to you."

"What things?" Jack asked, his anger being replaced by a feeling much closer to shame.

"If the Sea King's too powerful in the ocean, where do you think she wants him?" the girl asked him, her eyes burning with fury.

Jack felt a tug as Mako slapped his body in the face with his tail over and over, trying to wake him up.

"You're saying—," Jack started, but Lian interrupted him.

"The sword is just a tool, you idiot!" she yelled as the walled city began fading away. "Stop depending on it, and start using your *head* again!"

With that, Jack woke up to an extremely displeased Sea King.

A very displeased Sea King with a glowing golden trident aimed at Jack's chest.

"You invaded my lands, human," the Sea King said, his voice strangely calm. "You escaped from the cages I put you in. You attacked my soldiers." Abruptly the merman unfolded to his full height. "For those crimes alone, I might have granted you a swift death. But then you STOLE MY DAUGHTER FROM ME." His eyes flashed, and a bolt of solid light exploded from the trident, crumbling the coral floor just inches from Jack's chest. "For that, you and all your kind will be wiped from the face of this world!"

"Your Majesty," Mako said, holding up his hands. "It is possible that we do not know the full story. Your daughter has . . . left before, in the company of humans—"

"With that *prince!*" the Sea King roared, then turned to Jack. "Tell me truthfully, Eye. Is the human prince behind this?"

It wasn't easy to think under that kind of withering gaze, and Jack wasn't really in the best frame of mind to begin with. "Behind this?" he said bitterly. "There's the pirate who's working for him, we think, but Bluebeard's been pretty much useless in all of this—"

"He *is* involved?" Mako said. "But she . . . she said . . ."

Whatever else the merman intended to say was drowned out by the most horrifying roar of rage Jack had ever heard. The whales guarding the throne room fled in fear, and the remaining coral began to crumble to the floor, huge pieces falling with enough force to crush the life out of a merman . . . or Jack. Mermen and merwomen screamed, fleeing for their lives, leaving Mako and Jack alone with the Sea King, walls tumbling and crashing around them.

"We shall *wipe* their species from this *world*," the Sea King roared amidst the chaos. "Starting with the prince! FROM THIS MOMENT ON, WE ARE AT WAR!"

CHAPTER 31

Alone in what was left of the throne room, Mako roared in frustration, then smashed his fists down on the coral floor beneath him, cracking it.

"Bad day?" Jack asked, his own head beating like a roomful of drummers.

Mako turned to him with a furious look on his face, then abruptly sighed, shaking his head.

"I could help, you know," Jack said, pushing on the sides of his head, which made no difference. "I mean, I know where Meghan's going. If you let me go, I could—"

"Oh, there's no letting you go now," Mako said. "I don't care if you could end this entire invasion without so much as a bruised fin. The people demand your execution, so that's what they'll get."

"Execution?" Jack asked, his throat going dry, ironic considering how much water was passing through it.

"Publicly," Mako said. "Morale reasons, of course. Invading our kingdom and whatnot. If it's any comfort, I know that . . . that Meghan chose to leave. Plus, you seem far too stupid to be as evil as the Sea King believes."

"That's not really any comfort," Jack said. "Because, well, *execution?!*"

"You're going to need to move past that," Mako said, picking Jack up by his seaweed bindings and throwing him over his shoulder. "I can make it easier on you if you'd like."

"You can make getting killed in front of thousands of merpeople easier?" Jack asked. "Well see, now you've got my attention."

Mako smiled. "I like you, human. And for that reason I will help, even if you don't see it as such." Mako whipped his tail up and slapped Jack in the back, something sharp piercing his skin.

"That is my sting," Mako said as Jack's muscles began to convulse. "Sorry for any pain it causes, but in moments you won't feel a thing . . . or be able to move. At least you'll go to your great beyond painlessly."

"Painlessly?!" Jack tried to shout, but nothing came out beyond "Guuhhhh."

"You may not appreciate it now, but you will, trust me," Mako said as Jack's entire body went numb. "Now I have to hand you over to the execution team. The King wants his soldiers moving out within the hour for the invasion, so I won't be around to witness your death. That said, I wish you all the best in your afterlife."

Mako sighed as he handed Jack's unmoving body to two other mermen. As they carried Jack away, he watched Mako rub his eyes and shake his head. "All this pain, all this death, all for some stupid teenage crush. I really hope it's all worth throwing your life away again, Meghan."

CHAPTER 32

Cheers filled the ocean as Jack was carried . . . somewhere. It would have been nice to see where he was going, but not being able to turn his head or even move at all made things a bit difficult. Still, hearing the chants of "Kill the human!" did help set the mood.

All he could see as he was carried was the ocean floor, broken every so often by something squishing down over his eyes, something that looked like fruit, maybe. It might have felt like fruit too, but he couldn't really speak to that either way, considering he couldn't feel anything.

His merman guards didn't seem to mind the fruit, or whatever it was, being thrown at him, as they'd occasionally stop to apparently give the assembled mob a better shot. Overall, Jack actually did come to appreciate Mako's gesture. This would have been a lot worse if he could have felt it.

The mermen carried him up some carved stone steps in the ground, around and around in a spiral, each circle smaller than the last, until they reached the top of some sort of discolored rock platform, high enough for the crowds to see them. They twisted Jack over onto his back, and for a brief moment he saw how many merpeople had come to see him get killed.

Stretched out in every direction, thousands of civilian merpeople screamed and yelled for his blood.

Really? *That* many people wanted him dead? That many people he'd never met, never done anything to? For a brief moment he forgot about his paralysis and just yelled at the stupidity of the whole thing with all his might, going off on the bloodthirsty merpeople for a good minute before remembering that his mouth wasn't moving and he was just moaning out what really were some pretty harsh insults.

"By the order of the King of the World," a merman just beyond Jack's vision began saying slowly, as if he were reading it, "this human child has been accused of gross treason against the merfolk and their realm. The human has been found guilty and will therefore receive the maximum penalty: death."

A cheer rose from the mob, and Jack went off on them again silently. Stupid paralysis!

"Bring in the shark!" the merman yelled, and Jack's blood froze. Shark?

Behind him he heard two or three mermen yelling back and forth, and a *lot* of thrashing in the water, the sounds of metal chains clanking and straining overpowering the yells every so often.

The sounds grew closer and closer, then everything seemed to pause. For a brief moment Jack desperately wished he could move just to see what was happening, while a smaller, smarter part of himself realized he was far better off not knowing.

"Open its mouth!" the merman closest to Jack yelled. *Open its mouth?!* Jack's eyes opened wide at the idea of—

Wait, his eyes moved! He glanced around frantically but couldn't see much more than he'd been able to before, thanks to his head still being paralyzed. Still, Mako's sting seemed to be wearing off, if slowly, which could be very, very bad. There really was no worse point in the process for him to start feeling something, not with a shark's mouth opening behind him.

Above him the moonlight wavered as something passed over the ocean's surface. Jack shot his gaze upward but he couldn't make out what it was. It sounded as if the crazed mobs didn't have any more luck, as merpeople began muttering and crying out themselves. Like *they* had anything to be complaining about right now!

"I said get its mouth open!" the merman yelled, and the chains clanked as the shark apparently thrashed angrily.

"There!" someone yelled, and abruptly everything got darker as row upon row of teeth filled Jack's vision. His head had just been placed in the shark's open mouth, a mouth barely held open by some massive but straining rusty iron chains.

"Release the chains on my mark!" the merman said, the sound muffled by the shark's mouth. Jack wouldn't have thought that odors would really travel underwater, but the smell in the shark's mouth definitely did, reminding him vividly of the giant who'd tried to eat him. Not the most pleasant of memories to pop up here at the end.

The cries of the crowd intensified, but Jack couldn't make out what they were yelling anymore. The merman to his side began counting down from ten, the shark struggling against the chains with every count. Somewhere, Jack thought he heard the sound of metal striking metal. Was that the chains?

"Three!" yelled the merman, and the teeth inched closer to Jack's neck. Involuntarily Jack flinched, nothing moving—wait, a finger twitched. Now two fingers! Oh, please, not now!

"Two!" the merman yelled. Feeling returned to Jack's arm, but he couldn't move it. Something was tying him down.

"ONE!" the merman yelled, and Jack flinched, squeezing his eyes shut desperately as the chains released. . . .

And then the sounds of the crowds came crashing over him like a wave, light shining through his eyelids.

Jack hesitantly opened one eye to find a man with a black coat, a blue beard, and an upside-down glass jug over his head, attached by suspenders to his belt, smiling down at him with an enormous grin.

"Captain Bluebeard arrives just in the knickers of time once again!" Bluebeard roared, then drove a curved sword down onto the ropes tying Jack down.

Freed, Jack used his barely moving arms to roll off the platform, then threw a look behind him. There, three pirates wearing dirty clothes and glass jugs held the chains of the shark, pulling desperately against the struggling beast of a fish. Jack looked the shark, easily twenty feet long, right in the eye, and the shark stared at him right back.

"I would have been soooo tasty too," Jack told the creature, then laughed in its face.

Bluebeard held out a hand to help him up, so Jack took it, wobbling wildly as if his legs weren't quite done being paralyzed.

"Not the steadiest boy, are ye?" the pirate asked.

"I was stung by one of the mermen," Jack mumbled as best he could, glancing around to try to figure out what was happening, which apparently was nearly impossible, considering how crazy things were. Everywhere he looked, pirates with glass jars or jugs over their heads fought against mermen, sword to trident. And yet, that wasn't the oddest thing.

Was that the entire full-size pirate ship enclosed in a bottle?

"Ain't she beautiful?!" Bluebeard declared, following Jack's gaze.

"It's your boat . . . in a bottle," Jack said, his head rapidly not wrapping around the concept. "Wha?"

"The rightful name be 'ship' if ye be valuin' yer hide," Bluebeard corrected. "Don't be callin' my baby no boat, if ye please, you land-livin' lubber-buss! Not when we're bein' goodly enough to rescue you!"

"Rescue?" Jack asked, glancing around at the pitifully small amount of pirates fighting the incredibly large amount of mermen. "We might be in a little trouble, if this is all you've got."

"Don't worry about it, boy," Bluebeard said. "My boys have 'em."

One of the biggest mermen, this one wearing a black shark's head hood, pushed himself off the ground. "YOU!" the merman yelled, swimming toward Bluebeard. As he swam, he absently grabbed two of the pirates' jugs and smashed them together, breaking them and releasing the scruffy-looking men's air supply. While those two frantically swam back toward the ship's bottle, the shark's head merman headed straight for Bluebeard. "See if you can take me by surprise again!"

"Alrighty!" Bluebeard roared, then winked at the men holding the shark back. They immediately dropped their chains, releasing the shark straight at the enormous merman, who suddenly seemed a bit less intimidating.

The merman put both fists together, then swung them around straight into the shark's eye. The shark thrashed in pain, then changed direction and swam away for easier prey.

"Maybe worry a bit," Bluebeard admitted with a grimace. "That's a *big* fish-man, isn't it?"

And then the merman pulled out a glowing sword.

"Now, where did that fish get yer sword?" Bluebeard roared, bringing his own sword up and leaping down off the stone platform, pulling Jack along behind him.

"He probably took it when they decided to have me eaten,"

Jack said, watching the sword's light run in trails as the merman whipped it around much too fast for the pirates to keep up with.

"Well, holdin' on to yer sword will be a topic for later, then, you can count on that," Bluebeard said with a wide smile. "Still, since it be yers and all, why don't you go grab it?"

With that, the pirate hurled the still recovering Jack right at the merman.

Fortunately, the water's flotation magic slowed Jack down so that he landed on the ground just short of the merman, who, unfortunately, watched him land with a much too satisfied look on his face. "One way or another, you will die, human!" the merman roared, then leapt forward.

As Jack's sword came down, he focused inwardly, trying to slow time down, but his head was too fuzzy. He couldn't concentrate, and the sword kept coming . . .

Only to abruptly stop as Bluebeard neatly skewered the merman with the pirate's curved sword. The merman's eyes went wide beneath the shark hood, but he kept falling forward, straight at Jack. Moving as quickly as possible, Jack could still barely get his legs working enough to roll out from under the merman, stopping just inches out of range.

Finally having a moment to breathe, Jack dropped his hands

to either side and let out an enormous sigh, just as his sword dropped from the merman's limp hands into his own. Well. That was convenient.

Bluebeard again offered his hand, the wide grin still in place. "See?" he said, a dangerous look in his eye. "Nothing to worry about."

"Cap'n!" said Skinny as he came hobbling up to Jack and Bluebeard. "Cap'n! We need to be on the move! The fish armies, Cap'n! Lookout says they're preparin' to march this way!"

"Hear that, boy?!" Bluebeard roared. "There's no time fer yer lollygaggin', not unless ye want an army of fish on yer feet!"

"Uh?" Jack said.

Bluebeard shook his head sadly, then grabbed Jack by his shirt, dragging him as he raced back toward the boat. "Landlubbers. Always stupidin' up the place!"

CHAPTER 33

The sun had been up for hours now, as Meghan studied the Sea Witch's songbooks for the right spell to take them back to the Fairy Homelands. Time was quickly running out, but Jack had a hard time worrying about that. No, something else was *much* easier to worry about.

"You promised what?!" he said for the fifth time.

"JACK!" May said, snapping her fingers in front of his face. "I need you to focus here."

"You'd give him *anything*?" Jack said again. It might have been the seventh time, actually. He wasn't really counting. "I mean, did you even think about what that could mean?!"

May sighed, grabbed his head with both hands, and pushed her forehead against his, looking him right in the eye. "JACK," she said. "Seriously! Who says we even need to follow through?"

Jack stared right back at her. "You know that's not how things work."

May crinkled her nose, pulling away. "Ugh. I *hate* this place. Why couldn't I be from Greek mythology or something?"

"Why would you make the deal, May?" Jack asked, his voice soft.

She looked at him, then down at the floor. "Seriously? You have to ask?"

A pang of happiness twinged inside him, despite the situation. "I would have been okay."

She looked back up. "No, you wouldn't have. It sounds like you . . . you were about to . . . no. And even if you had been okay, I wasn't going to take the risk. Not on you. You and Phillip . . . you're . . . you know."

He smiled at her. "I can't even begin to tell you how stupid that was."

She glared back, then smacked him in the shoulder. "You've got a lot of work to do on your cheering-up skills."

"Maybe I can make a deal with a pirate to give him anything in the world if he makes you laugh till you snort by accident? Seems like a fair trade."

She smashed him with a pillow from the bunk they'd been

sitting on, then pushed him over and stuffed it into his face as he laughed. "I'll give you a pillow in the face!" May yelled right as Meghan pushed the door open.

The mermaid princess paused, staring at May, the pillow, and Jack's face, then raised an eyebrow. "Well, I can't say I expected this," she said.

"Can I ask what you did expect?" Jack asked, then shook his head when she started to answer. "It can wait. Have you spoken to Bluebeard?"

She sighed. "Maarten? No. I . . . don't know what to say to him. He . . . he's been gone for so long, but to him it's only been a few years since he last saw me. The rest of us have moved on, however, and realized . . . What I did, it was a youthful mistake."

"Speaking from the youthful side, not everything we do is a mistake," Jack said.

"Just most things," May said quietly.

Meghan smiled. "I've never forgotten anything. That year . . . I used to sit on the side of his ship and sing as he'd play a flute. This was back when he didn't hide his royalty, back before he became a pirate and had to associate with such . . . ill-bred men."

"The flute, huh?" May said with a snort.

"Maarten was the most dignified of princes," Meghan said,

sitting down on the bed." But after . . . after my father came to retrieve me, Maarten would sail out again and again looking for me, and each time my father would sink his ship. He lost several crews that way, until none of his men would sail with him, prince or no. Eventually he had to pay huge sums to anyone who'd willingly join him on the open water as he searched for me. That meant pirates." She shook her head. "That's when he took on his disguise, or else he never would have been able to lead those men. You see what he's become now, after so many years. I wish he'd just given up and moved on with his life, as I have."

"Speaking of moving on, Captain Mako's okay," Jack said.

"Excuse me?" Meghan said.

"Captain Mako," Jack said. "The merman who sacrificed himself to give us time to get away? He's fine. The Eye didn't hurt him or anything."

"Oh, Mako!" Meghan said. "Thank the Sea King. I'm relieved he's fine!"

"Yeah, so relieved that you hadn't even thought about him," Jack said with a grin.

"It must be hard to remember your merman boyfriend when you've got pirates on the mind," May pointed out.

"Shush," Meghan told them, but she was smiling.

"Yeah, shush, Jack," May said. "Let her think about her pirate in peace."

"I'm not thinking about Maarten!"

"What did you used to sing to him?" Jack asked her.

She glared at him, but with a smile. "I . . . I haven't sung it since."

"There's really no need—," May said, but the mermaid didn't seem to hear.

Instead Meghan looked down and began to sing a song with no words. It started softly, then swelled, much like the sea. Jack glanced at May, who was staring off into space with a smile, which made Jack smile as well.

After a moment he closed his eyes, letting the mermaid's melody wash over him like a wave. . . .

Only to be hit by actual water. His eyes flew open. "I had no idea music could literally wash over you!" he said, then realized the other two were staring at the round window in the ship, where water had sprayed in.

Phillip rushed into the cabin looking panicked. "We have a problem," he said, then ran out just as quickly. The three looked at one another, then followed quickly after the prince.

Back on the deck of the ship, water was raining down all over, as if a storm had appeared out of nowhere in the middle of a sunny morning. The ship was slowing down as well, despite the sails still billowing with wind.

"What's happening?" Jack yelled to anyone, but the pirates were running around, too busy to say anything.

The boat finally shuddered to a complete stop, then began sliding backward as an enormous roaring filled the air. Jack threw a look behind them, and nearly lost what little remained in his stomach.

Directly behind Bluebeard's ship was a wall of water at least three hundred feet high rising out of the ocean, heading right for them.

And riding that wall was the Sea King, his golden trident lighting up the sky brighter than the sun.

The trident was pointed directly at the ship.

"Oh good," Jack said to Meghan. "Your father's here."

"Don't worry," she said. "He's trying to sink the ship, but we'll all be far gone. I've been studying the Sea Witch's songbooks, and I believe I know how to get us to the Fairy Homelands. I'll begin the magic now." With that, she closed her eyes, and began to sing.

Again, it was beautiful. And again, just like the last song, this one took them nowhere.

"What?" Meghan said, stopping her singing. "Why isn't it working? It always worked when I was . . . below the waves." She stopped, watching the water. "Perhaps the Sea Witch modified her songs so they'd work below the water?" She cringed. "And *only* below the water."

"Don't worry, then," Jack said, watching the enormous wall of water coming straight at them. "Looks like we'll all be there in a minute."

CHAPTER 34

Oh, Fish King," Bluebeard said, striding up to the rest of them, a smile playing over his face. "You don't wanna be a'challengin' me. No, sir." He laughed loudly, then sprang to the wheel of the ship. "Get goin', ya lazy cow-eaters!" he yelled. "Batten down the hatches! Tie down whatever ye can, 'cause we're ridin' this wave all the way in!"

"We're *what?*" Jack said.

"Is 'batten' really a word?" May asked.

Phillip silently grabbed ropes, then pulled May and Meghan toward the captain's cabin, collecting their belongings from the ship's deck as he went.

Jack followed his lead, grabbing another rope and going after Phillip, who was busy tying the ropes to hooks on the boat's deck.

"Not inside?" Jack asked, tying one end of the rope to himself and handing another rope to Meghan for her to secure herself.

"Glass windows," Phillip said, pointing inside the cabin. "If they break, it might be a greater danger. I think we should just use the cabin's outer wall as a shelter." With that, he knotted the ropes, then tied one to his waist and handed the other to May, along with her bag.

"This is going to be bad," May said as she tied the rope around her waist. The roar of the tidal wave was getting louder, almost drowning out Bluebeard's excited orders shouted at the pirates, none of whom seemed to be sharing his joy.

"Little Eye!" Bluebeard yelled from above them. "Get yer sorry self up here before I make you walk the plank!"

Jack looked at the other three, then quickly untied himself and took the stairs two at a time. He reached the upper deck and stopped in shock as he had to look up, then much, much more up to see to the top of the wave, a wave that was easily twice as high as it had been before.

"The big fish up there might be a problem," Bluebeard admitted, despite his wide grin. "I need you to be takin' care o' him while I guide my ship here into safety on that there wave."

"I . . . what?" Jack said.

"Take care of him!" Bluebeard roared. "Distract him. Do whatever yer kind can do! I don't care. I just don't wanna be worryin' about a trident through my chest while I be steerin' her to shore!" He slipped a rope noose around Jack's waist. "There. You'll be secure now."

Jack glanced at the other end of the rope, and realized it was tied to Bluebeard's waist. "Wait, I'm secured to *you*?!"

"What could be safer?" Bluebeard shouted back. "Get ready, lads! Here she comes!"

And here she did come as the pirate ship began rising backward up the enormous wave. Bluebeard looked over his shoulder, steering and laughing maniacally even louder than the roar of the wave.

At the top the Sea King waited, his face contorted in rage as he stared down directly at Jack.

Jack pulled his sword, Lian's words echoing through his mind. Was this stupid, needless heroism again? It didn't feel like it. After all, he'd most likely be killed whether he was hiding or facing the Sea King. That being the case, there had to be a way through it, had to be a way to survive, using what he had, just like Lian had said.

Wait. Why was he taking her advice again?

Anyway, there was no time to think about that. No, now was

for facing down a hugely powerful King of the Seas that even the Wicked Queen was afraid of. And with what? The Sea King was powerful enough to completely shut down his sword, not to mention throw a tidal wave at them. There was no way to win, no way to beat the King.

Except it wasn't *about* winning. It was about surviving.

And that changed things completely.

Jack glanced down at the deck, then smiled. They just might live through this after all. But for that to happen, he'd need help, which is where Bluebeard came in.

The pirate roared with crazed laughter after Jack shared his plan. "Aye, you're insane, but I like it!" he shouted, then began barking orders at his pirates below. As Jack turned to face the wave again, he heard something heavy being dragged into the cabin below him.

If this was going to work, though, it was going to take some very careful, very dangerous setup.

"Ready, Little Eye?" Bluebeard said, smiling widely.

"Not even close," Jack shouted back, then climbed the tilting deck up to the back railing. The ship was steadily approaching vertical, so the railing seemed to be the most stable thing to stand on. Jack grabbed it, then swung himself up and over as Bluebeard steered them backward up the tidal wave.

Steering them right for the Sea King.

Just to test it, Jack tried focusing in, slowing things down, but just like before in the Sea King's presence, nothing happened. Even his sword's glow flickered and died again. This time he held on to it, though, as the ship steadily approached the Sea King.

"YOU WILL ALL DROWN!" the King of the Mermen roared, and a brilliant beam of light shot from his trident, straight at Jack. "THOSE TEARS MY DAUGHTERS CRIED WILL HELP YOU NO LONGER!"

Jack leapt to the right, and the beam passed through the spot he'd just stood in, just inches from Bluebeard, then exploded right through the mainmast of the ship.

"MY SHIP!" Bluebeard yelled as the mast crashed to the deck, narrowly missing about thirteen separate pirates. "I'm gonna kill that fish!"

"Just aim us right at him!" Jack shouted over the roaring of the wave as the ship continued its backward trip up the wall of water.

The Sea King roared, and light shot from the trident for a second time. This time Jack dodged to the left, and the light burst right past a wooden carving of a woman hanging off the front of the ship. Oddly, Jack thought he heard the carving yelp in surprise.

"A little closer!" Jack yelled, standing back up, then positioning himself right in the middle of the railing. He glanced down below him and saw through the cabin window that everything was in place. Skinny even gave him a morbid bone thumbs-up. Creepy.

"This is as close as I can get her!" Bluebeard yelled as the ship reached the wave's peak, the back of the ship facing the Sea King perfectly.

The Sea King smiled a horrible smile. "I WILL ENJOY THIS, HUMAN," he roared, bringing his trident up for a third time, aiming it straight at Jack's chest.

"Not as much as I will," Jack said quietly, returning the Sea King's smile. "FIRE!" he shouted at Skinny.

Directly below him Skinny struck a tinder, then lit a fuse on a cannon.

A cannon aimed straight out the back of the ship, and right at the Sea King.

The merman glanced down, his eyes widening. "WHAT—," he said, just in time for an iron cannonball to burst out the window of the captain's cabin and catch the Sea King right in the chest. The ruler of the mermen shot backward hundreds of feet into the air, his trident flying from his grasp to land on the deck next to Bluebeard.

The force of the cannon's blast combined with the wet footing knocked Jack off his feet as well. Frantically he windmilled, only to fall backward, tumbling end over end down the boat and into the massive tidal wave.

Only to stop abruptly, the rope around his middle almost cutting him in two. He heard Bluebeard shout in surprise, and then the rope sent Jack crashing into the deck, something fortunately breaking his fall.

"Hold on!" Phillip yelled, his own rope straining to keep him from tumbling down the deck after catching Jack.

Jack frantically sucked in air, smiling his thanks. Unfortunately, that's all he had time for, as the Sea King's magic controlling the wave abruptly stopped, and the wave crashed, throwing the pirate ship straight into shore . . . and straight at the walls of what looked to be a castle there.

Someone tumbled past him, but he couldn't see who. And then Phillip yelled out "MAY!" and Jack went cold with fear.

And then something struck him in the head, and everything went dark.

CHAPTER 35

May lost all sense of direction as the wave slowly broke, bringing Bluebeard's pirate ship almost vertical, then past *almost* vertical straight to vertical, and past even that. May hung out over nothing, and nothing held her back from that nothing except a very thin, very painful rope.

And then Jack flew by her suddenly, slamming into Phillip who'd let go to catch him just below her. Whatever Jack had been doing apparently had either been extremely successful or extremely unsuccessful. Knowing Jack, she knew which she'd bet on.

But what she didn't bet on was them living through crashing a boat this size, or a boat any size, really, into a castle five hundred feet below them.

"Hold on!" Phillip yelled from below, but holding on seemed like the least of their problems. You wouldn't hold on if your airplane were crashing. You'd grab a parachute and jump.

And just her luck, parachutes wouldn't be invented for another . . . infinite amount of years, probably. Stupid magic.

As the ship began to slowly slide away from the tidal wave and into more of a falling-type situation, May decided her last thought wasn't going to be anything so pessimistic as *Stupid magic*. No, it should be much more along the lines of—

MONKEY!

"THE MONKEY!" May screamed out as the little monster swung around the ropes just below her, holding the magic bottle that had sent the ship to the bottom of the ocean in its evil little paws. "SOMEONE GRAB THE MONKEY!"

Unfortunately, the roar of the tidal wave made her screaming useless, which just frustrated her more. Whether anyone could hear her or not, there was just no time. May pulled Jack's grandfather's knife out of her pack, judged the distance quickly, and then cut right through her rope.

"WHOOOOOAAAAA!" she screamed as she dropped into thin air straight at the monkey . . . then almost straight past him as she missed, the little demon giving her a confused yet almost satisfied look as she went. Not willing to give him the pleasure, May threw her arms out and managed to grab hold of the monkey as she passed, which didn't do much to stop her fall but did a lot to make her feel better. If she was going out, she was taking the stupid monkey with her.

"MAY!" someone screamed as she fell past Jack and Phillip, but May was too busy to see who, too busy falling, too busy trying to wrestle a stupid bottle out of a stupid monkey's paws, and too busy keeping the monkey from clawing her eyes out.

She managed to grab the bottle just as she tumbled down the long wooden spire sticking out of the front of the ship. Throwing a hand out, she shoved the monkey onto the log thing, then grabbed a rope and winced as it burned her hands, crashing her into the ship just inches from a rather lifelike-looking figurehead.

"Oh, hey. Sorry about this," she said to the figurehead. "I'm just trying to save us all."

"Apology accepted," the figurehead told her.

May blinked in surprise. "Wow, I hate this place," she said, then brought the bottle down hard onto the ship, just as she'd seen the monkey do.

The bottle promptly cracked in her hand.

The monkey slapped its forehead, then took the bottle and

made the EXACT SAME GESTURE, only to have the bottle blow up and suck the ship right into it, just as it had done last time.

"I DID THAT TOO!" May yelled at the little monster, but it just shook its head in disgust at her.

"To be fair, his method worked," the figurehead pointed out.

May screamed, but this time in frustration as the now rapidly bottling boat began to crash into the castle walls. It wouldn't be much, but the bottle's magic had somehow held the ship exactly in the center. So the bottle might protect it at least a little bit.

The impact was like nothing May had ever felt, throwing her off the bow and toward the glass of the bottle, only for something to halt her just a few feet away. The glass bottle slammed into the rock walls, breaking them apart like they were paper. The ship crashed into the glass bottle, held back just enough by the bottle's magic to keep it from exploding apart, its timbers splintering and cracking as they barely held together. Instead, all around them cracks ran through the glass, shrieking up and down like lightning bolts. It was like a perfect storm of breakage, and they were in entirely the wrong place to enjoy it.

Smashing through the walls of the castle, the bottled ship had landed in what looked like a courtyard, utterly destroying a decorative fountain. May wondered for a second if insurance covered this kind of thing, before realizing how stupid a thought that was. Of course it would.

The ship seemed to be done being murdered, having stopped in place, sticking about halfway in and halfway out of the castle wall. The glass, unfortunately, was cracking faster and faster, threatening to negate everything May had just done to save them, by slicing them all into pieces when it broke apart.

But maybe they could unbottle the ship first!

"MONKEY!" May screamed. "Get rid of the bottle!" She glanced around, but somehow was stuck looking straight down. What had caught her?

"Please stop struggling," the figurehead directly behind her said. "I might lose my grip on you."

May glanced down at two wooden hands holding her tightly, and scrunched her eyes closed, repeating to herself that the wooden figurehead had probably saved her life, and now wasn't the time to be creeped out by the fact that a wooden statue was alive. "Thank you," she managed finally. "Would you mind if I climbed back up to find that little monster monkey thing?"

"Not at all," the figurehead said pleasantly, which was almost worse. Why did all this magic stuff have to be so easy to deal with while still being a crime against nature?! Either way, the figurehead helpfully lifted her back onto the bow of the ship, where she found the monkey shaking with fear at the landing. For a second she felt sorry for the creature, but the second passed quicker than most.

"UNBOTTLE US!" she screamed as part of the bottle above her cracked, showering them with a fine dust of glass.

The monkey glanced at her, then at the ceiling, then back to her. It nodded. FINALLY. It slowly climbed up to the top of the bow, then made a particular gesture. The monkey paused, as if waiting for something, then made the gesture again, then a third time, each time more urgently. Finally it turned back to May, an expression of terror on its face as the glass cracked like an earthquake above them.

"NO!" May shouted, grabbing the monkey by its coat and holding it in front of her. "I don't want to die here! I don't want my friends to die here either! The rest of you, I could go either way, but I'd probably end up on 'live.' Even you! Please tell me you're kidding! PLEASE!"

The monkey shook its head desperately, then suddenly smiled maliciously, stuck out its tongue at her, and snapped its fingers. The glass bottle shot off the bow of the boat like a rocket, the ship popping out of the breaking glass as the bottle shrank down, boomeranged in midflight, and flew back to land right in the smirking monkey's hand.

"Okay, that's it," she told the evil, evil creature. "You're gonna pay for that one. I don't care if it takes a thousand years and a billion dollars, I will live to see that day."

"DO NOT MOVE!" shouted a voice from outside the boat. May sighed deeply and utterly, then turned to find at least twenty soldiers aiming spears at her.

One soldier stepped forward and gestured with his spear.

"PUT THE MONKEY DOWN AND RAISE YOUR HANDS IN THE AIR!"

"Thousand years, billion dollars," May said to the monkey. "You. PAY."

CHAPTER 36

Well, look who's back," a voice said. Jack rolled over, expecting to find the remains of a destroyed pirate ship, but instead found an oak tree, a warm breeze, and a calming grass meadow.

Instantly he was on his feet, his sword out . . . only to find someone he hadn't ever thought he'd be happy to see.

"Nice to see you too," said the Charmed One with a hint of a smile. "Is this how you treat your friends?"

"Who said you're a friend?" Jack said, glancing all around them. "Where's Lian?! She's been keeping you out somehow!"

"We have a little time," the Charmed One said. "Thanks to the Sea King, of all people. Lian will be back soon enough, but for now we can talk undisturbed."

"You picked a great time to leave me alone," Jack said, waving his sword around to make his point even more clear. "Thanks for that. Now we're on the run from the Sea King and just crashed a pirate ship into a castle, all with just a few hours to get to the Fairy Homelands before the Wicked Queen's dragons show up and kill everyone. Oh, except the mermaid princess can't sing magic out of the water, the Wolf King has the Piper, and May promised she'd give Bluebeard whatever he wanted at some point in the future, which I'm sure is going to end just fine."

"And?" the Charmed One said.

Jack just blinked. "And what? You want more?"

"I'm sorry. I meant to ask, where's the problem? The solutions to all those issues are inherent in the problems, are they not?"

"Now I remember why I hated you," Jack said. "It's your extremely clear answers."

"We don't have time to discuss your immediate problems, Jack," the knight said. "There's something more pressing that needs to be addressed before Lian returns. Your sword, and what it is doing to you."

Jack went cold. "It's turning me into an Eye, isn't it."

The Charmed One sighed. "It's not that simple. The sword isn't inherently evil in any way, as I told you when I first met you. It is just a tool, nothing more. But that tool gives you access to powers beyond what you're used to dealing with, and those powers can give you . . . opportunities."

"Can we maybe just skip to the end of this and get to the point?"

The knight stopped, then nodded. "The point is this." He waved his hand, and an image appeared of an older boy, maybe a year older than Jack. The image widened to reveal that the boy was dressed in the armor of an Eye, covered in the same midnight blue cloak the Charmed One and Lian wore. And as the image grew, Jack could see the boy standing next to a familiar-looking woman.

"That's the Wicked Queen," he said softly.

"More relevantly," the Charmed One said, "that is you next to her."

The meadow went silent except for the wind blowing through the large oak tree. Finally Jack cleared his throat and spoke.

"What . . . what is this? What are you showing me? A possibility?"

The Charmed One shook his head.

"This is you, the way the Wicked Queen saw you in her Magic Mirror." The knight looked away. "This is why she believes that you will betray May."

"'One of these boys will betray you, and the other will die,'" Jack said, repeating the words the Wicked Queen had told May three months earlier.

"I wanted to head this off, Jack," the knight said, letting out a deep breath. "Unfortunately, your refusal to be trained, and now Lian's interference, have ensured that whatever effect I might have had will be too late." He shrugged. "For all I know, this was meant to be exactly the way it's happening and I never had a chance."

"That . . . can't *be*," Jack said, his entire body and head numb from the idea. He would never, NEVER betray May, or join the Wicked Queen! How could this even be possible?

"It's not just possible. It will happen. You are heading straight for it," the Charmed One said, answering Jack's unspoken question. He glanced at the weapon in Jack's hand. "You are meant to take my place in more ways than one, it seems."

"But why?! And why tell me this?" Jack shouted. "I can make my own choices. I can CHOOSE not to do this!"

"Of course," the Charmed One said. "And right now you would choose just that. But at some point in the future, the near future, it seems that you will choose the opposite path. I have not seen how or why, and neither has the Queen. But I can't help but think it has something to do with Lian."

"Why? Why her? Isn't she just an Eye?"

"There's no such thing as *just* an Eye," the Charmed One said bitterly. "There's no more clever, strategic, or manipulative group in existence, each one surpassed only by their Queen in terms of cunning. But Lian—"

The Charmed One stopped abruptly, grasped his chest, then exploded in a cloud of smoke. As the smoke drifted away, Lian strode up slowly, what little Jack could see of her face unreadable.

"Well, that was unpleasant," she said to him. "I can't believe you crashed the entire ship."

"I'm sorry I didn't crash it into you," he said. "Next time I'll work on my aim."

"You'd still miss, even with something that size," Lian said, then shrugged. "But I get your bitterness. I heard some of what the Charmed One was telling you. Gonna be an Eye, huh? I knew it."

"You know nothing."

Lian smiled. "I know who you are, Jack, and right now I think that's more than you know. I know who *I* am, I know who the Charmed One was . . . and I know something that you've been dying to know, even if you'd never admit it to another living soul."

"You know how much I want to tie rocks to your feet and drop you back into the ocean?" Jack asked. "'Cause I'm happy to tell the world that."

"No," Lian said as the meadow began to fade out. "I know where your *father* is, Jack."

And then the meadow disappeared once more.

CHAPTER 37

Jack woke up to the sight of stones moving all by themselves below him. That was interesting. Apparently the world on land had learned some new tricks since they'd been gone!

Then feeling began to return to his legs, and he realized he was being dragged along the stone hallways of a castle.

A castle? They'd survived?! Jack almost laughed before the reality of the situation sank in.

Being dragged along by people with what looked to be swords was usually a bad sign.

"You are awake," Phillip said from his side. "I feared you were permanently injured."

"The day's still young," Jack told him, his head pounding with every word. It was hard to tell which hurt more, the real pain of what had to have been a horrifying crash into the castle, or what Lian had just said to him. His father. Everything he'd had to live with all his life, everything he'd gone through, the fact that he was seen as the son of a criminal and nothing more, and Lian knew where his father was.

"Tell the prisoners to be quiet," someone ahead of them ordered.

"Be quiet!" a guard holding Jack's right shoulder said.

"I like how they pretend we didn't hear the first guy," Jack said to Phillip. The prince, meanwhile, just shook his head, quieting down. A fountain of antiauthority, Phillip was not.

Being dragged as he was, there wasn't much Jack could see. From what he could tell, the guards had May in front of them, with what seemed to be a monkey tail growing out the back of her shirt. Okay, *that* was new. Behind him Jack could hear Bluebeard grunting and groaning, but given that he wasn't shouting threats at the guards, Jack assumed the pirate was still unconscious. More important than the pirate, though, was—

"Did you notice this one's eyes?" one guard behind Jack asked. "They're yellow. And she's got claws and fangs."

"Mermaid spy, most likely," whoever was in charge said from the front. "Tie her up and gag her. Can't take any chances with the king."

The guards did just that, and soon Meghan was being dragged along right beside Jack, her eyes flaring with anger as they passed through some kind of elaborate doorway into a tiled room.

"Your Majesty," the guard in the front said, "we've brought you the shipwreck's survivors, including what we believe to be a mermaid spy. The ship did indeed bear your royal seal, though we haven't had ships on the water for fifty years. Many of the crew escaped off the back, but we have guards chasing them down."

"Wha . . . me crew?" Bluebeard mumbled, still sounding asleep.

"Get them to their feet!" a man's voice said from a distance. "Who are these people?"

The guards roughly jerked Jack to his feet, and he looked up to find a middle-aged man who looked far too beaten down for his age, and far too small for a large threadbare robe and oversize crown missing half its jewels.

"Your . . . Your Majesty," said a shocked older man's voice from behind the crowned man. "Look! The man in the blue beard!"

"I recognize that voice," Bluebeard mumbled, then gasped. "Farnsworth! My old chancellor!"

"Maarten?" Farnsworth said. "By the sea, MAARTEN!"

"It can't be," the king said, striding forward to Bluebeard, then holding the pirate up by his shoulders. "Brother?"

"That robe never did fit you, Fford," Bluebeard said, then grabbed the man in both arms and shouted joyfully as he embraced him, several bones cracking in the process.

"MAARTEN!" King Fford shouted. "Guards, release these people! My brother has returned!"

The guards awkwardly released them, and Jack watched as the two least likely siblings in the world clapped each other's back and looked each other over, both seeming a little disappointed by what they saw, but both trying to hide it.

"Fford?" said a woman's voice from the doorway behind them all. "Who is *this*?"

"Ah, Marispoptia!" Fford shouted. "Meet my older brother, returned to us after almost forty years missing! After years of searching, we gave up all hope. Yet hope may always be rewarded if patience remains, as proven by my brother!"

"Yes, yes, I get it," Marispoptia said, looking over Maarten with some distaste. "He is not the rightful king, then, is he? I would hate to think I'm engaged to the wrong brother."

"That would be *truly* horrible," Fford said, looking everywhere but at Marispoptia.

"Engaged, Brother?" Maarten said. "I see that congratulations are in order!"

"Uh, indeed," Fford said, now looking everywhere but at Maarten. "Guards, take that mermaid to the dungeon. We'll want to question her soon—"

"YOU'LL DO NO SUCH THING!" Maarten roared, leaping over to Meghan and clutching her to him protectively. "If I have any authority left here whatsoever, you will leave this woman be!"

The guards glanced among themselves, not sure who to listen to. "You gave up your authority when you left the kingdom, Maarten," the chancellor, Farnsworth, said.

Fford and Maarten looked at each other, and Maarten frowned. "I did leave this kingdom in Fford's care long ago," he said. "Yes, it might be a bit worse for wear, but I'm sure he did the best he could—"

"Left it?!" Fford said, forcing a laugh. "You abandoned us to chase after that mermaid . . ." And then his voice trailed off and his eyes went wide as he looked at Meghan. "Maarten . . . what did you *do*?"

"Nothing I wouldn't again," Maarten said, wrapping his arms around Meghan protectively, despite her attempts to sneak out of them.

"That explains the warning we received," Farnsworth said quietly.

Fford nodded, his eyes still on Maarten. "This is so like you," Fford said. "You've been missing for forty years, and the day you come back, you bring a war to the very steps of your kingdom."

"I don't CARE what I bring!" Maarten shouted. "I would do anything for this woman!"

"At the expense of your people?!" Fford shouted. "Do you have any idea what is about to happen when the Sea King invades?"

"I have quite a good one," Maarten said, his eyes blazing. "Call the soldiers, I'll lead them myself—"

"You'll lead *nothing*," Fford said, glaring at his brother. "Fortunately for our people, I've already taken steps to protect them."

Maarten went deadly silent for a moment. "Tell me of these steps," he said finally.

"A visitor arrived just yesterday," Fford said, a smile overtaking his face. "A visitor at the head of his own army, an army that could have overtaken the castle easily. Fortunately for us, we recognized him as the hero he is, and he brought warning of an upcoming incursion by the Sea King. Proof came with the tidal wave that brought you here, and our spotters reported churning beneath the waves approaching shore."

"This visitor," Jack said, his eyes narrowed suspiciously. "Who was he?"

Fford barely looked at Jack. "A great man. An ally of the long-lost Snow White."

Jack swallowed hard as a rough voice laughed behind him, sounding like rocks scraping against one another.

"Oh, the boy knows quite well who I am, Your Majesty."

Jack, May, and Phillip all slowly turned around to find the Wolf King in human form standing in the doorway, two goblin guards flanking him. The wolf smiled at them, baring his teeth. "Good to see you again, children."

"Even without his heroism, it would have been hard to say no to the Wolf King's offer of alliance," Fford said with a hopeful smile. "After all, he didn't ask for much, just a favor."

"Indeed," the Wolf King said. "In return for destroying the merman army about to invade your shores, all I ask is that King Fford help me return some wayward children to their homes. Thank you for your aid, Your Majesty, but I can take them from here."

CHAPTER 38

"Bluebeard, we could use some help here," Jack said as he, Phillip, and May backed away from the wolf. One of the guards had Jack's sword on the other side of the room, which was the perfect place for it to be doing a whole lot of good.

"Goblins? Here?" Maarten said, pushing Meghan behind him. "But the Wolf King was a hero!"

"Some of those stories aren't as up-to-date as we'd like," Jack said. "He betrayed Snow White for the Wicked Queen."

"Preposterous!" Fford said.

"The children will say anything to avoid going home, Your Majesty," the Wolf King said with a knowing shake of his head. "I appreciate your assistance in this matter."

"Fford, do not do this," Maarten said. "There seems to be more happening here than we know. Goblins are the Queen's creatures!"

"You've left me no choice, Brother," Fford said. "Whatever he's done, the Wolf King is our only chance against the Sea King's armies." He snapped his fingers, and his guards advanced on them. "Marispoptia, you should come with me quickly. I don't think you'll want to be here in a moment."

"Too late," Maarten said as he bent down, picked up a wooden seat painted to look like gold, then threw it as hard as he could right at the wolf. "Time ta run, lads!" Bluebeard shouted, grabbing Meghan by the waist and plowing right through the Wolf King's two goblin guards.

Phillip and May scrambled to follow, the pirate monkey hanging tightly to May's neck as she ran, but Jack leapt backward instead, then ducked beneath two guards' hands and threw a shoulder into the guard holding his sword. The guard fell over as Jack grabbed his weapon, then turned to find half the guards and a very annoyed Wolf King staring at him.

"I'll get him!" the older man, Farnsworth, said, then clumsily grabbed for Jack. The man almost comically missed, tripping over another golden chair to fall at Jack's feet. Jack gave him an odd look, which Farnsworth returned with a wink. "The window," he whispered. "It's a short drop, and you'll catch up to Maarten just outside."

"Care to try your luck against me again, Jack?" the wolf growled, a wide smile of anticipation crossing his face.

"Nah," Jack said, then leapt backward, straight out the window behind him. At least, that had been the plan. Instead his shoulder clipped the side of the window, and a huge wave of pain crashed over him as he fell, surprising a blackbird sitting on the windowsill. Down he went, watching the bird fly away and wishing he could do the same thing instead of heading straight down toward whatever might be below.

Which turned out to be a large pirate captain. "Children be so plentiful that they be fallin' from the skies now?" Bluebeard roared, grabbing Jack by the shirt before he hit the ground. "Stay with the group next time!"

The group, with Meghan still under Bluebeard's arm, was currently running for what looked to be a drawbridge leading out into the forest. "Wrong way!" Jack shouted, and yanked on Bluebeard's arm to spin the pirate around. "We need to head for the ocean!"

The others just stopped and stared at him. "Correct me if I be wrong, little man," Bluebeard said, "but ye do be wishin' to live, aye? And ye do know that the Fish King will gut ye like a trout if he gets ahold a'ye?"

"Basically Bluebeard's calling you stupid," May translated helpfully. "We're not going back to the ocean."

"We are if we want Meghan to be able to sing again," Jack pointed out. "We need to get her back into the ocean. She'll do her thing, and we'll be off to the Fairy Homelands before the Sea King's armies even get here!"

Before they could argue, Jack ran the group back past a host of formally dressed royalty, who all leapt out of the way indignantly. Just past the nobles were the remains of a large open courtyard, once beautifully decorated, now slightly put off by the enormous pirate ship sticking halfway into it.

"There!" Jack shouted, running over to the ship. "We'll climb down from here, and—"

He stopped abruptly, his mouth dropping open and words refusing to come.

"What's the problem?" May asked, absently struggling to free herself from the monkey's grip. Then she noticed what he saw and fell backward, landing on her behind with a loud groan, her eyes still wide with shock.

Covering the shore in every direction, mermen with human legs marched out of the ocean in tight formations, each wielding an ugly-looking trident and weighted net. They extended as far as Jack could see up and down the shore, and there seemed to be no end in sight.

And the merman soldiers weren't the worst part.

As Jack watched, his mouth hanging open, enormous sharks emerged from the water, their mouths filled with teeth, mermen riding on their backs. And those sharks walked on legs, just like the mermen did.

Somehow the Sea King had not only given legs to his mermen, but to all the creatures of the sea.

Here and there eels slithered up the beach on centipede-like legs. Huge schools of piranha ran around the sand in a frenzy. And— No, that couldn't be real. No. No fish was that large. Its reddish orange body completely covered in mermen, the forty-foot-long monster's eight long tentacles walked it out of the ocean and up the beach, like the world's largest spider. Its beak squawked something angrily, and a moment later, a second, then a third spider-like fish followed it out.

"Those are giant *squid*," May said quietly, standing back up next to Jack. "They're . . . they're *huge*."

"They're attacking with the entire *ocean*," Jack said, not able to believe his eyes.

Below them the castle gates opened, and battalions of goblins, trolls, and ogres filed out in formation, spreading out to protect the castle. There was going to be a war here, and it stood between them and the water.

"We can't . . . we can't do this," May said. "We have to go back! She can dunk her head into a pond or something!"

"Too late," growled a voice from behind them.

They turned to find the Wolf King and a much larger group of goblin soldiers behind them, along with a host of uncomfortable-looking castle guards.

"Give up now, and I'll see to it that all three of you make it to the Queen unharmed," the wolf said. "If you fight, I *will* make sure it hurts."

Jack looked to Phillip, who glanced back and nodded, then to May, who, despite her wide eyes, also nodded. "Okay," Jack said. "Well, that's it, then."

And with that, he grabbed Meghan's hand and pulled her over the edge of the courtyard, down into the oncoming invasion.

CHAPTER 39

The fall wasn't long, but Jack's feet still stung as they hit the sand. Meghan seemed to be in more pain than he was, but given how new her feet were, that wasn't surprising. He quickly yanked her out of the way when, a second later, Bluebeard landed hard enough to shake the ground a bit, followed quickly by Phillip and May, who both landed relatively perfectly.

They'd been lucky. The goblins, trolls, and ogres in front of them were concentrating too hard on the approaching mermen to notice what was happening behind them. If they could just move fast enough—

"TURN AROUND!" the Wolf King shouted from the courtyard. "Take those children and that woman. Use whatever force is necessary!"

Immediately the closest hundred monsters whirled around and ran toward the group, about every other mouth drooling hungrily.

Goblins riding some kind of armored hairy monsters made up of half teeth and half fur galloped at them, black iron lances aimed directly for them. Jack pushed Phillip into the way of one of the monsters, nodding at the prince, then stepped into the path of the other. This would have to be timed just right.

The goblin aimed his lance directly at Jack's chest, smiling widely. Jack returned the smile, then sidestepped at the last minute, slamming the lance down with all his strength as it passed him. The lance hit the sand, knocking the goblins right off the back of whatever the hairy monster was.

"Get on!" Jack yelled, and Meghan quickly climbed up behind him. Jack glanced over at Phillip, who was already on his monster, with May behind him.

"GO!" Bluebeard yelled. "I'll take care o' these foul beasts meself!"

"Captain!" someone screamed, and Skinny and the rest of the pirates emerged from the rocks surrounding the castle. "Ye won't be fightin' alone!"

Bluebeard began howling with laughter. "BRING ON YER

WORST!" he yelled to the Wolf King, then waded into a group of goblin archers who'd been aiming at Jack and Phillip from a distance.

"GO!" Jack shouted, kicking at his monster, who tore off like an arrow from a crossbow . . . toward the castle. Jack yanked on the reins, but the monster didn't seem to be interested in listening, so Jack grabbed a spear from a nearby goblin as he passed, then braced himself and dug it into the ground, grabbing the monster as tightly as he could with his legs. The monster swung around in a half circle and began galloping toward the water, the goblin army, and the oncoming merman invasion . . . which, sadly, was an improvement.

Jack's spear didn't last long, as he quickly used it to bash a goblin in the face and the thing broke in half. The monster's teeth seemed to be a much bigger deterrent, as most of the goblins leapt out of the way as a creature with a mouth bigger than their head came running at them. One troll swung a club bigger than Jack right at Jack's face, but he and Meghan both ducked beneath it, and the club plowed into the group of goblins chasing after them.

They were past the first obstacle, only now they were heading straight for a much more toothish one.

"SHARKS!" Jack yelled, as if that would dissuade his ride, but the monster plowed right into the side of one of the enormous creatures anyway, knocking it over. The shark's little feet scurried helplessly as the shark pinned three mermen under its weight.

Tridents came flying at Jack from multiple directions as they ran forward, so he immediately slowed time down, grabbed two tridents out of midair, and stuck one into the ground. He dug his legs into the monster's body again as the creature slid in the sand, and Jack used the pivot to spin them back in the right direction. The second trident he used as a lance, ready for whatever came at them.

"You . . . move . . . fast!" the monster growled beneath him.

Jack almost fell out of his seat in surprise. "You can talk?" he said as he swept his trident into a merman's legs, clearing a path for Phillip and May right behind him.

"Most don't . . . understand us," the creature growled, and Jack realized that, much like with the fairy, it wasn't so much that the creature was speaking human but that he was understanding the creature's growling. The sword. It *was* changing him.

None of this was doing much to make him feel any better.

There was no time to think about it now, though, not with wave upon wave of mermen, both mounted and infantry, all standing between Jack, Meghan, and the ocean.

None of that mattered to Jack's ride, however. As he galloped full tilt straight at the line of mermen, all their tridents aimed right at the creature, Jack realized that this could end very, very badly.

"Wait!" Jack yelled. "We need to stop!"

"No stop!" the creature growled. "Fight . . . fish!"

Getting the feeling that arguing wasn't going to do much good, Jack twirled his trident around, desperately searching for an opening, somewhere to direct his ride toward, but the mermen left no gap, no weakness. . . .

And then out of nowhere, arrows began falling through the air right into the forward flank of the mermen.

"Get away from my love, you miserable day-old fish!" Bluebeard screamed from behind them, surrounded on every side by his pirates, each armed with a goblin bow and firing as fast as they could.

A few arrows narrowly missed Jack, which enraged Bluebeard even more, but the majority landed right on target, ensuring that the mermen were too distracted to worry about maintaining a united front against the charging monster.

His ride slammed into the line of mermen, and Jack quickly got lost in a sea of tridents, fur, and huge shark mouths. He swung the trident out, over and over, easily moving twice, three times as fast as the mermen, attacking anyone who interfered with their forward progress. Each strike desperately fended off teeth, blades, and claws as much as possible, but there were just too many to block entirely.

Not to mention, as bad as the sharks and mermen were, the monster seemed intent on racing straight at something much worse. The creature was practically galloping right toward one of the giant squids, whose tentacles launched out toward them with an alarming speed.

"NO!" Jack screamed.

"OH YES!" the monster growled, leaping onto the back of a shark, then pushing off and jumping straight at the giant squid, all four paws and his mouth spread wide. The monster, Jack, and Meghan all slammed into the squid, knocking it backward off its eight legs, sending mermen flying off in all directions.

"Watch out!" Jack yelled as the enraged squid hit the ground, its bladelike tentacles wrapping themselves around Jack's mount. The monster roared in pain as the tentacles squeezed, even as one of the squid's tentacles wrapped around Jack's waist and yanked him off the creature's back, his sword flying out of its sheath into the ocean. Meghan fell off as well, though where she landed, Jack couldn't see, as he was a bit busy being squeezed around the middle.

The squid tossed Jack's ride into the air as if it weighed nothing, then dragged Jack straight down toward its open-beaked mouth. The one eye that Jack could see was furiously watching its incoming meal get closer and closer.

"I'M NOT GETTING EATEN AGAIN!" Jack yelled, driving the trident down into the beak. The trident hit something soft in the squid's mouth, and just like that, Jack was airborne, flying out toward the ocean as the squid angrily tossed him away.

He landed hard in the waves, spraying water everywhere. His monster, meanwhile, was nowhere in sight. Jack turned back to the ocean—

And slowed down time just quickly enough to avoid getting his head cut off, a glowing white sword sweeping right through the spot where his neck had been a moment before.

CHAPTER 40

Jack landed hard on the sand beneath the waves, rolled to his side, and came up with the trident aimed at . . .

Well, nothing. There was no one there.

"It's a pity you never learned to use this properly," a deep male voice said from behind him. Jack pivoted off the trident, throwing himself forward just as something metallic rang out as it hit his weapon. He pulled the trident from the sand as he landed, glancing around frantically but still not seeing anything.

"I should have killed you when I had the chance!" the Sea King yelled from Jack's side, and again Jack threw himself out of the way of his own sword. The blade disappeared, then reappeared on his other side, striking out again, barely giving Jack any time to dodge.

"You need to listen to me!" Jack tried to shout, but something kicked him in the chest, and he flew backward, landing in a wave. He rolled into the water, coming up a bit deeper in the ocean, glancing around frantically for the merman.

"You and your Queen think you can tell me what I need to do?!" the Sea King yelled, and something hard splashed in the water to Jack's right.

Jack threw his gaze down at the water, then back up at nothing. And suddenly he knew what to do.

As the waves came in, they separated around two invisible legs. The glowing sword appeared right above those legs, slashing out at him, but Jack was ready, driving his trident up to block.

The legs disappeared from the water, but Jack felt the air move above him, and he drove the blunt end of the trident up, catching the invisible Sea King in the stomach. The King landed hard, the sword slashing out again, and Jack dodged, barely escaping the deadly blade.

"Here's where I end your pathetic little story," the King said from right behind Jack.

The sword came down just as Jack thrust his trident up behind him, capturing the sword in its tines. He twirled the trident, ripping the sword from the Sea King's grasp, then kicked backward, his foot hitting something hard and sending it flying, even as his sword fell from the air into his hand.

As the Sea King landed, fully visible now, Jack held the sword to the King's chest, trying to hide how fast his heart was beating. "No one ends my story but ME," he said, then cursed silently at how stupid that sounded.

Despite being an idiot, now that the sword was back in his hand, Jack felt stronger, faster, more energetic . . . and more aware of everything. What was the sword doing to him? Had the sword been changing him this entire time without him even realizing it?

And why didn't that scare him more?

"LISTEN to me," Jack said again to the Sea King. "Your daughter, she's somewhere out here! No one kidnapped her, she came with us to help save the fairy queens!"

"LIES!" the Sea King yelled.

"Why would I lie?!" Jack shouted back, his face exploding with heat as something in him just snapped. He growled in frustration and had to fight the urge to just start punching the idiot merman until he listened to reason. "The Wicked Queen WANTS you up here! She wants you on land, where you're weaker! That's why she sent an army here, to wipe you out!"

The Sea King started to say something, but Jack yelled over him. "NO! You don't get to talk anymore! You know why your daughter left the first time? Because she was in *love* with a human! No one made her come up here! The Sea Witch didn't convince her! SHE wanted to be with a human! SHE wanted it, not humanity, not the people in this castle, HER! And now you're about to lose her again because you're too stupid to know she's making her own choices!"

The Sea King's eyes burned white, and his face twisted into a sneer. The water around him began to boil, and Jack had to leap backward to avoid getting burned.

Maybe he'd pushed it a little much.

"YOU . . . ," the Sea King said, the water rising to lift the King to a standing position, the trident Jack had used glowing white hot as well, somehow in the King's hand, though he'd never reached for it. "YOU!"

"No, Your Highness," Jack told him, noticing something right over the Sea King's shoulder. "Her."

The most amazing voice began to sound from beneath the waves, harmonizing with the sounds of battle on the shore. The song was familiar, but the Piper's pipes, as magical as they were, couldn't compete with the voice of the little mermaid princess.

"Meghan?" the Sea King said, the rage draining from his face. "What . . . what are you singing?"

"It's fairy queen magic," Jack told him, lowering his sword. "She learned it from the Sea Witch, and she's using it to take us to the Fairy Homelands."

"FINALLY!" May said as she, the pirate monkey, and Phillip arrived and jumped off their creature. The monster, now freed of the humans at its reins, leapt for Phillip, but the prince easily grabbed the reins and looped the beast's front and back paws together in midair, crashing it to the ground without really hurting it.

The song grew louder, and Jack could see Meghan swimming just beneath the waves as the world began to swirl around them. This was it. They were finally going back!

"Meghan," the Sea King said. "You would leave me again?"

"I wouldn't worry about that," growled a voice a moment before a wolf the size of a horse slammed into the Sea King from behind. The Wolf King's teeth latched on to the Sea King's throat and bit down hard.

"NO!" Jack shouted, too far away.

"The wolf is mine!" Bluebeard roared, leaping into the fray.

And just like that, the armies of mermen and goblins, the

beach, the ocean, and the castle all swirled away into nothingness.

Jack, May, Phillip, Meghan, Bluebeard, the Sea King, and the Wolf King all dropped to the ground hard, just feet away from the largest, thorniest vines Jack had ever seen.

And there, waiting with a smug smile for them all, was Lian.

"Oh, so close!" she said, her smile getting wider. "But close only counts in horseshoes and dragon fire." And with that, Jack looked up to see a flight of black, red, and green dragons off in the distance, heading straight for the Fairy Homelands.

CHAPTER 41

Y ou said they wouldn't be here until sunset!" May screamed indignantly.

"Wait, you're telling me I tricked you into thinking you had more time than you did?!" Lian said, leaning calmly against the silver gate. "*That* doesn't sound like me. Does it? Oh wait, it totally does!"

"There is still time to end the spell," Phillip growled as he pushed himself to his feet.

"Nah," Lian said, kicking her legs out joyfully. "But I really should thank you for bringing me the one person capable of performing fairy queen magic, delivered straight to my waiting hands, and without me even lifting a finger. Not to mention a mortally wounded Sea King and my Queen's granddaughter, all together, just for me."

"Don't take more credit than you deserve," the wolf growled, standing over the wounded Sea King. "I played my part here as well."

"Sure, big guy," Lian said, rolling her eyes. "You did great, doing your whole wolf thing."

Jack slowly pulled out his sword and aimed it at her. "Phillip's right. There's still time."

"Oh, is there?" Lian asked, her smile widening. "It couldn't possibly be that I outwitted the great Jack the Thirteenth, son of Jack the Giant Killer and grandson of Jack the Hero of the Cursed Bucket. There's just no way I could have beaten THIS Jack, not when he comes from such *noble* and *fine* stock!"

Lian stepped forward, completely unconcerned about Jack's sword tracking her every movement. "And can we just go over all the ways you've helped me in the last two days? You freed the children of Hamelin from Pan's spell, leaving Pan with no one to play with." Lian smiled. "Well, until my Queen gave him some rebel prisoners. The Land of Never is the perfect jail, since no one can leave without the permission of their jailer. And Pan's happy now, with so many new friends to play with. Oh, and who else was there? Our favorite pirate-prince?" She grinned at Bluebeard, who glared back at her, strangely silent. "Why, it must have taken so much effort to convince *him* to take you to the Sea Witch. I mean, he's only been trying to get her help for, like, fifty years!"

Jack's throat tightened as he began to see Lian's hand in everything they'd done. Every taunt, every dare . . . Lian had goaded them right into where she wanted them to be, and to do what she needed them to do, including—

"Which led to war!" Lian shouted, her eyes wide in almost wonder. "I can't believe you were able to start a *war* between merman and human! Do you have any idea how long the Eyes had been working toward that? And you just waltz in, steal the mermaid princess, and accomplish in hours what we'd been working on for years!" She shook her head in amazement as the roaring of dragons got closer. "Your talent for serving our Queen really does know no bounds, Jack!"

"I do *not* serve her," Jack growled. "Not now, not ever!"

"See, there's where you're wrong," Lian told him, absently pulling out her own sword. "The Queen's old Magic Mirror told her. One of you," she said, pointing at Jack and Phillip, "will join her, betraying your little princess. The other will die by the Queen's hand." She laughed. "Did you really have to think that hard about which would be which?"

"That will never happen," Jack said softly.

"Keep on believing that," Lian said. "Though if I were you, I'd probably delude myself too. Honestly, Jack, this doesn't bring me any pleasure—"

May snorted loudly.

"I'm just satisfied at a job well done!" Lian continued, ignoring May. "This doesn't make me happy, humiliating you like this, outsmarting you at every turn, playing you for a fool *over* and *over*. . . ." She paused. "Okay, it makes me a *little* happy, if by 'a little' you mean 'a lot.' But that's not the point. The point is, the fairy queens and anyone who knows their magic need to die. So let's start with her."

And with that, faster than Jack could see, Lian turned and leapt at Meghan, her sword aimed right at the mermaid's chest—

Only to hit Jack's sword instead as he leapt to block her.

"Oh, you want to *fight*," Lian said, smiling wider. "Really, Jack? That's really what you want to do? 'Cause I promised I wouldn't hurt you, but if you're not giving me any choice . . ."

Jack took a deep breath, sighed, then stabbed five times in rapid succession at her in five different spots.

Each one missed like she had never been there.

"Oh, I think that officially qualifies as you asking for it," Lian said softly, then dropped low and kicked her foot out, sweeping

Jack's legs out from under him. Before he even realized he'd fallen, Lian had her sword pressed to his throat.

Had they really gotten this far only to fail? Jack glanced silently at May, who was inching her way over to Meghan. The mermaid had her eyes locked on her bleeding father, while Bluebeard was slowly circling the wolf.

None of that mattered, though. Not with Lian here.

"Jack's right," Lian said, her eyes locked on him. "You can all just stop your maneuvering. You've lost. Just let it go." She disappeared almost faster than Jack could see, kicking Bluebeard into the sleep spell and then swinging around to grab Phillip's arm and throw him in as well, returning the sword to Jack's throat before he could even move.

The prince and the pirate both hit the spell barrier almost at the same time. Bluebeard instantly went limp, snoring before he hit the ground, while Phillip . . .

Phillip stayed wide-awake as he landed, hard. The prince's eyes went big, then immediately shut as Lian glanced over to make sure he'd landed inside the barrier. Hadn't he? He must have. He was well past the spot where Bluebeard had landed, being much lighter than the pirate. But how was Phillip not asleep?!

"The funny thing is," Lian said, "I knew the mermaid wouldn't be able to sing on land. So I gave you the one thing she'd need, thinking I was being almost too obvious! But you of course chose the hard way instead, and had to get her back into water, wasting what little time you had before the dragons came."

"What'd you give us?" May asked. "Besides, you know, a blinding headache every time you open your mouth?"

"The pipes, you idiots," Lian said, shaking her head at their stupidity. "I left them on the Piper's tree stump! You even took them with you! They're magic, as Jack knew. He almost cast a spell himself before you guys went into the Land of Never, but apparently it never occurred to him that if *he* could play them, so could someone with actual magical and musical talent."

Jack flashed May an embarrassed smile while she just smacked her forehead.

"It hardly matters," Lian said, nodding at the dragons. "But still, pretty pathetic, guys."

"The spell," Meghan said, her eyes on Bluebeard. "It feels . . . familiar. It's fairy queen magic, isn't it?"

"Someone's got an ear for music," Lian said, turning to the mermaid.

"Even the fading harmonies of a musical spell," Meghan said softly. "It . . . it was meant to be a spell of death for someone, but . . . but it's been modified. The fairy queens must have changed it, lessened it . . . turning it into a spell that merely puts the victim and anyone near her to sleep."

"This is all fascinating," Lian said, "but it's far too late to cast a counterspell, if you even had the power to begin with."

"Oh, I don't," Meghan said, finally looking up. "This spell was too great for the fairy queens themselves. I would never have had the power to break it."

May let out a defeated groan as she slowly dropped to the ground, looking exactly like Jack felt.

"Which is why it's fortunate that the fairy queens added a means to break it," Meghan continued. "All one would have to do is wake the girl at the center of the spell, and the spell would be broken. So simple, actually . . . once you know how."

"That's the beauty, though!" Lian said, stamping her foot excitedly. "No one can get close enough! If they try, they get hit by the spell themselves and fall asleep!"

"You're right," Meghan said. "If only the fairy queens knew that someone would be along, at some time in the future, to find the girl and wake her up. But it'd have to be someone special, someone they knew was meant to be close to that girl . . ."

"The prince!" the wolf growled.

Lian whirled around to see what the rest of them already saw: Bluebeard lying alone in the sleeping spell.

Phillip was sprinting as fast as he could directly toward the enormous vines surrounding the Fairy Homelands.

CHAPTER 42

N O!" Lian shouted, and began to move so quickly she almost disappeared from Jack's vision. Instantly he was on his feet, running as fast as he was able to.

Which still wasn't fast enough. There was no way he could catch her before she caught up to the barely moving prince.

But he did have something that could.

Without a thought about what he'd do later (or at least without a *second* thought), Jack whipped his sword horizontally right at Lian's legs. As hard as he threw it, the sword still barely managed to catch just the tip of her heel, knocking one foot into the other and sending Lian sprawling forward onto her hands.

Her spill gave Jack enough time to catch her, which turned

out to be a bit of a problem, given that the girl he'd just caught now had both his sword and her own in her hands.

"Oh, Prince Phillip?" she shouted over her shoulder, both swords aimed at Jack. "I'd stop if I were you. Otherwise I'm going to kill your friend right here and now."

Phillip hesitated, then slowed to a stop, turning around to look at the situation.

"Phillip, GO!" Jack shouted. "I can handle this!"

"You have no weapon!" Phillip shouted, taking a step back toward them.

"I don't care!" Jack shouted. "Don't you get it? You're the only one who can fix this! You're the *hero*, stupid! Go do the hero work, while I take care of Little Miss Isn't So Clever here! GO!"

Phillip paused again, then turned back toward the vines.

Lian sighed. "I've never met a royal who can follow simple instructions." And with that, she stabbed at Jack with his own sword, then threw her sword directly at Phillip.

There was no time for a word of warning, no time for anything. Lian was just too fast, and nothing could possibly stop the sword as it flew straight and true right at Phillip's back—

Until an urgent, vibrant musical note sounded from behind them. A shimmering hand of crystal smashed down right on the sword in flight, pushing the sword straight to the ground mere inches from Phillip's back.

And just like that, Phillip disappeared into the thorns.

"NO!" Lian screamed again, and turned her fury onto Meghan, now holding the pipes May had just given to her.

The wolf roared, then grabbed the pipes out of the mermaid's hands with his teeth and bit down hard enough to break them apart. "You have accomplished *nothing*!" he growled at them. "The prince won't have time to break the spell, for the dragons are already here!"

Jack glanced up to see that the Wolf King was correct. Blotting out the sky were dragons of black, red, and green, some with riders, most without. The riderless dragons seemed wilder, more willing to fight, but the dragons with riders seemed to be herding the rest toward their goal, the goal they had now almost reached. It was only a matter of seconds before the fire started.

"C'mon, Phillip," Jack whispered, glancing between Lian and the wolf, but neither seemed interested in fighting. Like him, both were watching to see who would win, Phillip or the dragons.

The dragons drew closer and closer. They were right on top of the Fairy Homelands now, and several seemed to be ready to breathe fire.

"Now would be a good time, Phillip!" May screamed.

"He's too late," Lian said in an odd tone. Jack glanced at the Eye, but her face was unreadable beneath her hood. "He's just too late."

A tiny movement caught Jack's eye from beyond the silver gate. Had Bluebeard just twitched?

And then it *was* too late. The dragons reared back, then dove forward, letting loose a torrential hailstorm of fire, searing everything with an all-encompassing heat that was almost unbearable even at a distance. The thorny vines blackened and shrank away under the flaming onslaught, revealing the most beautiful city Jack had ever seen. Soaring spires painted with colors that had no name, crystal sculptures entwined with trees and bushes, a central pool that looked to be nothing more than water made from a starry sky . . .

It all burned.

May stepped closer to Jack, her mouth hanging open, no words coming. Jack knew the feeling. It was all he could do not to fall to his knees and cry.

"Phillip," May said, tears streaming down her horrified face. "He . . . he was in the middle of that."

Lian turned around, the fire burning behind her, and glanced at Jack, her eye suspicious. "That's true. There's no way the prince could have survived that, is there?"

The wolf growled low. "The fairy queens would have been worthy foes. It is . . . unfortunate that they had to be dealt with in this way. But what the Queen commands shall be."

"As the Queen commands," Lian said, her voice still suspicious. "Well, I guess it's time to get you two back to the Queen. You take the girl. I'll get Jack."

The wolf turned to May, who had her hands up as if she were going to fight him, despite the tears still streaming from her eyes. "You have no idea how not a good time this is," she said quietly. "You are *not* taking us anywhere, do you hear me?"

The wolf sighed. "As the Queen commands, so shall it be." With that, he leapt at May.

And just as fast, the wolf fell to the ground, unconscious from the hilt of a glowing sword slamming into his head.

May glanced up in surprise.

So did Jack.

Lian tossed Jack's sword a few feet away, then bent down to check if the wolf was still breathing. She nodded. "He'll be fine."

Above them the dragons began to circle, their jobs now complete, then slowly form back into a flight formation before heading off the way they'd come. Lian watched them go, Jack and May still staring at her in surprise. Finally she turned to look at them.

"Okay, *what?*" she said.

"Why *that?*" Jack said, waving vaguely at the wolf.

"You don't get it, do you?" she said, shaking her head. "I mean, I should expect that by now, but I always seem to give you the benefit of the doubt, and—"

"Get to the point," May said, her voice still quiet.

"You'll figure it out soon enough," Lian said, pointing out into the still burning Fairy Homelands. "And that means it's probably time for me to go, considering what's about to happen." She bent down and grabbed the Wolf King's paws, then dragged him a short distance away. "Tell Phillip I'm impressed," she said. "And Jack?" She smiled. "See you soon!"

She picked up her sword, blew a familiar-looking whistle, and disappeared along with the Wolf King.

Behind them Bluebeard groaned. "What is going *on?*" he said, pushing himself to his feet.

"Perhaps I can help," said a voice, and Phillip's head appeared out of nowhere . . . just his head. And his blushing, bright red face.

And then, like a curtain falling, the scene of a burning city fell to the ground, replaced by the beautiful, magical colors of the Fairy Homelands, completely safe and sound.

"Where to start?" Phillip said now that his entire self was visible . . . his face just as red.

CHAPTER 43

Where to start actually fell to healing the Sea King, as his situation seemed the most urgent. As they all gathered around the merman with human legs, Jack shifted impatiently from side to side, and noticed May doing the same thing.

"I'm waiting for something else to come along and ruin this for us," he whispered to her as a fairy queen in all green quietly hummed over the merman, his injuries disappearing with every chorus of the song.

"It's a fair bet," May said, looking at nothing. "Can you see Merriweather?"

Jack glanced around at the other five or so fairy queens standing nearby, and shook his head. "But don't worry. She'll be here."

"Will she?" May asked without looking up. "I mean, c'mon. You really think after all this that my grandmother won't have some way to mess with us still?"

"She's not your grandmother," Jack said, shaking his head.

"Prove it," May said, still not looking at him.

"I did what I did for Mariella," Meghan told the nearest fairy queen. "I would not have brought them back here for your sake."

The fairy queen, a smaller woman dressed all in purple, looked at her quizzically. "Mariella? Why, her spirit returned here years ago. She's a part of our lands now, as all fairies are once they pass on. So yes, you did this for her as well."

Meghan gasped, and lowered her eyes as tears began to fall. "I . . . didn't know."

"We welcomed her home," the purple fairy queen said. "She had been gone too long."

The Sea King's eyes fluttered open, and Meghan quickly pushed past the purple fairy queen to hug her father. He smiled at the sight of her, then did something exactly the opposite when he caught site of Maarten over her shoulder.

"YOU!" he roared, and was on his feet and leaping for Maarten before anyone could stop him.

Anyone except the green fairy queen, who barely hummed

for a second before the Sea King froze in place in midair. "Work out your conflict now," she said, her pupil-less eyes just as creepy as Merriweather's had been back in the Red Hood's cottage. "We will tolerate no violence here."

"You shall die for what you've done!" the Sea King said, quieter this time, but no less dangerous.

"See, Meghan?" Maarten said, staring at her father. "There is no reasoning with him."

"There is nothing to reason," she told him, wiping tears from her eyes. "My father and I will end this war immediately, then return to the sea and never again come to land. That is how it must be. You and I must not see each other again."

"I will not allow that to happen," Maarten told her, bending down on one knee. "I *love* you, more than myself, my kingdom, my world. I cannot bear the idea of living without you."

"Desperation doesn't look good on anyone," May whispered to Jack, who nodded.

"You just don't get it, do you, Maarten?" Meghan said.

"We are in your debt," the green fairy queen said to Phillip, Jack, and May, pulling them away from the domestic drama that was both more interesting and more disturbing than it should have been. "If there is any way that we might repay you—"

"YES," May said. "Tell me who I am."

"WAIT!" Bluebeard shouted, and strode over to them. "Ye made a deal with me, girl. And I aims to collect!"

May's eyes went wide. "You can't possibly be serious! This was what we spent the last three months doing, trying to find this place just so I could find out who I am!"

"Be that as it may be," Bluebeard said, "ye made a deal with me to save yer Little Eye here. Ye promised me any possession ye might own, and the fairy queen here just offered ye a favor. I want that. Ye cannot say no."

May stared at him in shock, her mouth moving but nothing coming out. The fairy queen tilted her head, then looked to May, who finally nodded, the hardest gesture Jack had ever seen anyone perform.

"Your favor, pirate?" the fairy queen asked, boring her white eyes into Bluebeard.

Bluebeard bored his eyes right back. "Turn me into a merman. For good."

About fourteen people gasped, it felt like, but that might have just been due to the volume of the gasps of Jack and May. Phillip looked speechless, while Meghan and her father looked doubly so.

"Meghan," Maarten said, turning to the mermaid. "Fifty years ago you gave up your entire life to be a part of my world, and to be with me. And after your father took you back, I sailed out to find the Sea Witch, hoping to do the same for you. But I found neither you nor her. Your sisters, they tried to help, but Pan found us, and—"

"You wanted to do that . . . for me?" Meghan said.

"I love you," he said. "There's nothing I wouldn't do!"

The fairy queen looked between the two of them. "You might not realize what you are asking. You will give up your humanity, your kingdom, your—"

"Yes, to whatever you say," Maarten said. "There is no price too high."

The fairy queen nodded. "Then so be it." She began to sing, a strangely soothing melody rising from her throat. Maarten turned to Meghan and her curiously quiet father in expectation . . . then doubled over in pain.

"What. . . ?" he said, then gasped as he hit the ground hard, his legs no longer supporting him. The reason for that quickly became obvious. As Jack watched with a combination of horror and fascination, Maarten's legs pushed together, his pants turning bright orange and scaly as his lower half turned into a fish.

"It is done," the fairy queen intoned. "You shall forevermore be a merman, with all that entails."

Meghan bent down to his side, a sympathetic smile on her face. "I know that pain, Maarten. I felt it myself. You truly intend to live below the ocean with us? And place yourself under the rule of my father?"

The Sea King's eyes went from enraged to gleeful, and for the first time Jack saw the monarch smile.

Maarten watched that smile with a certain dread, then nodded. "Of course. I would have done so fifty years ago—"

"You know that things can't just go back to that point," Meghan told him. "Mako loves me, and I have a life."

"I just want to be a part of it," Maarten said. "And whatever comes, comes."

Jack looked from Maarten to Meghan, then over at Phillip, who was watching the proceedings with a joyful smile. This was the prince's world, sacrificing everything for love, doing the noble deed, giving up yourself for others.

Doing everything that Jack couldn't. Yet here he was, like Maarten, trying to turn himself into something he wasn't ever since he'd met May. He was no Phillip. He was no prince. And there was no fairy queen spell that could make him one.

"If that is all?" the fairy queen asked, then turned without waiting for an answer and strode toward the city. Maarten tried to speak again, but a melody rose up around him, Meghan, and the Sea King, and all three began to float into nothingness.

"Don't forget to call off that invasion!" May shouted.

"We will," Bluebeard said. "But first we'll join human and merman soldiers to wipe out the Queen's goblin army." He laughed crazily.

"Good luck, Captain," Jack said as they disappeared.

The laughter stopped abruptly. "I'm gonna need it," Bluebeard shouted at him, then winked.

The pirate monkey realized that he was being left behind, and made a mad dash for his captain but was too late. Just like that, they were gone.

And just like that, someone else showed up.

"YOU JUST ABANDONED ME HERE TO BE BURNED BY DRAGONS?!" a tiny golden fairy screamed in Jack's ear.

"Oh, my fairy!" May shouted, grabbing the angry fairy and hugging her tight.

Meanwhile the pirate monkey dejectedly scrambled over to climb up on May's shoulders. The monkey and fairy stared at each other, backing away slowly, before the fairy took off and flew over to hide in Jack's hair. The monkey stuck out its tongue at her.

"Oh, GREAT," May said, yanking at the monkey again to pull him off her, accomplishing nothing.

"Speaking of annoying," Jack said. "Phillip, you never explained how you dispelled the curse."

At this, the prince went bright red and glanced around at the fairy queens and assorted lesser fairies as if he were watching for someone. "That . . . is a long story."

"PHILLIP!" someone shouted, then tackled the prince bodily and knocked him to the ground. Jack started to leap to the prince's aid, then realized Phillip's attacker was a dirt-covered girl about their age with reddish brown hair and a sleepy stare that, combined with her dazed grin, didn't exactly scream danger.

"This . . . is my long story," Phillip said simply.

CHAPTER 44

I'm Penelope," the girl said after all the tackling was done. She shook Jack's and May's hands, each step she took a bit more certain than the previous. It was as if the girl had just woken up after a long sleep but was still pretty out of it.

"Nice to meet you," May said, her eyebrows telling Jack that she wasn't exactly sure how nice it was. "And . . . who are you?"

"Penelope?" Penelope said, sounding as if she were asking herself.

"She is the, ah, cause of the spell," Phillip said, his blush growing. "As I guessed, apparently there was a curse on this girl, that if she were to prick a finger on a spindle, she would sleep forever and curse those around her to sleep as well."

May's eyes went wide, and she looked from Phillip to

Penelope and back. "Oh, wow. You're *her*," she said. "Sleeping Be— Wow!"

"Sleeping bee?" Jack whispered. "I'm glad you think it makes sense, because I've never heard anything make less. I mean, a spindle puts an entire city to sleep? If you're going to curse someone, why not make it something they can't avoid, like water, or air? Take a breath, and everyone for miles conks out, you know? A spindle? I've never even seen one!"

"Uh, yes, well," Phillip said, glancing uncomfortably from Jack and May while Penelope glanced very comfortably between the three of them. "Apparently Lian infiltrated the Fairy Homelands with just such a spindle, stabbed Penelope, then fled just ahead of the curse. The spell was so powerful, it knocked out the entire city, and you know the rest."

"We don't know how you woke them all up, Phillip," Jack said, a smile spreading over his face. For some reason he had an idea that his entire year was about to be made.

"Yes, right," Phillip said, apparently having trouble breathing. "Well, I . . . You see, to wake a sleeping girl—"

"Princess," Jack said. "Remember, from your story."

"To wake a sleeping *princess*," Phillip continued, his voice cracking, "there are certain ways—"

"My true love kissed me," Penelope whispered to Jack and May conspiratorially.

"He did no such thing!" Phillip objected.

"Didn't you kiss me?" she asked, staring up as if trying to remember. "I mean, I woke up and there you were, your face about an inch from mine, and it *felt* like you did—"

"YES, I kissed you!" Phillip shouted. "But I am not your true love!"

"The fairy queens tell me that only my true love's kiss could have broken that spell," Penelope said with a smile. "But do not worry. I won't tell anyone. Well, anyone else."

"I don't know, Phillip," Jack said, clapping a hand on the prince's and Penelope's shoulders. "If she's your true love, what are you waiting for?"

Phillip seemed to have no response, but fortunately for the prince, someone interrupted them. "Young sir," a tiny silver fairy said, shyly looking at Jack. "Merriweather wishes to speak to you."

"Finally!" Jack said. "So let's go—"

"To *you*," the silver fairy said. "*Not* the others. She said you, and only you."

Jack glanced at May and Phillip, who just looked confused. Finally their golden fairy put her hands on her waist and bent over to look at Jack from his head. "If a fairy queen says go, you *go!*"

Jack frowned. "I guess . . . I'm going," he said. "Merriweather wants to talk to me. Just me."

May stepped forward, a question on her lips, but Jack just smiled at her. "I'll find out what you need to know, May. No matter what."

May stopped, then smiled. She started to speak again, but instead just reached out and hugged Jack tightly. "Thank you," she whispered. "And if you mess this up, I will never forgive you."

He smiled at that, then followed the growingly impatient silver fairy away down the multicolored tile path toward the center of the Fairy Homelands.

All around him fairies buzzed happily, some singing, some chatting away, but all just happy to be alive. Somehow the mood didn't translate as well as their words did, because Jack had never felt quite so depressed as he did right now for some reason.

He followed the silver fairy into what looked to be some kind of elaborate organic tree-ish dwelling in the center of town, the tree growing up through crystal formations that looked just as natural as the tree, if in a different way. As soon as he walked in the entrance, though, everything changed, and he found himself in the middle of an enormous castle. He glanced out a window, expecting to see forest, but instead saw the open ocean. Because why not.

"Um, so where's Merriweather?" he asked as they walked farther into the castle.

"Thank you, Auriel," came a voice from down the hall, and the silver fairy smiled, then turned and flew away. "Gwentell, please bring your charge in." Jack's golden fairy, apparently named Gwentell, nodded in response, then settled herself down on Jack's shoulder as he followed the voice down the hall.

At the end of the hall, Jack found a woman in a familiar blue dress, her eerie white eyes just as disturbing as they'd been the first time he'd seen them. Still, Merriweather looked much better than the last time he'd seen her. Granted, she'd been locked in a life-and-death battle with a djinn at that point, so really anything was up from there.

"Come with me, Jack," Merriweather said, and Jack hurried along behind her as they walked down several hallways, passing by rooms made of gold, fire, and confusion, among other things. Finally they stopped in a room that looked to be made entirely of glass, from the chairs and the walls to the tapestries and doorknobs. Merriweather gestured, and Jack sat down in one of the glass chairs, a little surprised by how comfortable it felt.

"Indeed," she said, apparently agreeing with his silent thoughts. "But let us speak of what brought you here. As I told May, my obligation to her is complete. I saved you three from the Ifrit. But you . . . It was you who ultimately saved my life, and convinced my . . . sister . . . to rescue me. So it is to you I owe a debt, and therefore it is *your* questions I will answer. I owe nothing to the others."

"They helped save you too—," Jack started to say, but one look from her stopped him.

"None of that would have been necessary if any of you had been where you were supposed to be," Merriweather said, her white eyes crackling with energy and annoyance. "This world cannot hold with such wrongness. The Wicked Queen almost destroyed our homelands and us along with them today, all because we were forced to hide Penelope here! This is not where she belongs. . . . *None* of you are where you belong!"

"Where are we all supposed to be, then?" Jack asked. "Where is *May* supposed to be? That's the reason we came—"

Merriweather sighed. "I know but little, but I will share what I can, in payment of my debt. From what I know, May was born to a successful young merchant and his wife, loving parents both."

"Born . . . here, in our world? Because—"

"Yes, in the lands now occupied by the Wicked Queen," Merriweather said. "Unfortunately, her mother passed away when May was but a year old. As her father traveled far and wide to sell his wares and support his small family, he chose to remarry, giving his infant daughter a new mother, as well as two stepsisters, given that May's stepmother had two daughters as well. While her father traveled, then, May's stepmother began to care for her." Merriweather paused. "Or so she would have, if May had remained with her family. Unfortunately, the Wicked Queen stole her away from her stepmother for reasons unknown to me."

Jack frowned. "But why would she do that? The Wicked Queen wouldn't bother if May weren't important in some way. Though, I guess that does prove that the Queen and May aren't related, at least."

"Does it?" the fairy queen asked. "We know not how the Wicked Queen came to know of May. Perhaps she was the merchant's mother, and stole her granddaughter to protect her from what she knew was coming. Or could she be May's maternal grandmother, searching for a remembrance of her daughter? I'm afraid this tells us little about the Wicked Queen's motivations."

Jack sighed. "Okay, fine. So what would have happened if May hadn't been taken? What were you going to do for her?"

Merriweather's eyes grew hard. "I'm afraid May's stepmother was quite a wicked woman in her own right. Whatever money her husband had saved was quickly spent on frivolous luxuries and extravagant parties. If May had grown up under her step-mother, she soon would have been forced to serve the woman's every whim, once the woman couldn't afford to pay servants. Of course, May's father would have spent more and more time away from home in an effort to support his family, eventually passing away from sickness, leaving May at the mercy of her stepmother—"

"That's *awful*," Jack interrupted. "You're making it sound like she might have been better off with the Wicked Queen!"

"You forget that I was meant to play a role in these proceed-ings," Merriweather reminded him. "My magic would have saved May from a miserable existence, and given her a chance at a better life."

"Oh, right," Jack said, his anger dying as quickly as it had flared up. "What were you going to do?"

"If May had lived as fate intended," Merriweather said, "I was meant to help her win the heart of her one true love."

For a moment the room went absolutely silent, without even the sound of Jack's beating heart. Then, his chest strangely cold, Jack stood up.

"Her . . . her true love?" he said, his voice sounding like it was hundreds of miles away.

Merriweather nodded. "A prince, from a neighboring kingdom. May would have then become a true princess, and lived happily until the end of her days."

"But . . . her true love?" Jack said. "Maybe . . . maybe she could still be happy with someone different, just as happy as—"

"Just as happy?" Merriweather said, shaking her head. "No, nothing could possibly approach her love for this prince. A prince that most likely still awaits her."

"He's . . . out there?" Jack asked, having trouble thinking clearly for some reason. "Waiting for her? The prince, her true love?"

"In all probability," Merriweather said. "Despite May missing her appointment, such love was destined from the beginning of days, and would be extremely hard to put off entirely."

Jack nodded, his breathing shallow. "Who . . . who is this prince?" he asked finally.

"I do not know," Merriweather admitted. "Her prince was

destined to place a slipper on her foot, and at that moment they would both know of their destiny to be as one." The fairy queen held out her hand, and a translucent glass slipper appeared on it. "Only true love can transform this slipper from cold, hard glass. If her prince gave this to her, it would feel softer than a fairy wing on her skin."

"Oh," Jack said. "So that's it, then. She . . . she's meant to love someone else."

Merriweather nodded. "Why do you react in such a way? I thought you wished to know the truth."

Jack shook his head, not really focusing. "No, I did. I just thought . . . once this was all over, maybe . . ."

"You thought she might care for you?" Merriweather laughed. "Child, you were never meant to have even met her! If you had not interfered, the Wicked Queen would still be imprisoned. In fact, from what I can tell, your destiny almost appears that you were meant to *oppose*—"

"I get it, okay?!" Jack shouted. "I mean, I should have known." He reached out and touched the slipper, the glass cold to his touch. "I should have *known*. I'm not . . . It was all just a joke on me."

"As if *you* were meant for such things!" Merriweather repeated, shaking her head.

"As if I were," Jack said quietly, then turned to go.

"Child," Merriweather said as he left. "If it is of any solace, I would have thought your very presence would have doomed their mission to save our homelands from the start. The fact that Phillip and May succeeded in doing so in spite of you speaks volumes. But perhaps it is time to let them lead the lives they were meant to, without your interference."

Jack just stared at her, then nodded slowly. "Perhaps it is."

CHAPTER 45

The silver fairy led Jack to a room filled with blue silk to wait for May and Phillip. Barely noticing anything, he followed her in a daze, glancing out the window to see May, Phillip, and the new girl, Penelope, walking slowly toward the castle/building/whatever it was, the prince walking as much ahead of Penelope as he could without appearing rude. Penelope for her part didn't seem to notice that, or really anything else.

"I heard what Merriweather said," said a voice to Jack's right. The air shimmered, and Lian appeared out of nowhere, staring out the window as well. "Kind of harsh, even if it's the truth. Which it is."

"Thanks," Jack said absently, his eyes locked on May.

"Look at them," Lian said softly. "Phillip really is a hero.

There's no way around it. And May is as well, in her own way. But both will never defeat my Queen. They're much too . . . *decent*."

Jack started to argue, then went silent.

"You know I'm right," Lian said, and her voice sounded sad. "You know you three were just running to stay in place against my Queen. And Merriweather's correct. You weren't exactly helping."

"Is there a point to this?" Jack asked quietly.

Lian paused, then pulled her sword out . . . and threw it into the wall across the room. The sword slid in smoothly to the hilt, and Lian nodded. "*Now* we can talk," she said.

Jack gave her a confused look. "You don't want the sword overhearing?"

Lian pulled the hood off her head, revealing a face that wasn't the one she'd worn as a mermaid. In fact, she looked familiar, like he'd seen her before somewhere, but he barely cared enough to try to remember from where.

"I don't want my Queen listening," Lian said, turning back to the window. "Not all of us have had our swords fixed by the Charmed One to keep her out."

"*You* still managed to know exactly what we were doing," Jack said, turning back to the window as well. "Guess he didn't fix it as well as he thought."

Lian laughed. "You think it was the sword? How many times have you watched me disappear into thin air, you idiot? Eyes can turn invisible, Jack. You saw me do it right before the cave to the Land of Never, and, like, a million other times. Phillip even told you!"

"I try not to listen to him," Jack said, half-dazed. Could this be true?!

"You really think that I wasn't with you the entire time?" Lian continued. "Who do you think took the fourth mermaid tear? Your sword's light flickered every time you pulled it out. It sensed my sword and was warning you! Are you really *that* stupid?"

Jack's mouth dropped open, and he sat down hard on the bed, staring up at Lian. "You were there . . . the entire time?"

"Way to catch up," she said. "I had to make sure you didn't mess anything up, all while my Queen listened to my every word. Not the easiest thing to do, but I'm pretty talented."

"What do you mean, 'mess anything up'? You're trying to say you were *helping* us?!"

"You certainly didn't make it easy!" she said indignantly. "You were almost killed, like, five times by the goblins while getting Meghan to the ocean. I had to follow right behind you and protect you the entire time. Even the pirates almost hit you . . . such horrible shots! And the tidal wave?! The Sea King aimed for *me* once with his electricity, and almost killed me! I had to jump into the water. That meant I lost you for a bit."

"That's when the Charmed One came back," Jack said. "But you made things hard for us too. You made my sword go crazy in the Sea Witch's lair, and—"

"You *had* to be found, Jack," Lian said. "There were things that had to happen for you to succeed, so I *made* them happen. Mako never would have let you escape with Meghan, so he had to be removed from the picture. . . . I thought he'd *never* try to pull me out that hole in the Sea Witch's place. You needed Bluebeard to get Meghan in the first place, so I made sure you ended up in the Land of Never. I even made sure to leave you with a rope so May could pull you out when you first got hit by the sleeping curse!" She sighed deeply. "You have no idea how hard I've worked!"

Jack glared at her. "Right. And the whole time, you were able to get into my head."

"Because I was always close enough to touch your sword, which makes that easy," Lian said with a shrug. "I can teach you that."

"But why?" Jack said. "*Why* would you do any of this?"

Lian shook her head. "You really can't figure it out?" She straightened up, stepped around behind him . . . then pushed him hard in the back.

As Jack fell forward in surprise, the memory of a boy and a girl on a hill exploded in his mind, and he realized where he'd seen Lian before. The shock threw him so much, he slammed into the floor, not even making an effort to catch himself.

"Lian . . . you're that girl?!" he said, turning over onto his back.

"Maybe it's time you stopped using childish nicknames," she said, making a face. "If you're going to shorten Jillian, you might as well call me Jill like our dad does."

A chill shot through his body. "*Our* dad?"

"You fell down, Jack, years and years ago," Jill said quietly. "I . . . I pushed you down that hill. You broke that thick skull of yours, so our parents sent you to live with our grandfather, since he had magical items that could heal you over time. It was also quieter than . . . than our home."

"Our . . . home?" Jack said.

"You'll see it eventually," she said. "But this is what you've never understood, Jack. Our family? We're *not* heroes. We're not the noble princes who operate in the sunlight, winning the love of the people as we save lives and make it look easy. No, *we* do what needs to be done to survive. We steal from giants. We outwit our enemies, playing whatever card we can just to live. And we get the job done."

"And what job is that?" Jack said, barely able to concentrate. Lian was his sister? He *had* a sister?!

"What do you think?" Jill said. "I'm going to take down the Wicked Queen."

"But you're an Eye!"

Jill smiled. "You have so much to learn. But to do that is going to require going to some pretty dark places. You busy?" She stuck out her hand to help him to his feet.

Jack glanced up at her, then reached out and took her hand.

"Jack?" May said, opening a door into a room that took her breath away. The entire room seemed to be made out of blue silk, from the chairs to the bed to a desk in the corner.

And the room was empty.

"I asked you to bring me to Jack," she told the little fairies who'd guided her here. They just smiled and shrugged, pointing into the room, so May walked in to explore.

She sat down on the bed, looking around at the sheer softness of everything, then noticed something rolling toward her on the bed, something shiny and transparent she hadn't noticed before.

A slipper made of glass.

"What *is* this?" she said. A glass slipper? And only one? Wasn't there a royal ball or something missing here?

The monkey on her shoulder leapt to the bed and grabbed something else, something that'd been underneath the slipper. Something white and papery.

"Give me that!" she shouted, grabbing for it, barely managing to rip the paper from the monkey's hand. It screamed at her, grabbed the slipper instead, and climbed back up to its perch on her shoulders.

May started to open the paper, but a noise outside caught her attention and she pushed aside the blue silk curtains to find out what was going on.

At first she couldn't see much of anything. It was too dark outside as the sun set. But then she made out some fairy lanterns, off in the distance, moving away as if they were leaving town.

It was some kind of carriage, pulled by fairies. And on that carriage . . . She squinted hard, pressing her face against the window glass. There was someone on it. . . .

"Jack?" she said quietly.

"Princess," Phillip said behind her, his voice soft. "Where *is* he? We were led here."

May quickly sat down on the bed again, then unfolded the paper, a sheet from Jack's Story Book.

"Dear May," it said.

She began to read the note, passing along the important bits to the others. "Jack says I have a stepmother . . . and stepsisters! He doesn't mention my parents, though. Something about a prince. He's pretty vague. And . . . oh, wow. That slipper is—"

May abruptly dropped the note to the ground, her whole body going numb. "This is *Cinderella*," she said, an entire childhood and world of stories crashing over her at once. Was it possible? *She* was Cinderella?! With stepsisters, an evil stepmother, and . . . singing mice?

"What is a Cinderella?" Phillip asked her.

Penelope shrugged. "I think it's something you use to clean a fireplace," she told him, then bent down and picked up Jack's letter. "There's more on the back, only in a different kind of writing," she said, then read, "'And with a heavy heart, Jack left Phillip and May behind to join the ranks of the Wicked Queen's Eyes.'"

Penelope frowned, then looked up to find Phillip and May

staring at her in shock. "Well," she said, "at least it sounds like he's got something new to keep him occupied!"

Outside the window a large blackbird watched them, tilting its head as May grabbed the note from Penelope and began to read it again. The bird stared for a moment, then nodded and cawed "Jack!" loudly once, before abruptly flying out over the Fairy Homelands. It quickly located its prey, one of two people riding a carriage being pulled by fairies, then soared along above the carriage silently, following Jack once more as it had for the past four months.

Only this time, following him to the lands of the Wicked Queen, following him back to the blackbird's master.

JAMES RILEY

is the author of the Half Upon a Time series as well as many books too unwritten to count. He's met thousands of imaginary people, most of whom are more polite than you'd think, but less interesting than you'd hope. He doesn't believe fairy tales actually happened, mostly because he's never had tiny elves do his work for him at night, despite their promising several times. James currently lives in Los Angeles, but it's not like he's special that way . . . so do a lot of other people.